number
8

number 8

ANNA FIENBERG

Walker & Company
New York

Published in the United States of America in 2007 by
Walker Publishing Company, Inc.
Distributed to the trade by Holtzbrinck Publishers

First published in Australia in 2006 by the Penguin Group, Puffin Books

For information about permission to reproduce selections from
this book, write to Permissions, Walker & Company,
104 Fifth Avenue, New York, New York 10011

Library of Congress Cataloging-in-Publication Data
available upon request
ISBN-13: 978-0-8027-9660-8 • ISBN-10: 0-8027-9660-5

Visit Walker & Company's Web site at www.walkeryoungreaders.com

Book design by David Altheim
Typeset in Bembo by Palmer Higgs
Printed in the U.S.A. by Quebecor World Fairfield
2 4 6 8 10 9 7 5 3 1

All papers used by Walker & Company are natural, recyclable products
made from wood grown in well-managed forests. The manufacturing processes
conform to the environmental regulations of the country of origin.

For Judy Thompson,
with love and thanks for your wisdom,
commitment, and math panache!

number
8

1. Jackson

I think the best number in the whole universe is eight. The way I see it, eight has everything going for it. It's even, for a start. You can divide it by four and two—friendly numbers that come in pairs like brothers, or twins. I can't stand odd numbers. They're cold and spiky with nasty surprises inside them like sharp things you step on in the grass.

We used to have an eight in our address: 2–408 Trenches Road. How lucky was that! When people asked me my address, I'd write it out slowly, enjoying the way the numbers flowed smooth as cream.

I admire zero almost as much as eight. Nothing divides into zero so you can be ABSOLUTELY, TOTALLY sure you won't get messy fractions hanging over like bits of peanut butter spilling from the jar. My mom leaves the peanut butter like that all the time, dripping down from the lid, even though I tell her that's what brings the cockroaches.

Did you know that cockroaches can live for nine days without their heads? Mom knows because I told her, but it doesn't change her domestic habits. She just says, "*Nine*, huh? How very *strange*," and she laughs at me in her crazy Freddie Krueger way.

I loved the house on Trenches Road. Apartment, actually. It was small and high up, on a busy highway as loud as a war.

1

If you had a conversation on the street below you had to battle to make yourself heard against all the trucks and buses backfiring like bombs going off. We lived above a Spanish restaurant, but the waiters were all Chinese, and at night I could hear Liu and Chen calling to each other and Liu's brother had this snorting kind of laugh that made you laugh, too. Often I'd lie there in bed, chuckling myself. I'd wonder why laughter is so infectious, like yawning. The voices downstairs were company, a lot of round, even numbers grouping together in sets. When I listened to them, I didn't feel so much like the odd one out up there alone in bed.

There were lots of cafés and pubs on Trenches Road and dry cleaners and secondhand bookshops and music stores, and the other families in our apartment building turned their music up loud and argued and laughed. It was noisy and energetic, as if we were all strung together along some buzzing wire of electricity and we couldn't get off even if we tried. I didn't want to get off. I *liked* it.

It's so quiet here. 73 Valerie Avenue. Our new street is wide and leafy with trees planted every three seconds like exclamation marks. Silent ones. "Don't you love all this peace and tranquility?" Mom says. "You can really hear yourself think!" Yeah, I say, that's what worries me. Well, I don't actually *say* it, because Mom has her bright face on, and I don't want to see it fall. Mom thinks a quiet suburb where kids can ride their bikes without fear of being mowed down by trucks or drunks is heaven, and what luck, we didn't even have to die to get here!

The suburbs. I've never lived in a suburb before. I've lived in the middle of cities, in a tent when our money ran out, a trailer park, the desert, and once, for five weeks, in America when Mom said we should just take our courage

2

and toothbrushes and "make it" in the Big Apple. Rough end of a *pine*apple, that idea, if you ask me. When we went broke in New York, we had to stay in a crummy hostel for men. Mom wore a baseball cap all the time and spoke in a deep voice. It was good for her singing range, she said—you have to be able to get those low notes if you want to sing soul. Mom always tries to be positive. What I noticed were the stains on the sheets and the way you could practically pass out from alcohol poisoning if you breathed in fumes from the guy next to you at the sink.

Here it's so quiet, yesterday I heard our neighbor sneeze. I was going to say "bless you" but I didn't know if that was the right thing to do in the suburbs. Were you supposed to pretend you didn't hear, like the fence dividing you is soundproof or something?

In the suburbs there are only the polite sounds of lawnmowers on Saturday mornings and the thud of news-papers landing on neatly swept driveways.

I'm sitting outside on the back step, looking out at the lawn. We have a lawn. I suppose we'll have to get a lawn-mower. I'm so hungry I could eat one of those pigeons pecking in the grass. There's nothing in the fridge; I already looked.

Maybe some of those mangoes are ripe. Look, out there in our very own backyard is a mango tree. Mom thinks this is incredible. She goes like this: "Do you know how much people *pay* for those things in the stores? You'd never grow a mango tree in an *apartment*." (Well, obviously, Mom.) "Breathe deep, Jackson, the air is *fresh* here." She says this waving her arms around. She's always waving her arms around. Yesterday I noticed that the flesh at the top wobbles more than it used to. I didn't like thinking about that, so I looked away.

I've never eaten a mango. Mom says they taste like luxury. The fat green-going-golden ones are very high up on the tree. The ones on the ground are ripe but they have large gouges in them, so you can see the velvety flesh inside. It's the possums that do the gouging, Mom says. I've never even seen a possum in real life. Well, only as roadkill. I wouldn't mind seeing a live one.

When I get up off the step, I hear my knees crack. God, maybe the suburbs cause accelerated aging. Everyone just sitting around watching the trees grow. I crack my knuckles eight times for good luck. My thumbs are double-jointed, so I only do them four times.

I'm just looking in the fridge again, thinking maybe I've missed something, when there's a knock at the door. Ta ta *taa*. I jump in fright. Why don't people knock in reasonable numbers, like twos or fours? I take a deep breath as I walk up the hall. It seems to take ages. This house is so big. We don't need such a big house, I keep telling Mom, an apartment was more than big enough for just the two of us.

I open the door.

"Hi," says Esmerelda Marx.

I gulp. I can't believe it.

"Hi," she says again. "Remember me? I lent you my pen today."

I nod once, my mouth still paralyzed. Esmerelda *Marx*. I nod twice, to make it an even number. I look down at my hands.

Esmerelda laughs. "That pen must have been leaky, sorry! Mom's always bringing home the faulty ones from the bank. 'Waste not, want not,' she says. Of course you can't risk a leaky pen at the *bank*. Once, she thought a customer tried to cash a check for two thousand dollars instead of

4

two hundred, all because of this black smudge at the end. Claimed it looked like a zero. Ha! Can I come in?"

In her hands there is a plate with, let's see, ten cakes shaped like little boats. In each one there's a filling of lemony custard with sugar frosting on top. Suddenly, my mouth starts twitching and saliva dribbles out the corner so I look like some sort of lunatic.

I open the door wide, and she passes in front of me. Her long dark hair swings lightly against my cheek. She smells like flowers and something else. Fresh stationery.

I clear a space on the kitchen table. It's filled with pieces of paper—shopping lists and bills and little towers of CDs. I can hardly breathe. Esmerelda puts the plate down. I love the smell of fresh stationery.

"We've only just moved in here," I say quickly, waving at the cardboard boxes piled against the walls.

Esmerelda nods and says, "Mind if I look around? I find other people's lives *fascinating*." She wanders off into the living room before I can choose between "Sure" or "Go for it" or "There's not much to see."

"I live just across the road," she calls from the other room. "We're at number sixty-eight. My mom just baked these and when I told her I saw you getting off the bus coming home, she said I should take them over to you. We're lucky, Tuesday is her early day."

I stay rooted to the spot, as if struck by lightning. Sixty-eight! I'm filled with such a rush of envy. Talk about luck! Does she have any idea of her good fortune? Or the way her hair bounces into two perfect sixes? But how lucky am *I* that she noticed *me*! We live on the same street! Me and Esmerelda Marx. Maybe there is a God after all. Maybe there are a *pair* of them. I have so many thoughts and ideas and feelings that I decide I'd better just stand still like a bottle of soda that's been shaken up, and wait for everything to settle.

See, Esmerelda Marx was the only good thing that happened to me on my first day at Homeland High School. She was the eight seconds of awe and happiness that made me stop thinking about how terrible it is starting new schools. I spotted her in music, and then during math she lent me her pen. I watched her all morning. While I watched her I forgot to feel clumsy and too tall and that I'd scratched a pimple in the morning, leaving a red angry mark on my forehead.

The sliding door between the kitchen and the living room bangs open like a gunshot. My heart pounds in fright.

"Ve vill 'ave to do somezing about zat door," I say. I wince at the sound of myself. Why do I do this? Whenever I am truly nervous I go into this stupid Mafia boss act.

Esmerelda stands in the doorway, holding a framed photo. "Iz true, zis door it must go," she says, and draws a line with her finger across her throat.

We laugh and make karate chopping motions and shooting gestures at the door. I'm still killing the door when she holds up the photo.

"Who is this, Jackson? What a cool dress!"

"That's my mother."

Esmerelda's eyes open wide. It's like receiving an electric shock. Her eyes are green. I could fall into them, pools of green light. I haven't really seen her eyes before. I realize she keeps them half-closed most of the time as if narrowed against cigarette smoke.

"She's holding a microphone—is your mom a singer?"

"Yeah." I'm still looking at her eyes. There's something cat-like, a bit magical about her green eyes and black hair.

6

You don't see that combination very often. You'd see it on a witch maybe, or Wonder Woman. Esmerelda suddenly looks very intense.

"What does she sing? What is her name?"

"Valerie, like this street. That's partly why we moved here. Well, I guess that's what helped her decide, anyway. She sings blues, jazz. She's not famous or anything." I look at the photo. "That was taken at the casino in the city, just before she left. She used to do a midnight spot there on Saturday nights." I look closer. "Her eyes are all red because of the flash. Funny how a flash makes everyone look like the devil."

"The *casino*." Esmerelda draws in her breath. She studies the photo. "My dad went there once. Is it the Blue Moon?"

"Yeah."

"She looks like she'd be a great singer. Do you sing?"

I laugh. "No way. Well, only in the shower."

Esmerelda shakes her head. Her black hair catches rays of light from the window. It looks almost wet, it's so shiny. Suddenly she grabs my hand and pulls me into the living room. "So that's why you have a keyboard here, and the guitar, and the amp and microphone, and oh look, you even have those conga drums. Do you know what? I love to sing. I sing all the time. Yeah, in the shower, everywhere. I was in the school choir and last year I even did a solo. Well, it would have been a solo if Lilly hadn't insisted on sharing it with me. But I wasn't scared or anything. When I sing, I forget everything else."

"That's what Mom says." A sharp ache starts just under my rib cage. I think of Mom, how she looks when she's singing. Happy. She hasn't looked like that for a long time.

"Can we turn this on?" Esmerelda taps the keyboard. "I'm taking piano lessons, but we don't have one at home."

I switch it on and she tries out the different rhythms—swing, Latin American, rock.

"If you know how to play the piano, you can compose songs and accompany yourself as you sing them." She tosses her head importantly. Her dark hair is still moving as the rest of her stops. It's like a wave coming into shore. "Does your mother do that?"

"What?

"Make up songs."

"Sometimes." The living room is so different with Esmerelda Marx in it. "When Mom worked at the casino, before this new manager came, she used to sing her own songs. They're pretty mournful, you know, all in minor chords about people leaving each other and having no money, but dat's dem blues, as she says."

I remember how at Trenches Road I'd come home from school and Mom'd be rehearsing. I'd go and make myself a peanut butter and jelly sandwich and sit out on the balcony. Her voice would float out to me, as rich as hot chocolate. There were questions and answers in the music, no nasty surprises. I felt full sitting out there, satisfied, and it wasn't just from the sandwich. Once I told her she was like the number eight. I meant it as a compliment but she frowned. She thought I meant she was too round. "I'd rather be skinny and angular, like seven," she said. I told her she didn't want that, because seven is particularly mean-looking, like a medieval scythe. You could take someone's head off in one blow with one of those things. But she must not have been convinced about the scythe thing because after that I noticed how we had all this Diet Coke in the fridge and tons of lettuce. After work, though, late at night, she'd sneak up plates of french fries from the café below.

"It must be so great, your mother being a singer," Esmerelda says.

"Yeah, well," I say. "It means we move a lot. We have to go wherever she can get work." I think of Mom this morning and her bright face as she put on too much lipstick in front of the mirror. "Wish me luck, Jackson," she said, with a big false smile. I wanted to, but I knew the job she was going for wasn't what she really wanted. "We have to pay the rent," she'd said last night. "Dreams are expensive."

I could feel the black cloud coming down over me so I shook my head to clear it. I didn't want to spoil even a second of this miraculous afternoon. "Esmerelda sounds like a singer's name," I say, "or maybe an actress." I've read in Mom's magazines that women like you to ask questions about them and their feelings. And anyway, I was interested. "Is it Spanish?"

Esmerelda shrugs. "It was the name of a mermaid in a movie my mother saw as a child. She said she always wanted a romantic life, and there's not a lot of it in the banking world. I guess she wanted something different for me." She laughs. "'You've got to balance your accounts, Ez. Mind your deposits and withdrawals, otherwise the bottom line of life will reach up and swallow you.'"

When Esmerelda does her mother's voice she puts on this flat nasal tone and it's hilarious. She sounds just like the finance reporter on TV, the one mom throws her shoes at. I start doing it too, not throwing my shoes that is, but making my voice go down like hers at the end of each sentence, as if announcing a funeral. We start laughing, and we can't stop. I look at Esmerelda hooting away and suddenly I feel like I've known her all my life. She doesn't look like Wonder Woman anymore. Funny how when you laugh at the same thing, at the same time, you feel like you're not alone anymore. Suddenly I want to tell her everything, about the terrible quiet and the stinginess of odd numbers. But she gets started first.

"I've always lived on this street," she says wistfully, looking around the room. "I can't wait to travel. Have you ever been outside Australia?"

"Yeah, to the U.S. But we didn't stay long. I remember on our last night we went out to a diner and had chocolate cake for dinner. There's a photo of me somewhere with chocolate all over my face."

Which makes me remember the ten little boats sitting on the kitchen table. A growl of hunger swirls in my stomach. "Hey, let's eat, I was practically dying of starvation before you got here."

We go and get the cakes and Esmerelda suggests we sit outside. It's a balmy (not barmy, well, maybe just a bit) afternoon and we can smell the jasmine climbing all over the soundproof fence.

"That's nice, the jasmine," I say casually. "You never get that smell in the city. Where we lived it was mainly bus exhaust and paella."

"What's paella?"

I tell her about the Spanish dish, the shrimp and chicken, mussels nestled in their shells, and the greasy fingers you get when you eat it. She tells me how great it must be to know that sort of exotic stuff. While she's talking, I'm eating five cakes. They're light and lemony, with sugar frosting that melts on your tongue. I'm hypnotized by how good they are.

"I'd rather eat your mother's cakes than paella any day," I say, wiping my mouth. I can feel the sugar tingling on my chin. "It's not that great, you know, moving around all the time. You're always the new kid. You hardly have time to learn people's names before you have to start all over again."

"Mmm," says Esmerelda. "Will you forget mine, do you think?" She opens her eyes wide suddenly, and I get that feeling of falling again. Now I think her eyes are more like a stretch of grass, maybe a golf course: green, smooth, with no odd spiky bits. You could lie down in them, close your own eyes…

She's still staring at me, and now she's fluttering her eyelashes. She looks like an actress on TV. You can tell she's thinking about how she looks, and I wish she wouldn't. I liked how it was before, when there was nothing else between us.

"I won't ever forget *your* name," I tell her. Oh, how corny that sounds. Pathetic. I snort. "I mean, it's too long—there are four syllables before you can even draw breath."

We both look down at the plate. There's only one cake left. We stare at it. "Well, just call me Ez then if it's easier," she says, and takes the cake. "Everyone else does." I notice her eyes are narrow again.

There's a silence between us, the first one, I realize, that afternoon. I've said the wrong thing, but I'm not sure what it was. I want to get back to when we were telling each other things, without thinking.

"You know, I've moved fourteen times in thirteen years. Thirteen is a very bad number, but I guess seventeen is worse. I hope we don't get to seventeen. You know why?"

Ez doesn't say anything, but I think that's because her mouth is full. "See, the seven in seventeen is a really mean number. It's thin and sharp but you should see how they draw it in Europe. It looks even more dangerous because

11

there's a spike like a crossbow through the middle. I know because at my last school I sat next to this Italian boy who kept getting into trouble for drawing his sevens that way."

I glance at Ez's face. She's looking at the half-devoured mangoes on the lawn.

"Some people think seven is a really *lucky* number," she says. "When my dad went to the casino, that's what he played at the roulette table. He said it was an amazing place, there were all these men in gold chains and million-dollar suits, ladies in low-cut dresses." She turns to me, and her face is all eager again, and open. "Tell me about the casino," she says. "Did you ever go there? Why did your mom leave?"

Now I get it. Esmerelda wants to hear about the exciting, glittery side of things, like TV. I don't blame her, what with all this suburban quiet soaking up everything like blotting paper. I decide I won't say anything about being lonely or Mom's new job, that's if she gets it. Right now, Mom is probably wearing that smile and waving her arms around for the boss or whoever's interviewing her. She's telling him that sure, she's had years of experience in waitressing and serving beer, and really, all she's ever wanted is to work at this gorgeous Homeland pub. She'll do the dinner shift three nights a week, as advertised, and lunch and Saturday nights as well if they want. She won't tell him how she's decided that she'll give up singing and become a civilian if she gets this job. She won't tell him, either, how you've got to know when to give up on a dream, and get real. (That's what civilians do, she thinks, they have normal jobs and stop being crazy artists hanging onto crazy dreams.) And she won't say how it's about time she made a stable life for her son who thinks numbers have supernatural powers and has a nervous cough. Well, I *told* her the cough had nothing to do with Trenches Road and its backfiring buses, but she didn't listen and now she keeps telling me to breathe deep the fresh air. I don't tell her that the breathless thing is actually worse now, due to the quiet. In this place you can even hear yourself swallow. It's unnerving. But she's got enough to worry about.

"Jackson? How long did your mom work at the Blue Moon?"

"About a year and a half."

"Well, she must have seen a lot of rich people in that time, just like my dad did." Esmerelda nudges me. "Did she see that millionaire guy, you know the famous one who—"

"Oh, yes, and she got invited out to dinner by these guys in Ferraris and Jaguars. Once she got to ride in a Lamborghini, you know the car with the doors that open upward like wings." Actually, Mom only ever saw those cars as she drove out of the parking lot in our 1984 Ford Escort on her way home. But she always described them to me, because I collected model cars for a while.

"So why did she leave?"

"Oh, it's kind of complicated." I look at Esmerelda. I don't know whether I should tell the truth about it. I'm sure Mom wouldn't like it. But then I take a risk. Mom would understand. This is Esmerelda Marx, for goodness sake. She's waiting to be entertained. And boy, do I have a story for her.

"Well, see, it was like this. Mom got along really well with the manager—you know, the boss who employed her. Her job was to work at the bar and serve food but this guy, he was always trying to get more spots for her, singing. He said that's what she was born to do. He was such a fan, he was a real jazz tragic—"

"A what?"

"You know, someone who's crazy about jazz. He could

13

tell you the whole history of jazz if you sat there long enough. He loved the way Mom sang, said she was another Ella Fitzgerald, and no matter what was happening in the casino he'd make sure he came to listen to her. But then he had to quit—his wife got really ill—and the owners took on a new manager. That's when the trouble started."

"Why, wasn't the new guy a jazz fan?"

"No. He wasn't excited about anything except money. He kept stalking around, telling people to do their jobs quicker or they'd be fired. He kept a stopwatch in his pocket. 'Watch out, things are gonna change round here,' was his favorite saying. He even told Mom to sing more songs in an hour, so people'd get more value for their money. Can you believe it? He told Mom she didn't bring in a big enough crowd. Said she was getting old and her breaks were too long between sessions. Well, actually, Mom thinks she only takes about six minutes, just time enough to have a drink and pee. And I can tell you, Mom pees faster than anyone I've ever met."

"So does my little brother. He's always in such a hurry to get on with his game, sometimes he's still dribbling as he leaves the bathroom."

"Well, Mom wasn't happy, as you can imagine, but then a really bad thing happened." I stop here because I feel a cough coming on. I try to swallow it down but this familiar feeling like a door closing over my throat starts and I begin to bark. Honestly, I sound like a dog with emphysema. That's a terminal disease. I looked it up in the dictionary.

"Should I get you a glass of water?" Esmerelda's looking at me like I'm dying.

I nod, mainly so she won't hear me so loudly in the kitchen. Water never really fixes the cough, I just have to let it go till it's finished. It's exhausting.

I drink the water, and wipe my eyes.

"Have you got TB or something? There's a famous opera where the heroine dies of tuberculosis. *La Traviata*. Her last song is fantastic. She coughs up blood all over her lover's handkerchief. I know about tuberculosis because I sang one of the songs from that opera last year for the Christmas play. I had everybody howling."

The cough is still there. I take a deep breath, and hold it for four seconds. I count the numbers out in my head, watching them drift together into a set like gentle cows corralled in a field. I put a bracket around them like a friendly arm to stop them from getting out. My heart slows a little as they pair off inside their enclosure, cozy.

"Have you been to a doctor?"

I nod. "Yes, a few. I'm okay. They say I do it to relieve stress."

"Wow. Why don't you jog or do yoga instead?"

I shrug. How can you answer a question like that?

"So," begins Esmerelda with a little wriggle of impatience, "what was the really bad thing, or don't you want to talk about it?" She looks up at me again, wide-eyed, and flicks back her hair.

"It's okay," I say, watching the way her hair settles on her neck. "See, things were getting pretty ugly, especially when Tony—that's the mean manager—hired a new security guy. He was a brick wall with legs and he followed Tony everywhere, making sure the staff did what the boss said. He was even stupider than Tony, if that's possible. He's one of those guys with no neck, and shoulders like a gorilla. He had this habit of humming the theme to *Rocky* under his breath. Fancied himself as a boxer, I guess. Well, one night, Mom had a really bad argument with Tony and she left in such a hurry, she forgot her

15

handbag. When she got to her car, she realized she didn't have her keys. She dithered around for a while, because she was still so angry and didn't want to go back in and have to see Tony."

"Wow, your mom tells you everything, doesn't she?" Esmerelda cuts in.

"Not everything. I heard all this when Bev dropped round, her friend from the casino. Mom thought I was asleep, but it's pretty hard to close your eyes when there's all this loud talking and thumping of tables and swearing going on in the next room. See, Bev *hates* Tony, she says he's a WMD—"

"A what?"

"Weapon of mass destruction—he causes devastation in a wide radius wherever he goes. Well, finally, it's so cold out there in the parking lot and Mom doesn't have her coat either, so she goes back to the casino. She hurries past the slot machines on the ground floor and takes the elevator down to the basement, to Tony's office where she left her bag. But at the door she hesitates. There's a noise inside, a shuffling sound like paper being rustled. And then she hears someone humming the theme from *Rocky*."

"The security guy!"

"Yeah." Esmerelda's eyes are huge. The light through the window is shining right into them and now I can see little flecks of gold in the green. I'm not usually a gabbler—in fact, I'm used to keeping stuff to myself. But there's something about this girl. Maybe it's her eyes or maybe it's the way she's listening to me like she's about to hear the winning number to the lotto but I realize she's not the kind of girl you can disappoint. I have to find the right words.

I crack my knuckles twice. "So this Rocky guy, he gets really mad when anyone argues with Tony. But what can she do? She has to get her bag. Slowly she opens the door and

16

the first thing she sees is Rocky's fat shaved head. He has his back to her and she's so close she can see the rolls of muscle sweating like salami over his collar. She holds her breath, trying not to make any noise. She spots her handbag lying on a chair an arm's length away. Maybe, she calculates, she could grab it—quick as lightning—and go. She's looking at the bag, measuring the distance, when suddenly Rocky moves and she sees what's on the desk. She nearly chokes. There are these piles of small plastic bags filled with white powder, and stacks of one hundred dollar bills."

"Drugs!" breathes Esmerelda. Her eyes are wider than I've ever seen them. They're shining like twin stars. "My uncle is a policeman. You should hear him go on about drug dealers. Scum of the earth, he calls them."

I nod. "And lying smack in the middle of all this is a gun. So Rocky finishes scratching his butt or whatever he was doing, and brings out more money from a metal safe on the desk. Time to go, thinks Mom, bag or no bag, but just as she turns she sees something move on the floor. The Persian rug flips back and a trapdoor opens, right there near the desk. She's standing, frozen, not believing her eyes when a head looms up out of the hole in the floor. It's Tony, and he's staring right at her. She's trapped!"

"Oh, no!"

"Rocky turns to see what Tony is glaring at, and he leaps up, gun in his hand. 'That won't be necessary—yet,' says Tony to Rocky in an icy tone." *Icy* is good. I wish I could think of phrases like that in English essays. "Tony climbs up out of the hole in the floor and carefully closes the trapdoor. Then he smoothes the rug down. In one quick step he reaches out and grabs Mom's arm. His fingers dig deep. On his breath she can smell the cigar he just finished.

"'Tell me, Val, what have you seen here tonight?' Tony asks in this steely voice.

"'Um, well, nothing out of the ordinary,' Mom stammers. 'Just Rocky counting the night's earnings. You know my eyes aren't too good without my glasses.'

"'That's right. And you'll do well to keep your mouth shut, if you want to stay around to see your grandchildren,' says Tony."

"But she doesn't have any grandchildren—does she?" says Ez.

"No."

"Oh, I get it," says Esmerelda, her brow clearing.

"Anyway, so Tony lets go of her arm and she takes her handbag. 'Silly me, I forgot it,' she says.

"'Drive safely,' he whispers, real nasty, and she runs out of the room, out of there."

We sit looking at the lawn for a while. In the bright sunshine, sitting on the step and full of cake, it's hard to believe that night ever happened.

Esmerelda shivers. "Is that really true?" she says softly.

"Yeah, I wish it wasn't. But after that night, Mom never went back."

"Who would!" cries Ez with a shiver. "Pity my uncle lives so far away. Did she think of going to the police?"

"No. She didn't want to put us in any more danger. Big gangsters like Tony have a whole army of henchmen. The underworld of crime is like a giant octopus—tentacles everywhere. They strike quickly. You have to go into witness protection if the police investigate—it can take years to get evidence and you can never be sure you'll be covered. That's what Bev told Mom. She said it was better to move, and move quickly. She found us a cheap hotel and we stayed there until Mom found this place. She likes it because it's far away, on the other side of the city, plus there's a job opening at the local pub. And then there was the name of this street, Valerie. It's destiny, she thinks." I can't help rolling my eyes. Mom's decisions about destiny have had some weird consequences.

Esmerelda looks at me. Her eyes are fringed with lashes so thick it looks as if they're outlined in black.

"Are you on the run then, Jackson?"

I shift around on the step. Her voice is all husky with awe. In a way I'd like to keep the drama going, so beautiful Esmerelda Marx will keep looking at me with admiration and concern. But then I realize I'd have to keep talking about it all, which means I'd have to think about it, and actually the whole thing still makes me nervous.

"No," I say. "Mom and I are small fry. People like Tony don't bother with us. They know we'd be too scared to do anything."

Esmerelda shudders. "I'd be so freaked out if anything like that happened to me. The scariest stuff that goes on in our family is Mom threatening to ban TV if I fail a math test."

I don't tell her that that level of danger sounds like heaven to me. I don't mind math. "Well, now it's life in the slow lane, in the suburbs." I sigh like a Mafia gangster who's seen it all.

Esmerelda grins. "Yeah, but I've got a feeling you'll quicken the pace."

We talk a lot that afternoon. Esmerelda wants to know more about the casino—the dealers, the pit bosses, the entertainers, what it's like singing to an audience of gamblers on a losing streak . . . I don't know much so I tell her what I do know and then I start to make it up. I tell her about the guy who was banned because he counted the cards. It's legal, but the casino doesn't like it. He won forty million dollars in one night. Esmerelda says most people choose certain numbers to play because they're lucky, like when her Dad played a seven because she'd just had her seventh birthday. I tell her yes, many believe in luck and magic, but it's a common mistake. The only guys who can actually beat the casino are those who have systems. They count. It's actually quite interesting, I tell her, and I start to talk about the numbers—how in blackjack the aim of the game is to collect cards with a total count nearer to twenty-one than that of the dealer. Now if there are fifty-two cards, and you play with an eight deck that's four hundred and sixteen cards. I'm about to go on about how you can't possibly count all these but there's a way where you put like-numbers into sets, when she gets up and starts to fiddle with the keyboard again.

I guess she's not so interested in numbers. Hardly anybody is.

She keeps turning the conversation back to Tony and how many thugs do I think there are in the gambling world and is a security guy the same as a bouncer? I wish we could get back to the numbers, or even to discussing more normal things like the kids at school. When I ask her, she tells me a bit about Lilly, one of the girls who I noticed was plastered to her—at lunchtime the girls all seem to walk together in close huddles, as if they're guarding a secret, or a bomb. They're impossible to get at like that. She doesn't seem too keen to talk about Lilly, so she starts on about this kid they call Badman, the tough guy in our grade, but then she says how Badman reminds her of Tony and we're back onto the life of crime. Now I'm regretting ever having told her. I'm thinking: will I have to be this entertaining and streetwise forever? Will I have to invent bigger and better stories about the seething underbelly of corruption just to get her attention? It's my own fault, but by six o'clock I feel jittery and sort of empty under my skin, as if I'm wearing some kind of Superman outfit and she can only see that.

We watch the shadow of the mango tree stretching long across the grass. Suddenly she leaps up and says she has to go. I'm almost relieved. I've been dying to have another good cough. I walk her to the door. We don't say anything as we walk. It takes twenty-seven steps to get from the back door to the front. I wish it took twenty-six.

She stands there at the door.

"Oh, wait, you forgot your mother's plate," I say. I rush back the nineteen steps to the kitchen to get it. If I ever grow up to be an architect, I'm going to build houses using even measurements only.

When I hand her the plate she says, "Hey, Jackson, how come you're brainy *and* good-looking?" and she gives me this slow smile like the sun coming out.

I stare at her like an idiot. I can feel my cheeks burning. What should I say? No one's ever said anything like that to me before. What can I say?

"Well, see ya," she says, flicking her hair. I watch her run across the road. She doesn't look right and left. She doesn't look once. I guess you can do that in the suburbs. Do that on Trenches Road and you're instant roadkill.

I walk back down the hall and it seems like I'm floating. I don't even notice the number of steps. I go to look at my face in the bathroom mirror. It's still red and shocked looking. Then I go and lie down in my new bedroom. I hope Mom brings french fries back from the pub.

2. Esmerelda

"Hi, Ez, how's it going?"

"Oh, hi, Lilly." I weave the telephone cord through my fingers. It bends neatly over each knuckle. I'm not going to say anything about this afternoon. Let her sweat.

"Listen, I'm really sorry I couldn't come over. I know we said—"

"It's okay, don't worry about it. You missed out on my mom's lemon delights though."

"Oh, wow, the ones with the custard filling?"

"Yeah. You know I let the first bus go, waiting for you. And the second one was late. I thought it'd never come. I guess you found something more interesting to do." Damn, why do I say this stuff? What a pathetic whiner. Let her think you don't care, you idiot. You *don't* care, anyway; you decided that a long time ago in sixth grade.

"Well, Ez, you know we've got this assignment due on Friday? Mitch said he'd help me with the Ancient Egypt stuff. He knows a site on the Internet that's got all these cool pictures, and my printer's not working so—"

"Oh, *Mitchell*, well that explains it. Did you get your project finished?"

Lilly giggles. "Not exactly—his brother was using the computer and he said he'd kill us if we got in his way so we went up to the mall, got a drink, just hung around together. Oh, Ez, it was so great. Ez?"

"Yeah."

"What did *you* do? Is your assignment finished?"

My stomach is so tight. I want to tell her about all those amazing minutes between four o'clock and six, and I want to keep it just for myself. I've known Lilly since kindergarten. Now we're in high school and this torn feeling is still happening to me. Lilly calls herself my best friend, but often I feel like I'm just the carpet she walks on: always there, wall-to-wall, keeping her feet toasty. Well, *I* used to like Mitchell, too. I was the one who pointed him out to her—his awesome imitation of Mrs. Hatfield's voice, the cool way he faced up to Badman as if he didn't give a damn, his smile—when he turned it on, you felt like the only person in the world. But after I told her, she focused him on *her*, like the sun on a piece of glass. His face went red as fire when she spoke to him. He became her slave. I bet he would have worked on a pyramid like one of those Ancient Egyptians, hauled bricks for three hundred years in the flaming sun if she asked him to.

So what will she do with Jackson Ford?

"Ez, I've got to go now," says Lilly. "Dinner's ready. But I'll see you tomorrow and we'll talk then, okay?"

"Yeah sure, Lils. I gotta go, too. Bye."

"Ez, set the table for me, would you? Dinner's almost ready." Mom's in the kitchen and I can smell Bolognese sauce.

"What's for dinner, Mom?" calls Daniel.

I stand in the doorway of my little brother's room. He's playing PlayStation, his thumbs moving so fast they're almost blurred. Mom yells something back to him but his eyes never move from the screen.

"Oh, that's good," he calls but I know he hasn't heard. He's just died and the screen is going black, showing Game Over. Now he'll have to start the whole level again from the beginning. He starts whispering all the bad words he knows. I hear a couple even I didn't know.

"You'll beat him next time," I say, and tickle him under the arm.

"He's a poop-head STINKbug," he shouts, and thumps the floor. There are tears in his eyes. Mom worries about how much time Daniel spends getting killed on the screen. She thinks it must be bad for his self-esteem. Dad worries about how many men, animals, and monsters he murders with such a variety of weapons. He thinks Daniel may become a serial killer. I think Daniel's just found a way he can escape from the world and Mrs. Hatfield. I had her in second grade as well, and I know she is far more terrifying than any monster he'll meet on PlayStation.

"Let's go have dinner," I say to him. "You can fight better with some food inside you."

Daniel grins, and a tear squeezes out of his eye. He wipes it away quickly. "We must be having onions for dinner," he says.

"Yeah," I say, "I saw Mom sobbing her heart out in the kitchen."

When Dan and I have set the table, and Dad got home and put on a Mozart minuet (he thinks it will inspire us to have more intelligent conversations), Mom serves the spaghetti.

"Was that Lilly on the phone?" she asks as she sits down.

"Yes." The spaghetti is really good. I realize how hungry I am. Jackson ate far more cakes than I did, and they're light as air, anyway.

"So why did she leave you stranded?"

24

"Oh, she had homework and stuff."

Mom throws down her fork in exasperation. "Why couldn't she have let you know? Really, Ez, that girl just has no consideration for anyone else. What kind of a friend is that? I was worried when you didn't get off the bus."

I put down my head and eat. Mom goes on and on. I know what she means, but it's strange how when Mom badmouths Lilly, I want to defend her. I want to tell her Lilly's good points, like . . . and anyway, Lilly is my friend, she's *my* choice and we laugh together, and I don't want Mom butting in, giving me advice.

Now Mom and Dad are going on about interest rates and how they went up today by a quarter of a percent. A quarter of a percent of what? Why is everyone so worried? A percent sounds so tiny, like something the size of a mosquito or a sand fly. I don't say anything though because if I do they'll both launch into this long lecture about fixed rates and variable rates, and offsetting your home loan and negative gearing. I swear, all my life they've bored me to death about money and the need to save and considering the consequences of your purchases and all that crap that in elementary school I was the only one in the class that refused to have a bank book. "You'll have to spend a lot more time on your decimals," says our math teacher, Mr. Norton, "if you want to have a career in the bank like your parents." As if.

No, I'm going to be a singer. At least that's what I *want* to do. I might not be good enough but I'd really love to sing in a band. I read in a music magazine that the best way to learn is to listen to all different kinds of music. I'd like to know more about that jazz singer, Ella someone, who Jackson mentioned. But how am I ever going to do that? In this house it's practically impossible to listen to *any* music composed since the nineteenth century. Mom says "modern music rots the brain," wrinkling her nose as if someone's just made a bad smell right under it. She's like that mayor in New York who declared zero tolerance for crime—except Mom's got zero tolerance for rock or metal or hip hop or any other kind of popular music so I have to sneak around like a thief trying to snatch moments of listening time.

It must be so great to have a CD player in your room with headphones and all like Lilly does. You could shut yourself off from the world like a castle surrounded by a moat.

When I walked into Jackson's house this afternoon and saw the keyboard and mike and all those instruments I thought *yes*, this is where I belong. Jackson said his mom decided Valerie Avenue was her destiny. Well, meeting her might be *mine*!

I don't talk much about singing or what it feels like because my parents just get mad, and worry. "Making music is no way to make money," says Mom, and Dad always backs her up. "Musicians have tragic lives," he throws in as he goes to get a beer.

If I'm in the mood, I'll confront him with the holes in his logic. "What?" I say, frowning as if I can't quite understand, "all musicians, I mean every single one of them in the world, are doomed? Do you know them all? Or are you really just talking about two percent of them? Or one percent. Or maybe a quarter of a percent. Like, how would you know exactly what *percentage* of singers' lives end in tragedy? Maybe the percentage of sad singers is equal to that of sad bankers."

Then Dad always does his "I knew a girl once who was so rude to her father that she went to bed early and the night ended in tragedy" routine, so I usually just shut up and go to my room.

But really, how do I know what I'm going to do when I grow up, anyway? I'm only thirteen, and anything could happen. Why is everyone so obsessed with careers and the future and what may happen in a hundred years? I want to live my life now, this minute. What I love about singing is I stop thinking—I just let go, like a balloon cut loose. Right inside me, like the eye of a hurricane, is a silence I only hear when I sing. Listen, and it shows you what to do. Your breath goes in and out like the tide, flowing with the rhythm of the song, and the music rolls through in waves. If I close my eyes I can see them, dark blue and deep green and the happy notes, oh, they're like blinding sunshine on water, diamonds of light dancing on the waves.

Lilly-stings and math failures disappear when I sing. They dissolve like smoke on the water. That's an old Deep Purple song—just four notes, but a good guitarist punching them out can change the world. For a while, anyway. Badman can play it that way. You get goosebumps up your arms when he does. His father taught him all these old rock songs before he left for New Zealand. Pity Badman is such a loudmouth.

"So did you get your results back for the private school entrance exam?"

I almost choke on my spaghetti. I take a big gulp of water.

"Your mother asked you a question, Ez," says Dad.

"I thought you wouldn't mind if I finish choking first," I say. I *hate* this. Why does math exist? It's something human beings invented after all, not some random evil that the universe created, like blue-ringed octopus or stonefish that kill you within a few minutes of contact. Maybe math exams aren't as swift, but they can wound you slowly, torturously, over all your school years. If I become a singer I won't ever have to do math again.

"I got a Participation."

"Oh, *Ez*," say Mom and Dad together. They say "Ez" with a downbeat, like I've just lost both legs in a skiing accident. Sometimes I wonder if they'd rather have a dead math whiz for a daughter or a living dunce.

"Well, she got something," Daniel pipes up. "She got a Participle!"

I try to smile at Daniel. He's really good at English. He can spot a moving adverb at twenty paces.

"A Participation, Daniel," explains Dad heavily, "is just to say that Ez took the exam. Was present. Turned up. Now if she'd *tried*, she could have gotten a Credit, or a Distinction or a *High* Distinction."

"Like her father," Mom smiles at Dad.

"Like her mother," Dad smiles at Mom. Their voices sound as sickly sweet as melted chocolate.

Then they both look at me, and sigh.

I fidget with my knife.

"Don't fidget, Bridget," says Dad.

"Who's Bridget?" asks Dan.

"There are tryouts for the end-of-year concert tomorrow," I say loudly, changing the subject. "Everyone says I should get in but it's not easy, you know. Some of the seniors are really good and they only choose three groups from the whole school."

"You'll get in for sure, *Ez*," cries Daniel. He looks at Dad, frowning meaningfully. Then he turns back to me. "Are you going to sing with Lilly? Are you going to do that Britney Spears song?"

I sigh so hard that the little pool of salt that Dan spilled flies up into his nose. I wait for him to stop sneezing. "I guess so," I say. "Lilly wants me to. But you know, I'd really love to try something, like, oh, I don't know . . ."

"What, Ez?" Daniel's leaning toward me, concentrating so hard I can hear the snot from his sneeze hurtling through his nose.

I smile at him. Sometimes it's a little scary having a brother who is so much on your side he seems to care more than you do what you do with your life.

I lean toward him, and our foreheads touch. I whisper something I've only half thought about, and never said aloud. "I'd like to sing in a rock band with Badman. I'd like to go *wild*."

There, now, I've said it. I look at Daniel. He's shocked. I can see him struggling, trying to cope with the idea. He knows all about Badman, his Walls of Jericho wrestling holds in the school grounds, his practical jokes that send people to the hospital, his rattlesnake temper. But he's also heard him play.

"I think you would be great," he says loyally. "But you'll need someone there to guard you. That'll be me."

"Thanks, Dan." I start to get up. "Still, Britney Spears it'll be, I suppose. I'd better go and rehearse . . ."

"If you spent as much time on your math as you did on your singing, your grades would be excellent," says Dad.

I narrow my eyes until the world is a thin screen with black borders, like those foreign movies on TV. Everything looks better that way for a second, until I drop the silverware I've picked up.

"Oh, Ez, if you keep narrowing your eyes like that, you'll get a squint," Mom says. She turns to Dad, "Drives me crazy."

He nods. "She'll get crow's-feet."

"Crow's-feet!" Dan shouts, slapping his leg. He rushes around the table flapping his arms like wings. "Aark! Ark!" he cries in a very good impersonation of a crow. I always think that bird sounds like a swear word. Dan stops suddenly. "What are crow's-feet?" He looks at me in a worried way.

"Wrinkles around the eyes," says Dad. "And both of you can sit down and wait until your mother and I have finished our dinner."

In video clips, all the girls squint. It looks cool. Lots of singers even close their eyes during the whole song. You can drift off that way. The rest of the world disappears. Lilly can't do it for long. She's always too eager to see how the audience is reacting to her. Squinting plus singing are the only things I do better than Lilly. I put my whole heart into them.

As I watch my parents chew, I think about Lilly. I can hear Dad's teeth squeaking. It's actually quite hard being her friend. Lilly is tall and very slim—thin as a supermodel, like Kate Moss or someone. When she does stretches in dance, the teacher tells the class to copy her: "Bend like Lilly, our supple young willow!" It's nauseating. Everyone notices her. Lilly has long blonde hair and sky-blue eyes—she's like a postcard from an expensive holiday. She seems fragile, as if she might break if anything sharp happens to her. Badman never says the f-word around Lilly.

I look down at my thighs on the kitchen chair. They spread across the width of the plastic. When I press them lots of dimples appear, like the two on either side of Lilly's mouth when she smiles. Leg dimples are not considered attractive. And only witches have black hair.

Of course Lilly's voice isn't bad. I mean, she sings in tune and she hardly ever wobbles. She doesn't get stage fright, particularly if she's singing with someone else (like me). But her voice doesn't give me goosebumps. It's sort of sensible, like orthopedic shoes. Still, it's always Lilly who's picked for choir leads because she's so stunning that she lends class to any performance, just by being present. Just by turning up. Lills believes in the stars—she's a Virgo, with her bed made every morning and her room tidy—and she sticks all these Affirmations up on her mirror with Post-it Notes. The Affirmations say things like *I am beautiful* (as if she needs it) and *I can do anything*. Sometimes I think she likes hanging around with me because I'm fatter and darker than her, with hairy arms. I'm a good contrast to her fair beauty. I wonder when Jackson will notice how much more beautiful she is than me?

Finally my parents put their knives and forks together in parallel lines and we're allowed to clear the table. As we're scraping the plates Mom says, "So how's the new boy? Jackson, is it? Did he like my lemon delights?"

"Yeah, he was starving. There was nothing in their fridge, because they've just moved in."

I watch Mom's face wrinkle with horror. "Oh?" she says, "where was his mother?"

I know what's she's thinking. She's thinking any mother who doesn't work part-time in the bank and get home early on Tuesdays is neglectful and doesn't deserve to have children. Talk about zero tolerance. And now I have to tell her that Jackson's mother, the mother who had no food in the fridge, is also a *singer*. Another life ending in tragedy.

Personally, I can't wait to meet her. Jackson is so lucky. I can't imagine what it must be like to have a mother who plays the guitar and practices her vocal scales in red satin dresses instead of harping on about math exams. I bet Valerie doesn't even *care* about math exams. I bet she wouldn't ever expect her child to be a cardboard cutout of her.

I look at my mother's back as she starts washing up the dishes. Her shoulders sag a bit and she throws the frying pan down too hard in the sink so the gray greasy water splashes up into her face. She's saving for a dishwasher. Mom's finally convinced Dad that it's worth it. He argues that washing up together means that we have "quality family time." She says she'd rather do that sitting down. I feel guilty, gazing at her back. I know she's worried about money and being able to keep up the mortgage payments and that if she stops keeping her eye on the bottom line it will reach up and devour us all. But my math is not going to save this family. No matter how hard I try. I can see it plain as day. So why can't they? I'm just no good at fractions or long division or lattice multiplication. And I never will be.

I pick up the dish towel and Mom starts telling me about Doreen, this woman at the bank who has six children and a husband who just lost his job. But I keep thinking about Jackson. *He* can do lattice multiplication—can he ever! Today he finished ten problems in the time it took me to consider one. And he acted like he was enjoying it. I watched him out of the corner of my eye. There was a grin on his face, and he kept giving these tiny squirms of excitement—until his pen stopped working that is. Then I saw his face close up, and the little glow in his smile went out. It's strange, but I felt a pang, right up under my ribs, and I wanted to do something to bring the light back. So I lent him the pen. Pity it was leaky, but he didn't seem to care. Lilly would have been furious at being left with black all over her hands. Not Jackson. Sure enough, he got busy again, and the little grin came on slowly, like a campfire on a wet morning. He scribbled away until Mr. Norton said "stop" and then he sat there, quiet and self-contained, with the grin inside him. He looked to me as if he was singing a song in his head that he'd just made up.

It was then that Badman poked me in the back. "Check out the try-hard," he said, jerking his thumb in Jackson's direction.

We both looked at Jackson's double page, filled with neat columns of numbers crisscrossing each other. It was a perfect lattice, just like the stuff our neighbor put on the fence for his potato vine. I leaned out further across the aisle. On Jackson's page there were even more problems than those set on the board. He'd actually invented his own to solve! It was awesome—like watching magic happen, like the time I saw a magician open his wallet and it burst into flames.

I turned around to look at Badman's book. Only one problem done and redone and scratched out with big heavy dirty lines. Just like mine. Badman thrust out his chin. He glared across at Jackson. "Look at him, sitting there like he's got a firecracker up his butt."

On the other aisle next to Jackson there's Asim. He's the best in the class at math but I think Jackson might beat him now. Asim is like a walking calculator, but he's very quiet about being smart. He always looks puzzled, as if he's listening for something that might suddenly explain everything. His English is quite good now, but maybe his confidence is still low. It's strange, he lives only two doors down, but I've never really talked to him. Asim was watching the new boy, too.

I put the clean dinner plates back in their drawer and the

glasses in the cupboard above the sink. Jackson Ford. Jackson Browne. I like the music in his name. I like, too, the way he wears his hair a little longer than the other boys, the way it curls like a fallen question mark over his collar. I could make a list of all the things I like about Jackson Ford. He made me feel special this afternoon. With his musical living room, his streetwise life, his amazing story. When I think he was telling it all, just for me, I get a shiver inside. It's the same sort of feeling I have when I sing. But the shiver's never happened before without the music.

I remember when we were sitting on the steps, he pushed up his sleeves as if he was about to fight that security guy, Rocky. I noticed then the muscles in his arms. He's lean, but his arms are strong and hard. I wanted to accidentally-on-purpose brush my fingers against the skin, just to see what he felt like. But I took the last cake, instead.

Later, when I get into bed, I start at the beginning and go over everything that happened in the afternoon. I have this hazy, warm sort of feeling in my chest. It's like falling asleep in the sun, in the backyard.

Jackson is really brave. When I asked him more stuff about that casino boss, Tony, he just smiled at me. *Smiled*. I told him I'd be terrified if a guy like that was after me, it would obsess me completely.

"I just try not to think about it," he shrugged. "It's not so hard."

Jackson tries to handle things all by himself, I think. He's very mature. Mature *and* good-looking.

Oh, no, how can I have said that?

I sit bolt upright and throw the sheets off my legs. You should never say such things, even if you think them. You should never let a boy know you like him, right at the start.

Should you? It's like, well, jumping off a tall building and hoping this stranger'll catch you before you hit the ground. How can you know he will? It's just stupid. *He* thought I was stupid. He didn't even bother to reply. Just stared at me as if I was a complete fool.

"Brainy *and* good-looking." *Ugh!* I remember the words just coming out of my mouth, like a burp or a dream. My cheeks flame at the thought of it, as if I've stepped into a boiling bath.

I lie down again and try to close my eyes. But it doesn't work. What if he tells the other boys? How do I know he won't? What would Badman do with that? My life won't be worth living. Now I'll never get to sleep. And I'll be too tired to sing well at the concert tryouts. Oh, me and my *mouth*!

I've barely opened my eyes when Mom comes into my room. She sweeps back the curtains and the sun blares in like a trumpet.

"Ez, remember I've got an appointment with your Mr. Norton this afternoon."

"He's not *my* Mr. Norton." I watch her marching around the room like a Russian soldier, doing five things at once, as usual. She picks up my school shirt and dirty socks and yesterday's undies. Oh, why is she so . . . *her.*

"Why aren't these in the dirty clothes basket? You know I wash on Wednesdays. Really, you're so disorganized, that's your problem all over. So, as I was saying, I'm going to ask Mr. Norton about strategies your father and I can put in place to help you with your math. You know, Ez, I look at it like this: at the end of the day, it's your father's and my job to help you secure your future. That is the bottom line. We will assist you in the process of setting your goals and draw up a plan for working toward them."

"Will there be any interest involved? And if so, what percentage do you think?"

"I beg your pardon? I'm sure you'll find it all very interesting, if that's what you mean. Now, time to go and take your shower. It's nine minutes past seven."

Oh, why was I born?

Lilly is sitting with Mitch on the bench under the paperbark tree when I get to school. They're looking at color printouts, and a few kids are clustered around, peering over their shoulders. Lilly looks up and beckons me over. As I walk up to them, calling out "hi!" I spot Jackson strolling down the path toward us. I blush again, all over my body. What, is this going to happen every time I see him?

Jackson is walking faster now, toward the tree. I don't want to greet him, with everyone looking. I'm still red and sweaty.

I do a sudden dog-leg turn, miming something to Lilly about the bathroom.

But out of the corner of my eye I see Jackson raise his hand. "Hey, Esmerelda! ESMERELDA!" His voice is as loud as the school bell.

I turn back. All the kids look up at me. They glance from him to me and back again. But Lilly keeps her eyes on Jackson. I watch her take him in, from head to foot. And then she gives her neon smile.

"ES-MER-EL-DAAA!"

It's Badman, mimicking Jackson in a soppy soprano voice. He minces out from behind the tree, wiggling his stupid Badman hips. "Oh, Esmerel-*daaa!*" he calls again.

I'm paralyzed, as if lightning really has struck. My face

must be scarlet. Sweat is breaking out like a flash flood on my top lip.

I know I should just make some smart comment and ignore him. Normally, I would. I used to be queen of Badman insults. Now I should say "hi" to Jackson and smile back at him, cool as hell. But I can't. This has never happened to me before. I just can't take everyone looking. I mumble something no one can hear and start toward the bathroom. But as I turn I see Jackson's face. It's open and bewildered, with all his feelings rushing across it, clear as day. Then suddenly it closes over. He reminds me of those night flowers, the ones whose petals just fold up at dusk until you can't see the heart at all.

"Hey, where you going, *Es-mer-elda*? Can't you see the new jerk's in love?" Badman makes a kissy face, with his stupid fat lips pursed up like a chicken's butt.

I look at him and shake my head. That's all I can manage. I'm thinking about the way Jackson said "Esmerelda." No one says my full name anymore—well, only Dad when he's angry with me and then he says it short and sharp like bullets firing, and you can tell he can't wait to get it over. But Jackson, he said my name as if he relished it—he went the long way around instead of taking the short cut. He said it as if he was enjoying the view.

When I get back from the bathroom Badman and the rest of the kids are still gathered around the tree. Jackson is standing in the same position, his hands in his pockets. His face is red, too. Oh, why doesn't he just go? Maybe he's rooted to the ground with shame, like I was.

I hang back. I'd like to help but whatever I say here will only make it worse. Won't it?

"What's wrong, girlie?" says Badman to Jackson. He flicks back imaginary long hair and waggles his hips again. "Cat got your tongue, or maybe," he grins evilly around, "did you leave it with Ez?"

"Why don't you shut up?" says Jackson.

Oh, walk away! Leave it alone, Jackson!

"Why don't you?" spits Badman. His tone changes. He's not playing now and his voice is like gravel. "You're a jerk, Jack*ass*."

"You're a seven," says Jackson, real softly.

There's a strange kind of silence.

"A what?" says Badman.

Everyone is quiet, trying to think what new kind of insult this is. Deep, he must be very deep, this new guy. I remember the Italian crossbow story, and smile.

"You're dead, Badman," I call out. "He's just pointed the bone."

Badman is staring at Jackson. He's biting the inside of his cheek. "Whaddya mean?"

Jackson says nothing. He takes his hands out of his pockets and takes a slow step toward Badman. Only a few inches from Badman's face, he makes the sign of the seven with the crossbow in the middle. There's a moment of total stillness. Jackson's eyes are fixed on Badman. Jackson doesn't blink, and a weird wheezing sound comes from deep inside his chest. He looks as if he's possessed, haunted. As if he belongs to some mysterious martial arts cult. The seven samurais, maybe. His face is solemn like petrified wood. No one breathes.

The bell screams into the quiet. Badman jumps like a cricket. He starts to say something, tries to laugh, then lopes off toward the science labs. The rest of us follow. I look back to say "Good for you, Jackson" or maybe give him a high five, but Asim is there, slapping him on the back. How amazing! Asim looks so different when he smiles. I realize he doesn't do that very much. As they pass on the way to the classroom Jackson doesn't even look at me. He's too busy coughing and talking to Asim.

"What don't you like about seven?" Asim is asking. He doesn't seem to be scared of Jackson's wheezing bark or his weird cult impression. Just interested. "Is it because it is odd or a prime number or bad luck? Or is it because of the seven deadly sins?"

"Odd numbers make me anxious," says Jackson.

I'm glad Badman isn't around to hear that!

But Asim nods. "Have you heard of the idea of seventh heaven?"

Jackson shakes his head.

"Well, in the Muslim faith seventh heaven is the furthest of the concentric spheres containing the stars. It includes the dwelling place of God and the angels."

Jackson's face is all lit up. "That's really interesting. I always felt seven had a mystical sort of power. Negative, of course, being odd. Murderous, sort of. But maybe I'll have to reassess it—take this new angle into consideration."

Asim nods solemnly. "It is good to see all the evidence before you make a judgment. About anything." And he gives Jackson a long stare.

The way they walk into the classroom, you'd think they'd known each other all their lives.

"Hey, Ez, I've got the CD. Will we go to the music room and rehearse?" It's Lilly, tugging my arm at lunchtime. "Mrs. Reilly said the tryouts for the concert will be straight after lunch."

My mouth is full of peanut butter sandwich. I've been saving Mom's lemon delight cake for last. Nothing is going to stop me from savoring that. I know it will be the best moment of the day.

"Ooh, is that a lemon delight?" says Lilly, peering into my lunch box. "Could I have it? I forgot my lunch today, probably because Mitch came by and we walked to school together. I forgot *everything*." She giggles happily.

The light-as-air, custard-filled heaven is in her mouth and swallowed before I can even say, "Well, actually, I . . ."

She looks at my face. "Oops! . . . I did it again!" she sings.

That is the name of the Britney Spears song that we are about to go and perform before the entire school. It's hard to think of a more cretinous title. Lilly waves the CD in my face and jumps up.

"I'm so nervous," she says, hopping from one foot to the other. "Imagine, Mitch's never heard me sing before. Thank heavens you'll be there to keep me going. You know, Mitchell really likes you. He said we should go out in a foursome sometime. Who could you take? I know, that new boy. Jackson. He's very cute, Ez, isn't he? You know if it weren't for Mitch, well—" Her eyes go wide and impossibly blue.

"Oh, come on, let's get it over with." I throw my wrappings in the bin, stuff my lunch box in my bag and stomp off toward the hall.

I can hear her running prettily behind me. My legs feel like blocks of concrete. *Fat* concrete.

"Lilly Pierce and Ez Marx, come up to the stage now."

Mrs. Reilly peers down into the hall. We are sitting near the back with the other kids in our grade, so we have to pick our way through the crowd of crossed legs and feet. Mrs. Reilly has put her glasses on to read the program. She frowns.

"Lilly and Ez will perform a song by Britney Spears. It is called—"

"Oops! . . . I Farted Again," Badman calls out. The boys all around him break up, guffawing like hyenas. They make farting noises under their armpits.

"What's going on down there?" Mrs. Reilly's voice booms into the microphone. "Who's responsible for this noise?"

There's a sudden deathly quiet in the hall.

No one whispers or even scratches an itchy place.

Lilly and I are left standing on stage like cakes going stale.

"*You!*" Mrs. Reilly tears the silence open. She's pointing at Badman, her finger shaking with rage. I stare, fascinated, watching the way her jaw clenches, imagining her teeth locking into position behind the thin line of her mouth. It's like watching a snake—you want to run, but you're mesmerized.

"It was you, wasn't it, Bruce? *You* who made that disgusting comment!"

Badman is staring so hard at the floor, you'd think he'd fall through it.

"Stand up, young man."

He stands, clutching the neck of his guitar.

"Tell me, Bruce, do you think you can be so rude to another performer and still have your turn?" Her voice has frozen into ice, quiet and deadly. And then it cracks. "Well, that's not how Homeland High School works! Look at you, a seventh grade boy, and still behaving like a infant! Every-body, look at Bruce."

41

Three hundred pairs of eyes look at Bruce. I gaze over his head, out the window.

"I want you to apologize to your school, Bruce, for your rude and inconsiderate behavior."

Badman shifts his feet. His face has turned a dull purple.

"Do you understand the word 'apologize,' Bruce?" Mrs. Reilly speaks in slow motion, as if she's training a dog. "Maybe this is too hard for you. Can anybody be so kind as to tell Bruce what this very difficult word means? What about one of our little elementary school visitors?"

"Sorry," blurts Bruce.

"I beg your pardon, Bruce," sneers Mrs. Reilly. "We didn't hear you."

"I'm SORRY!" says Badman. His eyes are glittering, catching the sunlight from the window. He's holding them wide open so the tears won't spill. I know that trick.

Mrs. Reilly stares at him. I can see her hesitating. She really wants to stretch out the agony, see if she can totally break his back as well as his tear banks. But another teacher in the hall coughs restlessly and she pulls herself up straight.

"Well, Bruce, we don't accept your apology. Now leave the hall and go to the principal's office at once. Tell Mr. Phillips that Mrs. Reilly sent you. And leave that guitar here."

"No!" yells Bruce. "It's real expensive—it's my father's!"

"Do as I say or you will have another suspension! And you will have to apologize again to the school and to Lilly and Ez for disrupting our concert tryouts."

"Oh, Mrs. Reilly—really, it's okay," I say. "We don't mind!"

Mrs. Reilly whips around like a cobra striking. "You be quiet—*I* mind. Now, get out of my sight, Bruce Bradman."

We watch as Badman carefully leans his guitar against the wall, whispering something to the other kids sitting near it. He's probably telling them he'll stick toothpicks up their fingernails if they even breathe on it.

"OUT!" screams Mrs. Reilly.

He pats the guitar one more time and slouches through the door.

"Now, girls, quickly, get on with your song. We're running late."

Wow, what a great way to begin a performance. I glance at Lilly. She's taking a deep breath, going into fake-smile mode as if nothing has happened. Mrs. Reilly bends over the CD player. The instrumentals come on; it sounds like artificial sweetener, the kind that leaves a nasty, chemical taste on your tongue.

Lilly nudges me, beginning her first note. For a moment I'm so angry I'm scared I might blow up. My throat feels like concrete, too. How can you sing like this? I feel like a traitor—to music, to myself most of all. Badman was right: this stupid song deserves a fart in its title. But then I look at Lilly's face, and she's starting to wobble—she can't hold a tune on her own—and there are tears in her eyes and I burst out with the nerdy words.

Lilly gives me a shaky smile and as we sing I'm thinking about Badman waiting in the office. He's probably picking his nose, pretending he's not. I'm thinking what a damn shame it is that Badman is such a fool. He's the best guitarist this school's ever seen, but now he won't even be allowed to try out for the concert. There's no hope in heaven that I could sing with his band now. Even if *he* wanted me to. Which he probably wouldn't, seeing as, he says, like Bart Simpson, that girls have "cooties," and holds his nose clothes-peg style when any female walks by. Well, any female except for Lilly.

Truth is, I hate him and his crappy behavior, but I hate Mrs. Reilly and this song even more. It's weird that no matter how awful Badman is, it doesn't seem to make any difference to how I feel when I hear him play.

As we sing the last line, I realize that most of me has been absent for the entire song, sailing away into fantasy land. The rest of me is slogging away, getting the notes out right, dying quietly like I do in math.

And that's no way to make music. Is it?

3. Jackson

"Norton's given me loads of extra math homework," I hear Esmerelda groan behind me.

We're on the bus going home. It feels like a hundred and twenty degrees in here. My legs are sticking to the seat.

"Why?" asks Catrina, who's sitting next to Ez. "There's loads of kids worse than you at math. Me, for instance."

"My mother wouldn't think so," replies Ez.

"Oh," says Catrina. There's a little silence while she thinks this over. "Geez, Ez, I hope *my* mother never gets that interested in my school work." And she gives a kind of shiver that makes her knees dig into my back.

I clear my throat and turn around to Esmerelda.

"You can come over to my place if you want, and I'll help you," I say. I raise my eyebrows at Asim, who is sitting next to me, to see if this is okay with him.

He smiles, and nods. He likes Esmerelda, too. He likes the way she can mimic anybody's accent perfectly, even his, and make him laugh, and how she looks in her stretchy black gym pants.

Esmerelda groans again. "Thanks, but I have to report home first. I'm under surveillance, it feels like. Some nerdy cousin I've never met is coming over to coach me. He's some kind of math genius. Still, maybe later, if I say I'm going to study with you guys . . ."

"Why don't you come and study my firecrackers?" Badman calls to Esmerelda from across the aisle. "I got some new fireworks, too. There's one called Great Flaming Balls and it shoots fire thirteen feet high. It's the best!" He nudges Joe sitting next to him. "Come and see my *balls*, get it?" and the two of them laugh their heads off.

Ez just stares at him as if he's speaking Transylvanian.

"But fireworks are illegal, aren't they?" Asim says suddenly.

"Ooh, *cry* about it why don't you," sneers Badman.

Asim looks out the window.

Badman's a bastard. He makes that remark about crying all the time. Especially to Asim, who does cry a lot. He can't help it, after what he's been through. Badman wouldn't have lasted a minute, I think, in a real war.

Asim and I get off early, at the next stop, because we want to go to the mall. We wave to Ez and make our way to the front. When we're standing on the sidewalk, waiting to cross the road, I see Badman doing this girly wave back as he moves into my seat.

It's strange, I'm thinking, how Esmerelda acts around Badman. She couldn't like him, and she's so—well, queenly— the way she looks down her nose at him and narrows her eyes as if he's made a bad smell. But she never really lets fly with him the way I've seen her do with other boys who annoy her. It's as if she doesn't want to *totally* demolish him. There's something about him she likes, I'm thinking. Some- thing she wants.

"Have you ever wondered why girls seem to like the bad boys?" I ask Asim.

He frowns at me. "That is not my experience. Are you talking about Badman? It could not be true! Ez likes the Badman?"

"Mmm." I kick an empty can of Coke along as we walk. I'd really love one now, the sun is beating down like a hammer on my back.

"But he shows no respect to her. And he is cruel."

"Yeah."

Badman is a racist bastard. He makes fun of Asim's accent—not in a well-meaning way, like Ez—but spitefully, watching to see him break. Kids say that once, he shoved a firecracker up a cat's butt and lit it. Just to see what would happen. "Cry about it," he said when Asim protested.

And once, Asim told me, Badman walked out of school, just like that, and rang a neighbor's doorbell. The neighbor was this old guy, Mr. Wall. Everyone at school knew Mr. Wall had lost it—he was always out roaming the streets, looking for his wife who'd died twenty years ago. Kids often had to bring him back home. He was the type whose short-term memory had grown so bad he wore five shirts, one on top of the other. So when Badman rings the doorbell and Mr. Wall appears, Badman goes like this: Are you Mr. Wall?

"Yes, I think so," says the old man.

"Are there any other walls here?"

"No," says Mr. Wall, looking about in a confused way.

"Well, you'd better get out before the roof caves in! Ha ha!" And Badman shoots off, with poor old Mr. Wall running after him, into the traffic. Four cars piled up and the police came and everything.

Badman got suspended for that. And he already *had* a red card for blowing up the school garbage cans.

"But Ez has never been to the Badman house, has she?" Asim asked.

"No, I don't think so. She told me about his dad going away to New Zealand, but never about his mom or what his house was like."

"Yet she has been to *your* house," Asim reminds me, smiling.

"Yeah," and I smile back at him. "Three times. If she comes today it'll be four. Hope so, then it'll be an even number."

We buy a Coke each and some doughnuts. The ones with jelly and cream inside are delicious. We finish them by the time we reach home. I have to say that a really good bakery only five minutes walk from home is one of the better things about living on Valerie Avenue. The *best* thing, though, is eating the cakes with a friend. See, Asim lives just two doors down from Esmerelda, at number sixty-four. How lucky is he? A double whammy of luck. I told him that if he was anyone else, I'd be too mad to even speak to him. As it is, I'm just glad.

I let Asim and myself in with my key. Mom isn't home yet; she's got lunch shift at the pub three days a week, and dinner on Thursday, Friday, and Saturday nights. Lunch shift means cleaning up afterward and driving Polly home—an older waitress whose bad knees, Mom says, can't cope with public transport.

First thing, we go to the fridge and get another drink. We take apple juice and some rolls and cheese and lettuce outside and sit on the wicker chairs, looking out on the lawn. Mom bought the chairs at a sale last week, and we've covered them with some nice Indian cushions with little mirrors like cats' eyes. Plus there's an awning over the porch, which we've decorated with tie-dyed sarongs, so we have shade and atmosphere. Sometimes at night we eat out here, with candles and tall citronella flares stuck in the plant pots to keep away the mosquitoes. Mom says when she's saved a bit we can have a party for Christmas.

This is what Asim and I have been doing for two weeks now, sitting out here, watching the grass grow. When we finish eating, we kick a soccer ball, trying for a goal between the mango tree and the maple. Every day we look at the mangoes, and ask ourselves if those right at the top might be ripe. Neither of us has ever climbed a mango tree. I've got a feeling that today we might find out what it's like.

We go into the kitchen and find a big blue plastic bowl.

"You climb first," says Asim. "I'll hold the bowl."

I step up into the hollow near the base of the trunk where it splits off into three thick branches. The wood is smooth and cool under my bare feet but harder than I'd imagined. Hard as steel. Grabbing a thin shoot I lever my other foot onto a higher branch. Up close, I can see wrinkles where the branches bend. There are scars on the smooth gray skin, battle wounds. A green light wraps all around me, the sun filtered through the forest of lime leaves brushing my face.

"Can you reach the mangoes?" Asim calls up.

"Almost."

Where smaller branches have been cut off there are growths like eyes, ringed one circle inside another. I stare, mesmerized. It's like seeing into the eye of the tree, into its soul. As I look, I get the feeling some wizened creature, something wise like an owl or an ancient reptile, is holding its breath, looking out at me.

"Jackson?"

"You should come up!" I swing my other leg over and sit

for a moment in the heart of the tree. I've found a perfect seat. I could sit here forever; the silence is like a secret and I'm right inside it.

But when I stand, everything is different. My heart starts to hammer. I'm up too high. I can see over the neighbor's fence (the one who sneezes), right into her window. She's on the telephone, talking about the new driveway she's going to put in. Her voice is harsh like a red line. I hold on tight to the branch above me. Two, three, four mangoes are hanging near, but higher than my hand can reach. I go further, pulling myself up onto the next branch. Now my heart feels like it's going to jump out of my chest. My feet must be almost ten feet above the ground!

I've never been this high—well, only in the city, looking out from my window on Trenches Road, or an office block or something. But that's so different, another world, with that firm floor under your feet fooling you into thinking it's the ground. Here my toes can bend over the branch, into nothingness.

I fix my eyes on the mangoes and count them out loud, equal-spaced, in common 4/4 time. If you chant numbers long enough they turn into pure rhythm, a song. I lean against the solid branch at my back. It feels rough but strong as a man's arm. It doesn't sway with my weight. I like that. I know it can hold me and suddenly I feel incredibly safe with the hard living wood under my feet and the naturally occurring set of four swinging above me and the common time spreading through my body like warm milk.

The leaves rustle below me and I see Asim's face poking up.

"Hi! Put your foot here and then swing over to that branch," I say, pointing to my left. "You can sit there and we'll be on the same level." I finish the count at eight sets of four. Beautiful.

He's still clutching the bowl in the crook of his arm. I reach out and take it from him and he makes for the branch. When he straightens himself he breathes out in a long swoop.

"Amazing, isn't it?"

We look together out across the street. I can see the roofs of houses, all lined up neatly like dominoes. I can even see the bird crap and cracks in the tiles. Some have little attic windows with geraniums potted on the sills. The TV antennae stand loyally at attention on every roof. Suddenly I feel a pang of gladness to be here—I think of each family caring for their home, planting their gardens and painting their fences, and for some reason they seem like brave warriors, pushing ahead in the face of death and disaster. They're all making the best of things in the suburbs, being positive, as Mom would say.

"I got one!" Asim cries and holds up a fat golden mango. He reaches for a second, twisting the stem with one hand and pulling at the fruit with the other. He looks like an expert already. I hold out the bowl to him and he pops them in. Now I'm going for it, too—there is one near my head, and three just a little further along the branch. We're hauling them in like it's a sea full of fish, and the bowl is starting to overflow.

Asim takes out his pocket knife and we sit in the crook of the tree with our legs dangling down into the air as he slits the knife into a mango and licks off the juice. Then he cuts a big piece off the side and throws it to me. The flesh is a stunning yellow and I suck at it, the juice running down my chin in a river. Nothing has ever tasted so good.

The lemony leaves surround us in a canopy, and the world is green and cool. So we pretend we are hunters of old and we've just caught our food—we show our war wounds: scratches from branches and a big scar I have on my arm from years ago when I broke it.

"The possums won't like our hunting," I say.

Asim grins. "There will be plenty left for them, I think."

"Do you hear them thumping at night on your roof? They sound like a pack of soldiers doing their drill, up and down. And they pant so heavily. Mom told me it was the possums, but I didn't believe her at first."

"Sometimes we hear them. At first I was scared and ran into my father's room. I thought it was robbers. But now I just think possums and go back to sleep. You probably hear them more, with your mango tree. You supply their dinner!"

"Yeah. And then last night, they woke me up, it must have been oh, two o'clock—yes, I remember the digital clock saying 2:22 and I thought well at least if I'm awake that number is not the *worst* thing I could see. Could have been 3:33—"

"So what happened?"

"Well, the thumping was so loud, like heavy boots, and I got my flashlight and crept outside. I aimed it up onto the roof and I saw a furry animal with big dark eyes staring back at me. I guess it was stunned by the light because it just stayed there still as a statue and then, do you know what? I saw something clinging underneath. It was her baby!"

Asim was silent for a moment. Then he said, "That was a good thing to see."

"Yeah. It felt … good. But sort of sad, just the two of them. They looked like they were on the run. You know, suburbia eating up their habitat. Mom says they're not homeless, they're making themselves comfortable on our roof! I like that idea but she doesn't. Says they wake her up and she's not a good sleeper and then she has to go and make hot milk and pace and watch TV and by the time she's done all that there's only an hour before morning. No, she definitely doesn't like them." Suddenly I feel a twinge of fear, right where my heart is. "I hope she doesn't call the exterminator."

Asim tears a leaf off the branch and studies it. "Perhaps if you give them another house, they won't use your roof."

"How do you mean?"

"Well, I was thinking, we could *make* a possum house—a place just for them. We could build a little wooden house in this tree, or maybe the maple tree, it is better."

"But how would we do that? Where do we get the wood and how do we know—"

"My father has a shed where he keeps all his tools. There is everything we would need—I helped him make the bench where we have breakfast and a work table where we study. My father has much experience in these things. There is plywood left over, we have the hammer, nails, saw, even the electric drill . . ."

This is really exciting. We sit for ages in the tree, planning how we are going to build this thing. I still can't quite believe I have a friend who's happy to hang out every day, someone I can rely on. Seems I can talk to him about anything, as if we're brothers or something.

Strange, too, because Asim is Kurdish. He even has a different alphabet. The only "curd' I'd ever heard of was something Little Miss Muffet ate in that nursery rhyme.

When I told Asim about the curd thing, he laughed. That's how I knew I'd like him straightaway. And when I heard a bit about what he and his people had been through in Iraq, I admired him even more. I don't think I could ever have a sense of humor about those things. He told me the year he was born his family were driven out of their home and lost everything they owned. They had to escape to somewhere near Turkey and hide—just because they were Kurds. There was no shelter, or clean water or food for them. They were refugees.

And just before he turned one—it was a freezing November day—his mother died.

Asim doesn't remember her, but he has an album that tells her story in photos. His father made it for him, and it has a thin polished wood cover, with a gold lock and key.

When Asim first told me about what happened to him, I didn't know what to say. Only that, in a weird way, I felt like we had a lot in common: my father died when I was two. I don't really remember anything about him except a smell of fish and salt baked in the sun. It was a comfortable smell. And there was a blue T-shirt and lots of crinkles around his eyes. He had blue eyes like mine. Sometimes you don't know if you remember how a person looked because of photos you've seen. You make up a picture from there.

So I told Asim about my dad, and that I've had to move around a lot since then—"just like you," I said. How stupid did I feel as soon as I blurted that out! There's me in comfortable apartments or houses with heating and hot water and food and no Iraqi police spying outside preparing to take my family away—no having to run for my life. I felt ashamed after I'd said that. I went home and told Mom and she said she knew what I meant, but not to worry. "What you have showed Asim is empathy," she said, "and it is a good, decent human quality. It's a pity there aren't more people like that ruling the world." I asked her what empathy meant and she put down the potato peeler and took a deep breath so I quickly said, "It's okay, I'll look it up in the dictionary," because I knew one of her speeches about the government was coming on, and I just wanted to lie on my bed and think about things.

In that first week Asim and I talked about moving and meeting new people and how weird it all is, but most of all we talked about numbers. For Asim, although English was so difficult to learn, counting was the same in any language. He'd had to stay in a detention center for six months, and there were so many different languages and problems, the only way he could really communicate was with numbers. And he found he was good at it—he *had* to be, he said. He could add, multiply, entertain with math. He collected a class of kids there; they'd sit around in the dirt and he'd teach them how to add and subtract, play games with numbers. Mainly, the kids wanted to learn how to count the number of days before their release but no one ever told them when this would be. That was the hardest part, he said. Some people had been there for years. You should see him doing long multiplications in his head, or adding strings of three-digit numbers together in a few seconds. He's worked hard at it, he says, but I think he's just a natural talent. Any new school he walks into, he's a math star.

I'm not like that—I just enjoy making patterns with numbers. I like the way a math problem will always have a solution. Just one neat, tidy answer. No room for ifs and buts and maybes and what will happen? Just a single fact. That's cool. Something you can rely on. And then if you make up the problem yourself, you can make sure you get an *even* solution. Everything is in its proper place in the world. At least for a while.

Asim isn't so crazy about even numbers. He likes all kinds. Odds and evens, they all work for him. You can't have light without dark, ice cream without spinach, he figures. But he said a great thing about eight. The best I ever heard. He said eight was maybe the source of all life. It is the shape of DNA. The blueprint, the grand plan for living cells to grow. Isn't that the best?

Well, we're sitting in the tree, dreaming about the house we're going to build when suddenly a bang like gunshot cracks our ears. We both jump. Asim nearly falls off. We stand up shakily, hanging onto a branch and look out across the street. A heavyset boy with spiky hair is running down the road. Badman, with his shirt flying out behind him. He's shooting glances back as he runs, watching the smoke drifting from a brightly painted mailbox. The door has blown off, hanging crazily by one hinge, like a broken arm. We watch as an old lady comes out and wrings her hands.

Asim is trembling. Tears spill over his lids.

I reach out and touch his arm. "It's okay," I say. I don't know what to say, actually. Nothing seems right. When things like this happen I realize how different the two of us really are. On Trenches Road you got used to the sound of explosions. For us, they were harmless. Cars backfiring, kids lighting firecrackers in gutters. I made a kind of gun once by putting a firecracker inside a pen cap with a couple of pebbles on top. When I lit the firecracker, the pebble shot through eight pages of the *Herald* newspaper. I got a lot of respect for that in the neighborhood.

But for Asim, the sound of gunshot means something else.

He's wiping his cheeks. I figure he's only just realized the tears were there. "Happens when I get a fright," he murmurs. "Can't help it."

"It's okay," I say again. "Just bad old Badman." I think the only thing to do is change the subject. Get back to something more normal. So I start to talk again about the possum house. The maple tree is probably the better choice, I tell him, because I think we'll want to keep climbing the mango, and maybe the possums won't want visitors all the time. Asim nods, and takes a few deep breaths. Mom showed him how to relax his shoulders when he does this, and keep the breath inside for five seconds. I told him to hold it for four or six, if he can. Works for me, I said.

We're just starting to climb down when something catches my eye. A blue Mustang, purring slowly up the road. I love the growl of a Mustang, like a lion with its teeth bared. Don't you want the driver to just gun it, and roar? But the car creeps along, as if it's looking for something. As it passes under our tree, I read the license plate.

"Hey, Asim, check this out!"

We both watch it glide past.

"777," I shiver. "It's enough to give you the creeps."

Asim looks thoughtful. "I've seen that car before. Last week, I think. It was out front, going down Valerie Street. Slowly. Maybe there is something wrong with the engine. They are testing it out?"

"Looks in pretty good condition to me. But what a crap license plate."

Asim grins. "Think of the heavenly spheres."

When we go inside, the front door clicks and Mom is home. She trudges down the corridor with plastic bags of groceries. I quickly clear a space on the kitchen table for her to dump the stuff.

"Hi, Mom."

"Hi, Jackson honey."

She lets out her breath in a big sigh. Her face looks tired.

I always know what kind of mood Mom's in when she gets home. You just need one glance. Today she's hot and fed up and wonders what the point of her life is. She's probably had to serve paunchy businessmen who snap orders at her. Maybe the cook was rude to her. He is sometimes.

"How was your day, Mom?"

"Boring as meat without salt." Mom smiles and ruffles my hair. "Do you know that play from Shakespeare? Where the king asks each of his three daughters to describe how much they love him? Well, two of them say things like we love you more than gold, or diamonds or whatever, not giving it much thought, but the last one ponders for ages and says, 'I love you more than meat loves salt.' This is the best answer—think of a plain steak without salt, especially in those days when the meat was off half the time. But her father is a stupid vain man and he banishes her. He doesn't see the truth. Stupid question, anyway. Hi, Asim, how's it going?"

"Very well, thank you, Mrs. Ford." He is hovering in the doorway. Sometimes my mother is like a gale-force wind and you feel like a blade of grass in her path. Even when she's tired.

"Have you boys had something to eat?"

"Yes," I say.

Mom nods and flops down on a chair at the kitchen table. Her shoulders spread across the back of the chair.

"Would you like me to make you a cup of tea?" I say. "You can go and lie down for a bit."

Those nights Mom sang at the casino, she walked in the door a different way. She seemed to float, drifting around the kitchen lighting incense and humming to herself. If I was up, I'd stay a while and sit on the stool, soaking her up like a cat in the sun. We'd chat and she'd tell me the nice things people said about her voice. But the nights after Tony took over, she was like cement, her mouth set and heavy. So I'd make her hot milk with honey and tell all my best jokes. She'd try to smile but the cement got in the way.

"Thanks, Jackson. I've got some nice seafood pasta from work," Mom says as she walks up the hall to her room. "You'll stay for dinner, Asim? I've got enough for an army. You need some feeding up, sweetheart. I'm sure you've lost weight, haven't you?"

What, since yesterday? I roll my eyes at Asim, but he won't look at me.

"No, I haven't, Mrs. Ford. But thank you, I would like to stay very much."

She grins at us and hesitates there in the hall. Then she sort of lunges back and hugs Asim. "We'll have a lovely dinner," she blurts, "made of jellyfish and sea snails and puppy dogs' tails!" She makes a Frankenstein face, and disappears into her room.

"Sorry about that," I mumble.

"It's okay." Asim smiles.

Ever since Mom met Asim, she's always trying to pat his hand or hug him or make him laugh. She can't get over the fact that he's lost his mother. Mom thinks she has to fix everything up all the time, she just doesn't realize there are some things you can't fix.

Mom annoys me, often, but I worry—often—about losing her. I don't know why. I mean, she's always been there for me. Trying. But sometimes I imagine her just taking off somewhere or, oh, I don't know, disappearing. And sometimes she's there too much, like an octopus with all these arms and words and advice, like ten mothers at once. Well, at least I know Mom will never get lost at sea. That's how Dad died—he was a fisherman and his boat went down in a freak storm. Mom suffers from seasickness; she can't even go on a ferry without throwing up. Which maybe is a good thing, if you see what I mean.

"Do you mind if I use your telephone?" asks Asim. "I'd better tell Dad that I'm staying at your place for dinner."

"Sure, will he be at work?"

"Yes, he's doing Thursday nights at Franklins. He tries to get any extra shifts he can."

Asim's dad worked as an engineer in Iraq. His qualifications aren't recognized here, and the government has only given him a temporary visa. Asim doesn't know if they'll be able to stay here when the visa expires. He says his dad thinks about this all the time and the two lines between his eyebrows have grown heavier. His frown lines are actually the first thing I noticed—so dark and creased they look like someone drew them on with pen. Mom says what she can't understand is how Australia can go to war against a country, and then not help the people they were supposed to be fighting for. I don't get it either.

I listen as Asim slips into Kurdish with his dad. He looks so comfortable, standing there, his voice burbling along like a river. He must be describing something funny to his dad, because he's starting to laugh and making wide swooping gestures with his hands. Funny how people do that on the phone, forgetting that the other person can't see them.

When he hangs up he turns to me and says, "Dad thinks the possum house is a great idea. And he says do we think the possums would like some curtains, too, for privacy, and what about a little table and chairs for them to sit at while they eat their mangoes?" He grins. "Just joking. He must be getting very bored at Franklins."

I take Mom in her cup of tea and we go outside again and sit out on the porch. The shade is good here—the afternoon seems to be getting hotter instead of cooling down before night. Cicadas boom and the air seems swollen, throbbing. I'm thinking how good it will be to make something with my own hands.

"Did you build a lot of things with your dad, back in Iraq?"

Asim nods. "Yes, Dad had to build again our house when we returned from Turkey. Some friends helped, and the kids did, too—we used to have, how do you call them, working groups? I liked to bang in the nails. I got very strong! And afterwards, we'd cook up a big meal and eat it all together."

"I'd really like to learn how to use a saw and stuff. I think my dad used to do that kind of thing, when we lived up north. Mom says he was always either out sailing, hauling in bait, or tinkering around the house, fixing things."

When Mom talks about Dad she gets this faraway look, wistful, like when you smell next door's dinner wafting on the breeze.

"You boys got any homework?" Mom's voice comes crashing in.

"A bit," I call back.

We go and get our books. There's just two pages of math—fractions into decimals, problems using percentages. We both do the problems in ten minutes, timing each other. We enjoy doing them, although neither of us would admit it to anyone else. Asim has always been good at math. I haven't, and the feeling of success instead of failure is still a surprise. It's still like an unexpected gift when my answer comes out right.

We're packing up our books when I hear that low purr of the Mustang again. It's out front this time, stalking up our street. Why ours? The skin on the back of my neck prickles. 777 snakes behind my eyes . . .

Mom serves the pasta up in front of the television. The news is on. We sit in a row on the floor, cushions under our butts, bowls on the coffee table in front of us. The seafood is delicious—calamari and tender bits of fish all mixed in together. We're relishing it in silence, spoons scraping away when the prime minister comes on.

Quickly I go for the remote control but Mom snaps, "Leave it."

"You have not been listening," the prime minister is saying patiently, as if the reporter is a naughty little kid. "I'll restate it for you. Australia has a perfectly good immigration system, and people should use it. If they want to come to Australia they should make an application and proceed in an orderly way. We will not allow line jumping or any other illegality. That is the law of the land."

Mom chokes on her calamari. She's spluttering something, banging her fork on the table and I'm just glad the seafood is muffling her vocal cords.

"Bloody fool," she gets out, "how do you stand in line in the middle of a war? Or a famine? You just have to run, don't you? He thinks the world is like a sleepy little post of-fice—"after you, oh no, after *you*!" Smug little man, wouldn't know what hit him in the real world . . . Don't you agree, Asim? God, what you and your father must think of this country!"

She's shouting now. I look at Asim. He's glancing around nervously, patting the air near Mom, trying to calm her.

"No, it is okay, this is all okay, I love Australia." And he actually puts his hand on his heart.

Asim once told me that after his father, he loves math and Australia more than anything. Or Australia and math would be the right order. He thinks everything about Australia is good, even the thorns in the grass and the lethal snakes. He says there's nothing as lethal as chemical gas. Or racism. Or hate.

Mom snorts. "Oh, right. You love Australia, with our stingy selfish policies, punishing refugees, locking them up in jails? Even their kids? As if it's *their* fault they happened to be born in a country where they were hunted down and tortured!"

"Mom, shut up!"

Asim has tears in his eyes. *Cry about it*, says Badman.

"Oh, I'm sorry," cries Mom, flinging her arm around Asim. "You don't need to hear all this. I just get so riled up, with this f—"

"Mom, *don't* say it. You're just making things worse. You know Asim and his dad are on a temporary visa."

"That is right," whispers Asim. "We have three months more. We maybe need to be careful. What if the government hears bad things about us? But if we are good then maybe, maybe it comes true, and we will be Aussie citizens!"

We all smile and Mom gives Asim an extra squeeze. I turn the TV down, and I can see Mom taking a deep breath. I know she wants to protest that the walls don't have ears and in a democratic country we're *supposed* to be able to say what we like. She wants to throw her shoes at the screen, the way she did when the Pakistani children were hauled back to the detention center in the desert after they'd escaped. But she controls herself. I smile encouragingly at her. There is a small silence while we all try to think of something harmless to say.

"Well, you'll be glad to know that Polly's knees were better today and the cook was charming," she begins, making a face. "Turns out he's a Scorpio whose moon has been in Uranus for the last year—"

I snort and look at Asim.

"—making him cranky and now his moon has come out the other side or whatever it does and he's a different person." She laughs. "He even asked me out on a date, can you believe it?"

"Why don't you go, Mom?"

Now she snorts. "Let's clean up these plates. Chocolate ice cream for dessert?"

"With sprinkles on top?" I say.

Asim follows Mom out to the kitchen with his plate. I trail behind with the glasses and hear him talking quietly to her. ". . . but deep down my heart is glad when you speak like that. Good to know Aussie people feel strong this way."

We're finishing our ice cream and Mom's taking in the washing when there's a knock on the door and Ez comes flying down the hall. You can see she's been crying—her eyes are scratchy red and there are smudgy tracks on her cheeks.

"Two hours I've been doing this math, and I still don't get it!" she cries, and flops down on a kitchen chair.

"Hello," I say.

"What about the math genius?" Asim asks.

"He only stayed half an hour—had some super important conference to go to. I didn't understand a thing he said, anyway. There was this wart on his chin sprouting hairs and it was too distracting." Suddenly she throws her head into her hands and we hear a wet sob. "I am never, ever going to get any better. I'm just stupid and all my life I'll be spending useless hours pretending I'm not."

When Mom comes in with the washing basket, she takes one look at Esmerelda and tells her to calm down, girlfriend. "You've got to take a deep breath and hold it for five—"

"Six!"

"Seconds. Feel all the tension run out of you. *Then* look at your problem." She puts her washing basket down and pulls up a chair next to Esmerelda. "You know a secret? Whenever I feel like you do, I listen to Aretha Franklin. Full volume. And I sing along at the top of my lungs."

I roll my eyes. Here we go. Each time Esmerelda's come over, Mom has been home. I hardly ever get five minutes alone with her. It's this singer or that singer—"Have you heard this one, Ez, listen to the driving bass line, can you hear it? Guitar played like drums. Needs a deep, soulful tone."

Mom goes to put Aretha on the stereo. Aretha Franklin, her hero. Aretha, in my mother's opinion, is the best soul singer the world has ever seen. She was right behind Dr. King, fighting for black rights in life and music. It doesn't matter that she was singing forty years ago, she's like a classic, Mom raves, she'll be around forever.

I try to pull Asim into my room, but he wants to listen, too. Plus he's looking at Esmerelda in her black jeans as she slides out of the kitchen after my mother. We hear the first bar of "Respect" starting up. Reluctantly, I follow Asim into the living room where the stereo is booming.

Esmerelda is smiling now. She doesn't notice us come in. She's just watching Mom turn on the amp and switch on the mike.

She practically claps her hands with joy. Mom puts the

mike to Ez's mouth and straightaway Ez starts to sing—made-up words and sounds that seem to float out of her throat without her checking. I know she hasn't heard the song before, but she dives in without looking, singing away as if all the rest of her life—math, teachers, cousins, school—was just a silly pause, a glitch in the main melody.

Asim and I glance at each other; his mouth is open in amazement and he's stamping his foot in time with the rhythm. You can't help moving if you're in that room. He nods at me, and looks back at Ez and Mom, a huge wide open grin on his face.

Esmerelda is working up to the climax, layer by layer, like an artist putting on color until, now, listen to her, she's pumping her heart out with Aretha, asking for more *respect*, dammit, just come on and *give* it to her.

I have to say, Esmerelda is really something. Her voice throbs, gravelly, deep, and her notes don't have just one color, they sort of burble like water over rocks and now she's shooting upstream in a spurt of high sound that sends goosebumps springing out on my arms. Who would have thought a girl so young could sing so deep, make you shake?

Mom and Ez start the next song, "I Never Loved a Man," a slow spiritual, falling into a harmony together. Mom has that shiny look on her face, as if she's blaring out over the night sky. They've both flown to another world, far from ours.

Mom puts "Respect" on again, and turns it up louder. She calls to Asim, "Congas!" pointing to the drums standing against the wall. "Come on, try it!"

Asim shakes his head and hops from one foot to another. But then the hopping becomes stamping, and to my surprise he's suddenly over at those congas and beating them for all he's worth. He uses his palm and fingertips, with complicated little rhythms in between the main beat. He's such a surprise of a person—he must have played before and I never knew.

When the song finishes, Mom puts the track right back on, and they go again. I wander over to the piano. I hack out the melody. I know it firstly because I've heard the song probably 2,650,000,000 times and secondly because Mom insisted long ago on accompaniment. I must say, feeling the rhythm pounding through my fingers, the voices stitching the whole evening together, Asim's backbone of a beat, well, it's not a bad song. It makes you feel strong. Like nothing could possibly get you. At least while the music is playing.

At last Mom gives the stereo a rest. "That's better!" she says. "Now, Ez, why don't you tackle that math with the boys. And I'll make a soothing cup of green tea."

We go into the kitchen and Ez spreads the books out. Homework like we had, only fifty times more of it. What's the point of that? I wonder. Looking at Esmerelda's scribbles and erasings, she obviously has never gotten the hang of the very first principles. This happens a lot. It happened to me until one magical day in fifth grade. You just have to be lucky enough to meet the right person, at the right time, to help you understand the steps. Then you can climb up into the light.

"Hmm," I murmur, like a doctor making a diagnosis. I look around for Asim, but he's trickled back to the living room. He's got himself a chair to sit on, and has wrapped his legs around the big drum. He's tapping away, his eyes closed, so I leave him to it.

"Well, let's make a fresh start," I say, as if I know what I'm doing. I close the book.

"Hey, hold on, what are you doing?"

I get a new sheet of paper and some apples from the fruit bowl. I write out a problem involving just the first mathematical step and a group of granny smiths at ten cents each.

Ez stares at the fruit for a while. Then she picks up the pencil. After a minute she says, "This is too easy, Jackson! What do you think I am, a first grader?" Her voice is full of scorn, but a smile is tugging at the corner of her mouth.

I look at her answer and smile back. "That's great. If you can do that, you can do any of Norton's homework. That's the basis of it."

"So give me another one, smarty pants."

I make up two more, just like the first, with different fruit. She does them in sixty seconds flat.

"Excellent! Now try this one." I tell her to do that first step, then show her, taking my time and cracking a joke, how to do the next one that builds on it. I act really casual, as if we're discussing the weather. We do some more like that together, and then others which include further steps. We do them slowly, going through each step one at a time. The stereo volume has crept up again, and Ez is tapping the paper with her pencil. But the music doesn't seem to distract her. She's filling the page, concentrating. I tell her that soon she'll be able to do those first steps mentally, and she won't even notice. For the first time, she looks as if she believes it.

I'm really reluctant to start Norton's homework now. She's feeling confident and relaxed, and that load of two pages might be overwhelming.

"I guess I should start the real homework now, huh?" says Esmerelda.

We open the book and look at it. Her shoulders droop.

"What about this: we just do two problems together now, and then if you like I'll finish the rest but we can do them again, slowly, tomorrow afternoon, or on the weekend."

"Oh, you're an angel!" sings Esmerelda, springing up. She pretends to hold a mike, and sings some line about a bird that is really an angel sitting on her shoulder.

"Hey, that's gospel singing," says Mom coming into the kitchen. "Gospel was the root of soul—you know, that inspired kind of singing the African Americans did in church. Where they shake and holler."

"Really?" says Esmerelda. "Even Aretha?"

"Yeah, her father was a reverend. Those singers from Motown, they all learned how to sing in church. How to whip up feeling. Soul is all about feeling—putting your *soul* into the music. And you've got that, girl."

Esmerelda smiles like the sun has just come out.

"Thanks, Mom, can we get back to this homework now?" I say. I stab the paper so hard with the pencil that the lead breaks. Why does she *always* have to butt in?

"Sure, sure, don't mind me."

We finish the first two problems and Ez wants to do another. She's excited, I can tell by the way she's breathing. I know she's flying now and suddenly the mom-blues vanish and a tide of happiness rushes over me. Ez just needed someone to sit with her and help her not be afraid. I'm so glad it was me!

Mom's playing CDs in the living room. Tina Turner, Patti Smith. Esmerelda finishes the third, and we check it together. Then I take over. I can hear Asim pattering away on the congas. Esmerelda drifts toward the music.

I've nearly finished when Wilson Pickett comes on with "Mustang Sally." You might not know it—it's a track from the sixties that Mom plays at least once a day. It's a real funky rhythm and blues, with a bite to it. I grin to myself—Esmerelda will probably like it.

I'm humming along to this guy singing about his girlfriend and the Mustang he gave her, when I remember the blue Mustang we saw this afternoon.

If only I hadn't said the next thing, this whole night would have been the best of my life. Everyone was happy—me because Ez said I was an angel, Asim because he was playing his heart out on the congas, Mom because she'd shared Aretha with someone, and then, well, all of us were happy, I think, just because we were here together making noise against the dark. But then I have to go and say this dumb thing.

"Hey, Mom," I call, "we *saw* a Mustang today, and it had such a creepy license plate. Can you guess what it was?"

Mom appears in the kitchen. She isn't smiling. Her face is pale. "Where? Where did you see it?"

"On this street, it was just cruising along."

"What was the license plate?" She snaps out the question like a police interrogator.

"777," I say, trying to laugh. "Like a horror movie!"

I wanted her to laugh, too, and say "how very odd," or make one of her dumb jokes about my obsession.

But she just gets paler. She's standing under the kitchen light bulb and I can see the purplish shadows above her cheek bones.

"What were the letters?"

"I don't know, I got all caught up with the numbers, you know how it is."

Asim is staring at Mom. "What?" he says quietly. "What is it?"

Asim is wired like me. He knows at a glance when a mood changes.

Mom laughs. She ruffles his hair. "Oh, nothing, I'm getting as bad as Jackson here. The evil seven!" and she does a fake shiver that's supposed to be funny. No one laughs.

Esmerelda bursts into the kitchen humming "Mustang Sally."

"Oh, no!" she cries, looking at the oven clock. "It's 9:17. Mom'll kill me!"

I gather up her books. "Not if she sees you've done all your homework."

Esmerelda grins. And then, simple as anything, she takes my hand and squeezes it. She rubs her thumb across my palm.

"Thanks for everything," she says, but she's looking at Mom.

"I'd better be going, too," says Asim.

"All right, well, I'll walk you," says Mom.

We all stare at her. "But it's only across the road," I say.

She laughs her new, strange laugh. "You can never be too sure what's lurking around the corner!"

The phone rings, crashing through the quiet. Mom doesn't reach for it even though she's right there.

"Should I get it?" I say.

"No, no!" Mom says quickly.

She picks up the receiver. I see her draw in her breath. But she says nothing. Slowly she puts it down.

"No one there," she says. "Must have been a wrong number."

As we all walk out the door I see Asim studying her, frowning. It's he who gently takes her arm, crossing the road.

I guess when you've experienced so much danger, as he has, you see it everywhere, even where it doesn't exist—in the suburbs.

71

4. Esmerelda

It's Saturday morning. Sunlight seeps through the curtains like lemon tea.

My heart sinks. Even as I blink awake, lemon deepens into gold and little stars sail across the room to make a constellation on my comforter.

The weather is never on my side.

I know the whole world, or at least my part of the world, must be waking up, going, "Oh, great, it's going to be sunny for the weekend, what luck!" Sunlight is supposed to make you cheerful. Personally, if I could order the weather, I'd choose cloudy, thank you, or even better, stormy, with gale warnings. Today, at least. Then I could say to Lilly and Mitch and Jackson, "Isn't it a bummer how it always rains on weekends? Pity, the beach is out of the question now. Why don't we go to the movies?"

Don't get me wrong, I love the beach and big buffeting waves and body surfing. I always have. I just hate wearing practically nothing in front of other people, especially when one of those people is Lilly.

The bus to Pelican Beach is on time, too, and doesn't break down or smash into any random runaway four-wheel drives.

I arrive safely at the north end, on time, to meet my doom. As I stroll up to the surf club in my careful, carefree manner, I see Lilly and Mitch holding hands.

No sign of Jackson.

Lilly beams at me with her thousand-watt smile. She's still wearing it from a moment ago when she was gazing at Mitch. She's not wearing much else, either, just her gold suede bikini that matches her hair. I bet she takes boys' breath away. She's certainly stolen mine. I look down at the jeans and T-shirt that cover my bathing suit. How did she have the guts to leave her house that way?

"Hi, Ez, isn't Jackson with you?" She's looking past me, the smile dropping like a brick from a skyscraper.

"Hi, Lills, hi, Mitch." I shove my beach bag onto the other shoulder. "No. I thought he would be on the bus, actually. Must be running late. Slept in maybe."

We stand around in Lilly's shadow, watching the seagulls. A really bold one dives for a sandwich crust right near Mitch's foot. He lunges out, pretending to kick it. We laugh as the seagull yells at him, outraged. The sun is killing. I can feel sweat sliming down my legs, gluing the jeans to my skin. I wish Jackson would come.

I spot him first, coming from the north end. He must have missed the early bus. He's wearing faded orange board shorts and a black T-shirt. He's taking his time walking toward us, looking over his shoulder at the beach. Even from here I can see him frowning. His walk has that distracted feel, as if he's not in his body but far away, lost to the scene he's watching. I've never seen him out of school uniform, out in the world. He makes me feel shy all over again. Practically paralyzed.

As he turns and waves, he looks straight at me. In the dazzle of sunlight his eyes are electric blue. He's like a sudden lick of guitar, shocking. There's a smear of vegemite at the corner of his mouth. He smiles at me, and my heart flips.

"Hey, Jackson, glad you could make it," says Lilly before I can say a word.

I'm having trouble swallowing, what with my heart in my throat.

"Yeah, well, sorry I'm late," mutters Jackson, looking hard at the seagulls. "Asim dropped over earlier and it was sort of hard to leave, you know."

There's a fidgety silence. I let my bag slip onto the ground between my feet.

Last Tuesday, when we arranged all this date-at-the-beach business, Jackson asked me if Asim could come. So I asked Lilly, whose idea this was in the first place, but she said no, definitely not. I told her that Asim happens to be Jackson's best friend (you have to point these things out to Lilly because unless she's directly involved she doesn't notice other people) but she just said, "What has that got to do with me?"

I explained that Jackson would probably enjoy the day more if his friend Asim was there.

"But you'll be there, Ez, isn't that the whole point? It's supposed to be a foursome, a real date. That's what I planned—a romantic *date*."

"Don't worry, Jackson," says Lilly now. Her smile is back on, the pink gloss on her lips catching the sunlight. "We've only been standing in the boiling sun for half an hour waiting for you."

Jackson starts to smile but his mouth wanders off like a dead-end street. He looks down at his feet.

Lilly gives a little laugh and suddenly reaches out to grab his hands. She holds them both in hers and gazes into his eyes. She's giving him that special Lilly look, the kind that burns.

I glance at Mitch. His face is heating up, his lips thin.

"It's okay, Jackson," Lilly purrs. She wipes the vegemite tenderly from the corner of his mouth with her finger. His head jerks back as if struck.

"Did you bring any CDs?" she goes on in a low voice. "I brought my stereo."

"*I* brought CDs," says Mitch quickly, glaring at Jackson. He steps forward, standing in the space between Lilly and Jackson. He looks like one of those Bible-thumping guys trying to get his foot in the door.

Lilly turns to smile at Mitch, but her hand lingers on Jackson's arm.

Jackson is staring at Lilly. He can't take his eyes off her. The arm she touched is still floating in midair the way she left it. He doesn't even look at me. Maybe it's just as well. If he doesn't look at me all day he won't see the way my stomach rolls over my bikini bottom when I sit down.

We find a space on the sand and spread out our towels. The beach is so crowded it looks like vanilla ice cream. Or maybe M&M's. Oh, why am I so hungry already? I try to hold in my tummy. You can't breathe properly if you do this. Soon I see stars behind my eyes. I think I'll faint.

I look at Lilly. She's lying back, leaning on one elbow. She's a honey brown all over. Her stomach dips into a flat warm pancake between the rise of her hips. There is a hardly there gold chain glittering around her waist.

She lies on the sand looking like a present at a birthday party.

"Nice tan," breathes Mitch. I bet he wants to unwrap her.

I peer at her stomach from under my hair. It's real. The tan. She must have been working on it out in the backyard. Last year we both experimented with the fake tan in the bottle business and our legs went this outrageous shade of orange. Plus I found out Lilly was on some kind of diet, only eating carrots, which can turn you very orange and dangerously ill, too, if you persist. (I hid her carrots at lunch time and made her eat my Nutella sandwich.) What I want to know is, if the experts are so on about the sun being bad for you, why don't they come up with a real-looking fake tan? Maybe I'll work on that when I grow up, as well as my singing.

It's so hot, we're cooking here in the sun. I'm sweating like crazy. The waves are booming out there, bursting and washing onto the shore. I can't imagine why the boys don't just say *let's go, last one in is a festering dog dropping* or something. But Lilly is raving on—about some new dress her mother bought her this morning and the kids she saw at the mall.

The boys go on looking at her and sweating into the sand. I just don't get it—boys never sit still, even in class. They get detention for not sitting still and here they are now, lying around like garden gnomes while the great goddess Lilly speaks.

Well, I can't stand it anymore. "Who's going in?" I say, looking at Jackson.

He hesitates, glancing back at Lilly.

"Not yet," says Lilly. She's frowning, annoyed at being interrupted. "I like to get totally fried before I do." And she strokes her smooth, silky stomach. "I want to get so hot, you could fry an egg right here," and she points to her perfect navel. Everyone has to look of course. Mitch is staring, then he has to rearrange his board shorts.

76

She smiles her special smile at Jackson. He smiles back. Oh, God almighty, she's got him, too. It's just not fair— what's she going to do with the two of them?

"Well, I'm going in," I say and stomp off. I don't look back. I'm not going to think even for a nanosecond about whether my bottom looks like a blob of shuddering custard as I run. Screw them.

I'm halfway down the beach when Jackson catches up with me.

"You've still got your sunglasses on your head," he grins.

I feel the top of my head. My face gets even hotter. Oh, I hate this dating business. It makes you do such stupid things. Why can't we just hang out like normal people?

"I'll take them back for you," he says, and sprints off.

I keep going. I can't wait for the cool silence under the waves.

When I was little, I was amazed by the way the world changes as you dive underwater. At first, the quiet is like dropping off a cliff. Sharp. Voices disappear as suddenly as a door closing. It used to scare me. Now I look for it. My mind goes as clean and empty as the silence. I keep my eyes open underwater and look at things. Tiny fish flit past my fingers, weeds grow like lettuce, open fields stretch to New Zealand. I let it fill my mind. It's a bit like singing. You only hear the notes, nothing else.

Jackson reaches me just as I come up. We're so near, my chin almost grazes his chest on the way. I move back quickly.

"Oh, you're beautiful with your hair wet," he says in a rush. He reaches out and touches the hair lying plastered over my neck, across my shoulders. "You're all outlined in black—like a painting! You look even more like *you*, if you know what I mean!"

I'm nervous and I don't know what the hell he's talking about. But I've never felt such a stab of pure happiness as right now. I give a snort of laughter and splash him.

He leaps back, gasping. He's only in up to his waist. Spray makes tiny pearls on his chest. He hasn't been right under yet.

"Dive in," I tell him. "It's so good." This jittery excitement makes me want to leap around, be an idiot. I dive under another wave, and feel the glide of sea on my skin. The water parts for me and I hold my breath, swimming deep as a fish, so deep my stomach almost scrapes the sand. When I pop up, I'm far away, two sets of waves ahead.

"Hey there, Jackson!" I shout. I can see him, still in the same spot. He's hugging his arms. The waves jolt him, but he's standing his ground. His toes must be digging into the sand. I start to make my way back.

"Why don't you come out further?" I call. "We'll go out the back and catch some waves."

I'm only a wave away now. He looks hesitant. He's peering back at the beach. Oh, it's not fair, how does Lilly's power stretch this far?

Then it dawns on me.

"Can't you swim?"

He makes a rueful face, his lips twisting to one side. "Yeah, not that well. I'm okay but not great. I don't know how to catch waves."

I thread my way back to him. I'm thinking about all the different places he's lived. The city apartments, the desert, he's even flown over the Atlantic. But I've never heard him talk about the beach.

He laughs. It's an uneasy laugh. "I was late this morning because Mom was going off at me. 'You're not a strong swimmer, Jackson. In fact, you're oceanically challenged. Who's supervising? What if there's a rip, a hurricane, a tidal wave? I won't be there to save you! Can't I come, too?'"

He does this hysterical croak at the end, and we crack up. He's caught her worried expression perfectly. "*You're all I've got, Jackson!*"

I look at him and think again how different he is. Since kindergarten we've all pretended we're so tough we don't even hear what our parents say. Badman says "What's eating you? Wake up on the wrong side of your mother?" as his regular insult.

I suggest we head for the next set of waves where we can still stand, and watch for a bit. We look at each small wave as it swells, rises into a peak (or a *crisis*, as his mother would say), breaking into foam. I teach him to look for the moment just before the break—that's the best time to leap onto the wave—no use when it's already broken. I catch a couple to show him how to keep your head down, one arm out straight, the other paddling for speed.

After a while we try a wave together. He stays on and almost reaches the shore with me. He's grinning all over his face.

"Look how far we've come!" he shouts, shading his eyes like a sea captain.

"You're a natural!" I say, and cuff him on the shoulder.

He grabs me and lifts me clean out of the water with both hands. We're staring face to face and his teeth are so white and his mouth so wide. I don't think he knows what to do with me then so I jump out of his arms and leap back into the water. He follows me into the next set of waves.

"You're a good teacher," he says. He's so pleased with himself he can't stop smiling.

"Well, you just need someone to show you the first steps."

We laugh together. The surf is behaving perfectly. Maybe for once the weather is on my side.

Isn't it strange the different things people are afraid of? For me it's fractions and decimal equivalents, Lilly in a bikini, *me* in a bikini—so much scarier than a six-foot wave.

We go out farther. I peek at his face as a bigger wave looms above.

"Dive under now!" I yell. I find his hand in the water and we pull each other through the waves.

Now we're catching loads of them. We're flying, dodging people like bullets.

"This is faster than public transport," he jokes. "Miss one, there's another right behind it!"

I bump into a man built like a canoe. I stop, winded for a moment, and watch Jackson shoot past, arm pointing straight as an arrow, his feet kicking madly. He really is a natural.

While I wait for him, I float on my back. It's so lovely, letting your body go with the swell. I feel as boneless as a jellyfish, a piece of seaweed. My heart slows down. But my ears are beginning to ache from the cold water.

"Think I'll get out now," I tell him when he comes back.

His face falls.

"You don't have to, though. Keep going if you want, you're doing great!"

"I just have to catch one more wave. That'll make a set of four." He shrugs, laughing at himself. "It's one of my challenges—I have to do things in sets, and finish on an even number."

"Okay," I smile at him. "Whatever gets you through the night."

"That's a line from a song, isn't it? An old blues number."

"Yeah. Have you ever noticed how truly great lyrics say everything about life in just a few words?"

We smile at each other.

I decide not to tell him about Badman's favorite line: "Eat crap and die." It's from some heavy metal band, Knife Edge, or something. Sad, really. But on a bad day, I know exactly what he means.

The sand burns my feet as I pick my way through the towels and umbrellas. I find poor old Mitch still sweltering on the sand. And his shoulders are pretty red.

"The surf is awesome," I say. Energy is tumbling through me. I feel bold, electrified by the waves. "Come on, Mitch, I'll go in with you again if you want."

Mitch sits up, his eyebrows going *yes*!

"Oh, no, I'm just about ready," Lilly says. She turns to Mitch. "You want to come in with me, don't you?" And she starts playing with his hand, stroking his fingers for a second before letting them drop onto her leg.

We buy fish and french fries for lunch. I'm starving, and the french fries are just about perfect. Delicious! I like them best when they're crispy like this. I hate those cushiony fat ones, with no crunch. Tasteless. Especially when they're gray and mushy at the ends. "Hate is a very strong word," my mother always says, frowning. Well, I hate a lot of things, with a passion. It's okay to say you *love* things though, isn't it? Then you're being positive and polite, and everyone approves.

Jackson seems to *love* the crunch factor. I watch him carefully peel off all the golden fry and leave the naked fish in the box. Slowly, he devours the strips of crackling batter.

"Aren't you going to eat the fish?" Lilly asks him, peering over his shoulder.

"No, do you want it?" he says.

"I've eaten mine." Lilly picks up a piece of Jackson's batter and examines it. She studies it like a food scientist. "This stuff is lethal for me—just total fat. I haven't eaten calories like that for ages. Doesn't it always just go straight to your hips, Ez?" and she looks with sympathy at my midriff.

My mouth is full of french fries so I don't say anything for a moment. I just go on chewing, hoping the moment will disappear. I hold my breath, trying to suck in my stomach seeing as everyone seems to be so busy examining it right now. Unfortunately, the mushed fry decides to go down with the gulp of air and I start spluttering and coughing like a blocked drain. I sound just like Jackson on a bad day. I think of Valerie telling me about Mama Cass, that folk singer who died from choking on a ham sandwich. But at least the old Mama had a few hit records before she kicked the bucket.

Jackson jumps up and starts thumping me on the back. Mashed potato shoots out of my mouth. Relief floods me—maybe I can still have a hit record. I look down at my knees covered in white goobly spray.

"Ooh, gross," says Lilly, wrinkling her nose.

Mitch laughs till he just about wets himself. Jackson is still thumping away, although the thumps are turning into concerned pats, making neat circular patterns on my back. I smile at him. He's doing them in sets of four.

When we're about to go home, Jackson asks me if I want to come back to his place.

"Hey, can we come, too?" asks Lilly, giggling at him. "Ez tells me how great your house is."

"Oh, no, it's not that great," I say, right away. I'm shaking out my towel and catch Jackson's expression over the top of it. Oh, God almighty, what have I said? "No, what I mean is, oh sorry, well . . ." I stop. It's useless, blabbing on. I fold the towel over and over, smoothing it down before I stuff it in my bag. How can I make it better?

Jackson just shrugs. He doesn't look at Lilly or me. "Yeah, whatever," he says.

We walk along the asphalt path, past the surf club. The sun glints like a welder's hammer, sparkling on metal bits in the road. I find my sunglasses. Sometimes the sun is just too much, making your feelings heavier, louder, booming away, blinding you. There's no shadow, no shades of meaning, nowhere to hide.

I didn't *mean* it that way.

All the way home in the bus I'm fuming. I want to scream like the dying lady in *La Traviata*. I could punch myself in the mouth. Damn Lilly. It's just—I can't bear the thought of sharing Valerie with her. She won't see how special Valerie is. She'll just spoil it somehow, dull it. Make it hers. I consider trying to tell Jackson this, that I wasn't badmouthing his house—oh, but some things are just too hard to say.

I sneak a glance at him. He's quiet, looking out the window. I can only see his profile. The long straight line of his nose, no little bump of indecision. He can play dead, like a statue. Scares me sometimes, the way he closes up. Mostly, he's so open, tumbling over himself to tell you about his past, his ideas, his number thing; but if you hurt him somehow, or he disapproves of you, you won't find him anywhere. He disappears inside himself like those little soldier crabs that burrow into the sand at the bay behind Pelican Beach. No matter how hard you dig or how loud you call, you won't find out what he's thinking.

We troop through the front door in single file after Jackson, and he goes to the fridge to get drinks. He tells us to throw our things down in the hall. We stand around in the kitchen, looking at him pouring lemonade. It's stifling inside—the windows and the back door are closed as if no one's been home all day. But I saw Valerie's car outside.

"Phew, it's like an oven in here," says Lilly, wiping her face.

I lean over the kitchen table to open the windows.

"Open the sliding door, too, will you, Ez?" says Jackson. "And you can turn on that fan in the living room."

That's better. I like it when he singles me out, acts as if I'm one of the family. He must have forgiven me.

As I come back into the kitchen, Valerie is wandering in from her bedroom. She looks dazed, as if she's just woken up.

"I was just reading," she murmurs. "What's the time?"

There's a crease along her cheek where she must have fallen asleep on her book.

Jackson hands her a glass of lemonade. "Five o'clock."

"Heavens!" she says, her eyes widening. "And you've been at the beach the whole day?" She grabs his shoulders. "You're okay?"

Jackson wriggles out of her hold, turning his back on her. "Yeah, yeah," he mutters. "Didn't you go to work?"

"Yes, but I left early. Told them I was sick. I am, actually. Exhausted." She smiles around the room. "Hi, Esmerelda, how are you doing?"

Jackson introduces Lilly and Mitch and goes into the living room. I smile at Valerie and together we watch Lilly as she follows, swaying across the cork floor, her hips pausing for just a beat at the left and right. A sarong, flecked with golden thread to match her bikini swings gracefully over her perfect bottom. Valerie grins back at me and ruffles my hair. I know it's stiff with salt.

"Oooh, the beach," says Valerie and leans down to bury her nose in the top of my head. "I love that smell. Sand squeaking under your toes, skin toasty, white salt tracks drying on your legs—"

"Fish and french fries—"

"Sunsets falling into the water, salty kisses." Valerie stops and wrinkles her nose. "Sorry, I got carried away. Was it lovely at the beach? How did Jackson do? We haven't lived near the beach you know since his dad . . ."

"It was a great day," I tell her quickly. "Jackson caught some waves—he was really fine."

"Jackson did?" Valerie's smile opens up, disappearing her eyes. She reminds me of Jackson after he'd ridden his first wave.

"Yeah," I feel my own grin widen with pride. I can tell how happy she is because her face transforms for a second, and she doesn't look tired anymore.

"I'm so glad he has you as a friend," she says softly. "He's very lucky."

We beam at each other and I'm about to say to Valerie

that she should go to the beach more often, in fact why doesn't she come with us next time, when Jackson calls from the living room.

"Esmerelda? What are you doing?"

"He sounds a bit desperate," laughs Valerie. "Go on, honey. I might go back and lie down. Don't know why I'm so tired."

In the living room Jackson and Mitch are sitting on either end of the sofa, not saying anything. Jackson is tapping out a nervous rhythm on his knee. I can hear him clearing his throat. I wonder if he's getting ready for one of his coughs. Lilly is drifting around the room, picking up things and putting them down. She yawns and looks up at me.

"Jackson's mom is a singer, you know," I tell her. "Did you see the mike and amp? They've got all sorts of instruments here." I start to babble, I don't know why. Now that she's here, I somehow want to impress her, make her see what an incredible world she's walked into.

Lilly looks around and shrugs. She's holding a photo of Valerie wearing a baseball cap with her hair all tucked up inside it, and a man's shirt. She stares at it blankly for a moment, and puts it down. It's a funny thing but Lilly seems to have absolutely no curiosity. Why is your mother dressed as a man? she could ask Jackson. Isn't that the Empire State building in the background? Did you take the photo? What's America like? But Lilly just moves on. I think of the green caterpillars on Mom's gardenia bush, the way they just munch and fill and move on to the next leaf, without ever a backward glance.

I show Lilly the amp and mike in case she's missed them, and the keyboard and guitar.

"Mmm," she says, picking up the guitar. "My cousin's got

an electric bass, brand new. It cost one thousand three hundred and ninety-nine dollars. And he got a new amp, too, really loud, excellent quality. It's a Fallen Angel, you know? With built-in reverb and boost option. Top of the range. But he's a professional, so I guess . . ."

She lies the guitar down on the sofa next to Mitch and touches his knee. "You haven't met my cousin Jason yet, have you, Mitch? He's away a lot, touring. You should see his place, it's so cool, he's got this stereo system that cost five thousand dollars, it'd blow your head off."

We sit for a while, staring at the air, and then Valerie wanders in.

"I suppose you're all hungry after a day at the beach," she says, looking around the room. "Jackson? Have you asked your friends if they want something to eat?"

Mitch looks up at her hopefully.

"Oh, don't worry, Mrs. Ford," says Lilly, "we pigged out at the beach." She pats her stomach. "I've eaten enough for two weeks!"

Valerie frowns. "Don't think I've got anything very interesting in the fridge, actually." She closes her eyes for a moment, and I notice the dark smudges under her eyes. It could be smeared mascara, but it looks more like weariness to me. When she opens her eyes I notice they are veiny and red. My mother looks like that when she hasn't slept.

"But you boys ought to eat something . . ." Valerie says, looking at Mitch.

"I'll go to the store and get a few pastries, okay?" I say. "It's on me, I've got money."

Mitch's eyes dance.

Valerie starts to say no, then changes her mind. Energy just seems to drain out of her. "Thanks, love, that'd be great."

"I'll come with you," Jackson turns to me, starting to get up.

"You've got guests, honey," says Valerie. "Ez won't be long."

I charge off up the street. I'm glad to be alone for a bit. There's so much to walk off, so much to think about. The hill climbs steeply and the sun is blaring full in my face. My T-shirt is sticking to my back as I pass Badman's house.

Ivy grows wild over his fence, jungle green and bushy, curling out toward the sidewalk like a forest. My mother always sniffs at it, shaking her head. "Needs a good trim. So neglected-looking, that house. Such a shame." Mom says the ivy problem is because Badman's father has gone off to New Zealand and no one has time to look after things anymore. I like the ivy. It's a spot of wilderness in suburbia, a green pause in the rush of things.

I slow my pace, dawdling under the ivy shade. I lean my back against the wall for a moment and in the quiet a tumble of notes float out toward me. Badman must be tuning up. He licks through an E-minor scale. Sounds like water flowing up a set of steps. A streak of excitement shivers through me. Then three chords crash through the air and I feel as if my body might split open. "Smoke on the Water." That chord progression goes straight to your heart, bypassing your brain. I close my eyes and my legs start to thump in time against the wall. How many watts does *his* amp have, I wonder.

I sink back into the ivy, curling the darkness around me. Badman veers off the main track of the song and slides into a moody guitar riff that lifts the hair off the back of my neck. The rhythm is quickening, climbing higher. I can imagine his fingers flying on the neck of his guitar. The high notes are a scream, stinging like a cut in lemon juice, scraping the skin off the back of your throat. I'm singing for him, about fire burning in the sky, making the gravel rust in my throat. In the dark under my lids I weave my voice into his notes, becoming the treble to his rhythm. Another riff morphs into Led Zeppelin's "Whole Lotta Love," climbing into "Stairway to Heaven." His playing comes at you like wave sets and you keep diving under, into the trance of his music. He must be going under, too, because I hear his voice let loose, roaring with the guitar. His pitch is terrible, raw and wild and out of key, but somehow it swells the fever just right as he starts to punch the power chords of a heavy metal song, "Tainted Love." My heart is the pulse of his song and suddenly I feel a longing that's almost unbearable. I want to sing out loud, wrap myself in that music, be inside it, not outside, looking in . . .

"Bruce, will you turn that thing down! Damn noise, can't hear myself think!"

There's sudden quiet, so thick you could slice through it with a knife. A door slams, final as a pistol shot.

I walk on quickly, starting to run.

Jackson cuts the apple Danish and cherry strudels in halves, and arranges them on a plate. We bring them into the living room and sit around munching. No one seems to have much to say. I can hear Mitch's jaws moving, and Jackson's swallow. But mostly, like a soundtrack to a movie in my head, I can hear the sting of Badman's guitar.

"Anyone want a cup of tea?" calls Valerie from the kitchen.

Lilly and I do, and when Valerie brings them in, perching on the arm of Jackson's chair with her mug, I ask her if we can hear some of her soul music. "Aretha Franklin or Wilson Pickett or that Otis guy, whoever," I say.

Lilly looks at me strangely.

"What about Bo Diddley, ever heard of him?" Valerie asks me. "He played his guitar like it was drums. Had a back beat he called *sanctified*. It was, I guess—he got it from the black churches of America. You know, gospel music. There were drums, saxes, singing—in church people went into trances, got happy the way you see people do on the dance floor or at a concert—"

Jackson rolls his eyes. "We don't need a lecture, Mom. Why don't you go back and lie down. You look really tired." He's squirming there on the sofa.

Valerie grins at him. "I seem to have woken up."

"And that black gospel music really started in Africa, didn't it?" I put in, ignoring Jackson. I just wanted to dive back into music again—talk it, hear it.

"Yes," nods Valerie. "Way back, Africans were brought to America to work as slaves—they had no rights, no possessions, but boy, did they bring their music! No one could take that away from them. And drumming in Africa has a whole other dimension, you know—it's a way of communicating and helping people get close to their gods. There are these sacred drums, called *bat'a*—"

"Oh, Mom not the *bat'a* thing again, no one wants to know—"

"*I* do," I snap.

"Well, in Africa these *bat'a* drums act like signals to the gods to come on down and get with the people. The drummers can shift their rhythms to guide a dancer into a particular trance. It's amazing. And you know that hypnotic beat in rock music? Same kind of thing. Back in the sixties a lot of white people in America were scared of it. Said rock music was voodoo—you know, African magic, and it was hypnotizing their children on the dance floor. Ha! They wouldn't let black music be played on radio stations, said it was dangerous—"

"Did you know we sang 'Oops! . . . I Did It Again' for the concert tryouts?" Lilly says to Valerie. "We really hope we get in, they haven't told us yet. I think it's tomorrow we hear. Do you know the song? It's by Britney Spears?"

Valerie just opens her eyes very wide.

Lilly lets out a squeal. "Oh, Ez, why don't we show Mrs. Ford! We could do the song right here!"

And show off for the boys, is what she means. I couldn't think of anything I'd rather do less.

"We don't have the backup song here," I say.

"Oh, I could probably pick out the notes for you," says Valerie. "Hum it and we'll see."

Lilly stares at me. *Go on*, her eyes say.

I press my lips together hard. There's an agonizing silence.

Then Lilly starts to hum, faint as the fly buzzing behind the sliding glass door. She's turning red, her mouth quivering. I can't bear it any longer. I pick it up and we hum the first few phrases.

"Okay," says Valerie. "Got it." She plays it through on the keyboard, adding rhythmic chords and flourishes. She could make the Lord's Prayer rock.

"Stand *up*," Lilly whispers to me. She prances into a spot in front of the boys. I drag my feet after her.

"One two three *four*!" Valerie counts, and we start to sing.

Out of the corner of my eye I see Lilly starting up all the

dance routine hand-waving garbage as well. I keep my fists bunched tight in my pockets.

When we finish, the boys clap politely.

"Very sweet," smiles Valerie. "Have you ever tried harmonizing?"

"No," says Lilly, annoyed. She wanted straight praise. Her mouth pulls down at the corners.

But Valerie doesn't seem to notice. "Listening to other performers can really help grow your singing," she says earnestly. She starts sorting through the CDs near the stereo. "Have you listened to any a capella groups—you know, voices singing in harmony? Each voice acts like a different instrument, or the chords of a guitar. If you have more people, you can even sing percussion."

Mitch laughs, nudging me. "Remember that song 'Kookaburra Sits in an Old Gum Tree'? We had to sing it in rounds in third grade. Badman kept messing it up. But even without Badman, it was really hard. I put my fingers in my ears to shut out the others but then I lost track of where everyone else was up to—"

"And Mrs. Hatfield threw the chalk at you," I add.

Valerie nods. "It *is* hard, but worth it. You have to learn how to keep your own melody, while listening to the others. It's a bit like life, really." She sifts through the CDs. "Listen to this now, The Supremes—their harmonies are divine, gives you goosebumps."

Jackson groans as the first bars of "My Guy" begin. He's caught Lilly's raised eyebrow and he's wriggling again on his chair. "I don't think everyone is into the time warp, Mom."

But Valerie has her eyes closed, listening.

When the song is over, she says to Lilly, "Do you see

what I mean? But you'd do that with *your* song, of course. One of you could take the melody and the other do the harmony—you know the other part of the chord. So for example Ez may be singing in A, you in C. It's like a weaving, two strands dancing with each other."

Lilly stands up and stretches. She gives a loud yawn right in Valerie's face and goes over to the sliding glass doors leading out to the garden. "Do you have someone to mow your lawn, Mrs. Ford? The grass is very long, isn't it? My mother has this boy Richard come every two weeks. He's pretty cheap. We could give you his number if you want."

I stare down at the carpet. There's a stain the shape of Tasmania near my feet. Red wine, it looks like.

Lilly steps out into the garden and wanders over to the mango tree. Mitch gets up, too, pretending to stretch his legs, and follows her.

Jackson snorts into the silence. "There's harmony for you—drives people away. You might not have any trouble keeping your own tune, Mom, but do you know how to listen to others?"

Valerie gives a shame-faced grin. "Can't help myself. Sorry."

"Well, I'm not," I say. "I wouldn't mind trying that, if you feel like it."

Valerie goes over to the keyboard and we're just beginning on a new song, "A Natural Woman," when Lilly and Mitch drift back in.

"We'd better be going now," says Lilly loudly over the keyboard.

Valerie stops midnote and turns around. "Okay," she smiles, "it was lovely to meet you."

"Thanks for having us," says Mitch, and shakes Valerie's hand. "And thanks for the music—I enjoyed it."

I always liked Mitch. We stand smiling at each other for a moment.

Then into the silence the phone rings like a siren. We all jump.

Jackson rushes into the kitchen to get it.

"Don't!" calls Valerie, but we hear him pick it up.

"Hello," he says.

We stand around, listening. The clock on the wall ticks like a heartbeat. Valerie's strange reaction—fear, it looked like, her face tightening at the first ring—makes us hold our breath to hear.

"Hello?" Jackson repeats. "Hello hello, *hello* . . ."

Another pause, then the firm click of the phone back on the wall.

"No one there," Jackson announces as he walks into the room. He looks at Valerie. "Just that slow breathing again."

Valerie nods and looks down at her hands on the keyboard. When she looks up her face is exhausted, the light switched off.

"It's happened before?" asks Mitch, frowning.

"Yeah," says Jackson. "About five times a day—not a good number. Just this breathing, in, out, in, out, as if the person's waiting for something, but they never say what. It's freaky, especially when it happens late at night."

"Why don't you call the police?" says Mitch. "They could trace the call maybe."

"No, no, we don't want police involved," Valerie says quickly. "It's probably just kids, they'll get sick of it soon, I'm sure."

"Kids, you think?" says Mitch thoughtfully. "I know exactly who it might be."

We all look at each other. I'm guessing we're all thinking the same thing. Everyone remembers Badman and Mr. Wall.

"No!" I say. "He wouldn't do anything that bad, would he? That's harassment; you can be charged for that."

"He's done worse," says Mitch.

"Yeah, so I hear," grunts Jackson. I notice his jaw clenching tight.

Suddenly the phone rings again, tearing open the quiet. In the split second it takes to register it, Mitch has dashed to pick it up. Valerie's hand, flung out to catch him, drops to her side.

"Listen, you idiot," Mitch yells into the phone, "we've called the police. We know who you are. You do it again, you're dead meat!"

"Oh, don't say that!" shouts Valerie, running into the kitchen. She grabs the phone from Mitch and crashes it back onto the receiver on the wall.

Mitch looks at her in surprise.

She tries to smile but her lips finish in a straight line. "I don't want to scare them too much . . ." she shrugs apologetically, "they're only kids."

"Well, I bet they won't do it again now."

Valerie nods slightly. "Thanks, Mitch."

We stand around awkwardly on the cork floor, until Valerie gives us a funny half-wave and trudges up the hall. I watch her slow progress and imagine something huge and monstrous has just climbed on her shoulders, bending her back beneath its weight.

After Mitch and Lilly take off, Jackson goes really quiet. He's staring at the floor, picking at a loose thread. His shoulders are slumped, his body folded up. The way he's sitting, he looks burdened, a bit like Valerie. He couldn't still be mad about my comment at the beach? Or is he thinking about Badman and the phone calls? Or maybe he's just deciding what a crap afternoon this turned out to be . . .

"I better be going, too," I say finally.

He just nods.

He walks me to the door, out to the garden. I hear him sigh a couple of times. At the gate, I have to say something or I'll explode. "Are you okay?"

"Yeah," he frowns. "It's just—oh you know, Mom goes on and on, doesn't she."

"I thought she looked really exhausted, actually."

"Mm. She hasn't been herself these last few days."

"I guess she must get tired standing up all day, serving."

"Maybe." Jackson kicks at the weeds springing out from cracks in the path. Then he kicks his foot another three times.

"That makes four," he whispers to the grass.

"You could make dinner tonight," I say.

Jackson breaks into a grin. "Yeah, I've already thought about that. I do a mean pasta with chilli. Enough to blow your head off. We've actually got chilli growing in a pot on the porch. Did you see it? Red-hot pasta with garlic is Mom's favorite dish."

We smile at each other and I think of my mother telling Daniel that the fried egg messes he makes on Sunday mornings are *her* favorite meal.

"Hey, thanks for today, Ez," Jackson says, and takes my hand. His eyes are electric again. We both look at my hand

96

lying in his, and my heart starts to beat too fast. I don't know what to do. How long should I keep my hand there?

Suddenly he leans forward and his lips bump against my nose.

I laugh out loud. I can't help it. I'm so nervous I just want to run.

He grins back at me, opening the gate. He's about to say something more but he stops. I follow his gaze, out onto our street.

There's Badman, doing a wheelie on his bike in the middle of the road. "Hey, Ez," he waves.

"Hi," I mumble, looking away.

"You should see my new fireworks! I got a new Golden Eagle and a Dragon Slayer, and tons of Black Cats. When are you gonna see them?"

I shrug, wishing the road would open up and swallow him.

"When are we going to see the back of *you*?" yells Jackson. He puts his arm tight around my shoulder, staking his claim like that explorer we studied last term.

Badman does a wild Freddie Krueger laugh, then takes off, pedaling like a maniac up the hill. At the top he does a wide circle and flies back down, his feet in the air. As he nears us he looks straight at Jackson and gives him the middle finger, shouting something about a fire burning in the sky.

5. Jackson

I don't like Mondays.

Monday is a mean day, almost as mean as an odd number.

"Forget the weekend now," teachers say, "you're here to work until your brain blurs and you can't remember who Homer Simpson is." Well, not really, but that's how it feels. Have you ever been to a school where they do *sports* on a Monday?

Mom thinks Dad hated Mondays, too, says that's why he became a fisherman. "No Mondays at sea, just dawn and dusk." Mom has a special pile of songs for Monday-itis. "Drives out the evil spirits," she says, "makes you dance instead of moan!"

Well, I don't dance, but sometimes I hum a little to "I Don't Like Mondays" by the Boomtown Rats. Mom's favorite is a sixties song, "Friday on My Mind" by Stevie Wright, which I have to say isn't bad, but after Mom showed me a recent photo of poor Stevie in the *Good Weekend*, I decided I couldn't listen to it again. There he is at fifty, all worn out and medicated because of a golden staph infection he got in the hospital, and he's just sitting staring out from this threadbare old armchair, his hands all empty in his lap, his feet in grandpa slippers.

I felt so sorry for him with his empty hands. He looked as if his whole life was now one long Monday.

There are so many people to feel sorry for in the world, if you stop and think.

And I've got enough to do just getting through Mondays since Norton came up with his new "Cooperative Math." He's been moaning how 5/8 of the class were so far behind (expressed as a percentage that's 62.5) and he thinks he's going to divide us into groups so that those who've got a clue (3/8 or 37.5%) can help the others.

This would have been okay but he went on to choose leaders in the groups, like me and Asim. In the practice run last week he strolled around the room, slopping praise thick as maple syrup all over the leaders, telling the rest they should listen to us and be grateful for our "advanced comprehension."

Somebody should tell him that a better title for his Cooperative Math would be "How to Make Enemies." Or maybe "How to Make Even *Worse* Enemies in Case Yours Don't Hate You Enough."

Just because you can do certain kinds of math problems doesn't mean you know how to explain them. And it doesn't mean you can do all kinds of math. (Well, maybe Asim is an exception here.) But if you're Jackson Ford, you can't cope with *any* kind of math when someone like Badman is in your group.

I couldn't believe it when Norton read out the names. "Jackson Ford, leader of yellow group." He pointed at a small huddle of glum math-haters. In the middle, towering over them by a head, was Badman. He stood with his legs wide apart and his arms crossed against his chest. He looked like a bull tied at a post. (You couldn't help wondering what he'd do when someone let him go.) He glared right at me and thrust out his chin. Muttering something to Joe, who seemed to be in yellow group, too, they looked at me and laughed.

I took a deep breath and held it for four. Yellow all right. I'm as scared as mustard. Cowardy custard. You're gonna get busted. *Bad.*

This morning Mom played the Boomtown Rats and a new song, "Blue Monday." It has bass heavy riffs to give me courage. I didn't tell her, but nothing made any difference. I sat on the kitchen stool and listened to the three-note bass pattern like she told me to, and ate my Wheaties.

She ought to know I don't like sets of three, anyway, even if they *are* the most common rhythmic pattern in rock and roll. Mom thinks a dose of loud rock will fix anything. I just want to get Monday over with. I hope I can do it without my lungs collapsing in a coughing catastrophe.

As I'm putting my bag down in the corridor outside our classroom, Asim walks up. He starts to say something but the bell screams just then and all I can see is his mouth moving like an actor in a mime show. I make out "math," or at least I think I do, and see the frown between his eyes. He doesn't need to say any more.

I know Asim doesn't like the new system either. He hates being singled out, negative or positive. He thinks the kids sneer at his ability, as if it's something peculiar about him, like his accent. He doesn't want to be different. I tell him it's just Badman and his sidekick who think like that, but because they're so loud, it's as if they're holding the only microphone in the band.

"We could see Norton at recess," I whisper close to him as we walk into class. "You know, tell him we just want to change some people in the groups—"

"No, no, no," Asim is shaking his head in this agitated way. I let it drop.

He doesn't like making waves. He thinks any change is sure to be for the worse. Or maybe I'm the one who thinks that. In any case, his Temporary Protection Visa is coming up for renewal and he's still in limbo land. The government could decide not to extend it and send him and his father back to Iraq. In a couple of months, his whole life could change. Even though I know him so much better now, I still can't understand how he lives with that. What I do know is he thinks any trouble, no matter how small, could go against his character assessment. *You* try and tell him that some kid protesting about a dumb math class is hardly going to get the government's attention. No, he just wants to put his head down and melt into the background. Sometimes I think he feels he's still in a war, and he has to get up and pull on his khaki every morning for camouflage.

Anyway, I understand how he feels. And he's my friend. I just wish there was someone to stand with me on this. Norton won't listen to just one kid.

As soon as we're settled at our desks, Norton gives us a lecture on scale. A tickle starts in my throat. I'm not great at scale and measurement and space. I just like numbers. I clear my throat and try to breathe deep. "Don't cough or you're a dead man," I tell myself. Next thing I know everyone's scraping back their chairs. We're dividing into the groups and I've heard nothing Norton said.

"Red over here," yells Norton. "Yellow at the back. Leaders, come and get your papers."

I look at the questions on the paper. *The distance between town A and town B on the map is 9.5 inches. If the scale is 1:100,000, then they are how many miles apart?* and *I have a 1:40 scale model of a car. The real car is 13 feet long. How long is my model?*

I start to panic. Calm down, I tell myself. You're over all that. You can do math now, remember? But 40 what? 100,000 *what*? How do you know what to multiply or is it divide by? I try to think what Norton was saying before the cough got in the way.

I make my way over to the table at the back. Badman and Joe have already taken up two chairs each. That leaves the rest of the group, three girls, cramped together on the other side of the desk. I decide not to mention the unfair seating arrangements and sit at the top.

"Good mo-r-n-i-n-g, Mr. Jack-a-s-s," Badman says in that long drawn out chant we use for teachers. Joe smirks and the others giggle nervously.

I ignore him. "So who knows how to do this first question?" I say quickly.

There's a short silence while the girls study the paper. Badman is slowly tearing off the corners of his paper and putting them into a little pile. I look at the question again. "I don't really know where to start, myself," I begin. "What's the unit of measurement here?"

Something wet and hard hits me right in the eye. A small scrunched up white ball lands on the table near my hand. Badman's flicking spit balls. I can feel my right eye starting to water.

"Cry about it," says Badman.

He and Joe get busy, like assembly workers at a car factory. Or a spit ball factory. I watch as they tear their paper into tiny shreds, and put them in their mouths. They chew until the paper is soft and wet and then, taking a straw each from their pencil cases, they stuff the white mess in. Staring right at me, Badman puts the straw to his mouth and blows. I duck, but the ball hits me on the side of the cheek. I can smell his skanky saliva.

"What I mean is," I go on, "if the scale is 1:40, what do we put after the numeral? Forty what?"

"Forty jackass try-hards," says Badman.

The girls are studying their papers hard. I guess they think if they keep their heads down they won't have to take sides. Joe is laughing like a maniac. The drool from his spit balls is dribbling down his chin. But I'm thinking about Badman's random choice of units.

"Thanks, Badman, yes, that's right, the unit can be anything: jackasses, try-hards, feet, inches. Well, anyway, whatever we choose, we have to then convert them all into the same unit. 1:40 means one jackass try-hard on the model car is equal to forty jackass try-hards on the real car. Get it?"

Badman has stopped filling his straw. His mouth hangs open like the lid of our school garbage can.

"So if we choose inches, then do we have to make 13 feet into inches so they're all the same?" asks this serious girl called Robyn Graves. She's tapping her pencil nervously on the paper, but her face is all lit up with that excitement you get when you think you're onto something.

"That's right!" I smile at her. I stop smiling as a spit ball lands smack on her mouth. It leaves a patch of wet goo on her bottom lip. She sits frozen. I can tell she doesn't know whether to suck her lip to get rid of it or wipe it with her hand. Either way she'll have Badman germs inside her. I hand her a tissue from the pack in my pocket.

"Well, well, and how are we doing here?" Norton suddenly looms over us, rubbing his hands together.

Out of the corner of my eye I see Badman hastily sweeping the little piles of wet paper onto his lap.

It would be so easy to say, "Badman's shredding his paper and making spit balls, sir." I can feel the girls boring their eyes into me. The tickle in my throat is ballooning. I can hardly swallow.

"Fine, sir," I mutter.

"Good, good, that's the way," he bellows heartily and strides on.

Spit balls catch me and Robyn Graves at the same time. Robyn looks at me and then at Norton's retreating back. Her eyebrows go up in this pleading expression.

I look away. I want to explain to her that if I report Badman it will only be worse for us. Well, if I'm honest, mainly it will be worse for me. My life won't be worth living.

But then you couldn't say it's exactly heaven right now. I let out a couple of little coughs, hoping that will ease the tension. Robyn has given up looking at me and is scribbling busily on her paper. She's converting inches and the others are looking over her shoulder, working away. I try to concentrate on my own paper now, but the numbers are blurring, forming into a cloud.

Spit balls land on my neck, my legs. My face is smeared with Badman saliva. I'm so hot inside it's choking me. I hate my insides. They're all weak, squishy, like the little polystyrofoam balls that fill a soft toy. Badman stomps on me any time he feels like it.

Why does he hate me so much? Every day, the insults—*jackass, nerd, try-hard*—other kids smirk, hiding their grins behind their lunches. Is it the math? I don't think he cares all that much about being good at math. Maybe it's me and Esmerelda—he's always trying to get her attention. But he seems keener on Lilly. He doesn't ever swear around her or make those crappy sex remarks. I heard that last Christmas he gave her a CD. Except it was some heavy metal band she hated so she told everyone she gave it away to her cousin. Then Badman told everyone the CD was only a freebie anyway that came with his *Australian Musician* magazine.

My ankle suddenly burns like fire. I look at Badman.

"Oh, sorry, Mr. Jack-a-s-s, my foot slipped," he chants, chewing away.

I say nothing. I look back down at my paper. In my head I start to do one of my challenges. This is how it goes: you have to count by fours, tapping your right foot in time to the first four numbers, 4, 8, 12, 16, then change to your left as you do the next set. On every tenth multiple you have to blink your right eye, then your left, and so on. The object of the challenge is to see how far you can go in the time allotted, doing everything right. Once I got to 1,264 in two and a half minutes. That felt really good.

The cough eases and everything starts to drift far away. The cloud is quilting the space behind my eyes, and it's soft and floaty. Sometimes I see the numbers in my mind, and they soothe me with their familiar faces. Numbers such as eight are like family members, or maybe pets. I can lay eight on its side so it becomes the infinity symbol and trace the loops back and forth, over and over. It's like stroking a cat that stays still for you. Don't you love numbers, the way they

105

just lie where you put them and let you bend them into any shape you want?

For Esmerelda's birthday, Badman gave her his two favorite fireworks, Overwhelming Joy and Hallucinations. They exploded rainbows 13 feet into the air. He said his father got them on the black market, but they were really expensive just the same.

When I look up, the girls have nearly finished the questions. Soggy bits of paper cover the desk. A gob of spit hangs off my ear.

"All right, class, time to move back to your seats," bellows Norton. "Leaders, collect the papers from the group and hand them into me. Well done, everyone."

Badman pushes a soggy mess of spit balls toward me. "There you go, Mr. Jackass. That's mine."

You know something? I used to hate math. Numbers gave me the shivers. Especially when they were mixed up with really nasty problems. Why *invent* problems, I'd rage at the textbook, when there are so many in the world occurring naturally?

Mom says, "Life is a daring adventure or nothing at all." She tries to look at things positively. When I told her it was Helen Keller, a deaf and blind person, who said that first, Mom said, "See, and you think *you've* got problems!" What can you say to that? If you start thinking about all the people in the world who suffer from terminal diseases or life-threatening poverty, your own worries look pathetic. Positively ridiculous. You can end up shouting at yourself in the mirror. I know that. But other people's problems don't make your own any easier.

Fifth grade at Milson Elementary was the worst year of

my life. We had this teacher, Mr. Kemp, who gave us math problems every Monday. It was enough to make you mental. Sometimes, looking back on it, I think Mr. Kemp may have been mental himself. For sure he was the meanest guy I ever met, anyway. He was tall and thin as a fuse wire, and he'd whip around the classroom flicking problems at us and choosing the slowest kids in the class to answer them. He'd tap out the seconds on his thigh, and the rhythm would get faster and faster the longer he waited. He had a short fuse, all right, and as the seconds went by and no answer came it was like watching a lit line of gunpowder travel toward its terrible conclusion. He had the loudest shout on him I've ever heard.

How can you think with a demon breathing down your neck? You could imagine fire coming out of his mouth. You know that expression "his blood ran cold?" Well, that's how it felt: my body would seize up and go rigid, like concrete setting on a suburban driveway. Mr. Kemp saw the blank look in my eyes and he went in for the kill. He hated me.

That year the problems set for homework were real heartbreakers. One I remember went like this: *In a barn there are a number of animals, insects, and spiders. There are some chickens with 2 legs, some cows with 4 legs, some beetles with 6 legs, and some spiders with 8 legs. Guarding this group is a dog who lost one of his legs when he was run over by the farmer's tractor. If there is a total of 113 legs, how many chickens, cows, beetles, spiders, and dogs could there be? Give at least 3 answers.*

Well, I got stuck on the misery of that poor dog. How's he going to guard all those animals when he's running around on only three legs? And what kind of careless or maybe *mean* farmer was this to run over his own dog? All I could think about was how no one seemed to look after their helpless pets anymore, and I tried to feed any dog or cat that came onto our street, particularly the ones that looked like strays with no collars.

And what about those division of fruit problems? Once I was fuming over one of them and Mom left the potatoes on the stove to come and see. Over my shoulder she read out: "If Tom had 24 apples and he sold them for 6 cents each to his friend Ben, but he gave a discount to his brother of 3 cents each, and Ben bought 6, how much did Tom receive?"

"What I want to know," I told her, "is how angry Ben would be about having to pay the full six cents. And what kind of a friendship is that, anyway? Why the hell wouldn't you just share your apples with your friend and your brother? They're only apples for heaven's sake."

Mom nodded enthusiastically. "I agree, that's a typical capitalist sort of question where everyone is trying to rip off everyone else, even their best friends. Human beings can be better than that, can't they, Jackson? People with apples should share with those who don't, and they should set a better example in children's textbooks."

Well, all through dinner and into the washing up, Mom was still talking about social injustice. By the time *Everybody Loves Raymond* started on TV she was onto the disappointment of the Russian Revolution.

Good old Mom, she takes on my problems as if they were her own, but so often, I wish she wouldn't. After the fruit problem she must have realized that I was having real panic attacks over math, so she jumped right in to help. Trouble was, she didn't ever just tell me the answer to the question I was asking her, she had to go on and tell me the whole history of fractions and their deeper significance in the world. Like two thirds of the world's population are so poor they never even get to use a telephone. How's that for a weighty fraction? Then she'd move on to decimals and the division of money by the World Bank and suddenly it was ten o'clock and I could hardly keep my eyes open and there'd still be a page of math to go.

We used to have a lot of arguments about math. She'd go on and on like a laundry tap, and I'd start to fiddle with stuff and look out the window. This made her really mad and when she was tired, she'd start to yell. She goes all red in the face when she's angry and she looks like a different person. Her transformation used to make me think of the evil queen in Sleeping Beauty, so kind and sweet one minute and a witch the next. She'd tell me how she'd already *done* school and now here she was having to do it all over again with me. Did I think she *wanted* to be sitting here listing the factors of 164 when she could be lying on the sofa with a glass of wine listening to Neil Young? When she'd calmed down, she was painfully sorry. That was almost worse. She'd be so mad with herself that you couldn't ever be.

I think she realized how bad it was getting because she stopped checking on my math homework. She said she had never been any good at math herself and was only making it worse. That was the middle of fifth grade and when she started going out with Dan Smart. (I used to call him Damn Smart, although he wasn't, really.) Mom hasn't been out with many men since my dad died, but I think she chose old Dan because she thought he might be helpful. He was a high school math teacher, and very enthusiastic about his subject. She must have told him I was having problems, so as soon as he saw me, without even a hello or a handshake, he'd go, "What's nine times seven?" He'd hide behind the bathroom door and leap out as I walked past, calling, "If Mary was twenty-seven and her brother was twenty-nine, who is the president of Lithuania?" or something like that.

Well, as you can imagine it didn't work out, and we went back to the old ways. But Mom started to do yoga and learned to breathe, and I tried to concentrate. Sometimes she'd still get angry and bang the table. I'd go really quiet then, inside myself. I'd imagine I was a snail and all that was left on the outside was my shell. I was waterproof, her words bouncing off like bullets of rain.

And then, one beautiful day in the last term of fifth grade, Mr. Kemp left Milson Elementary (carried away in a straitjacket the rumor went), the sun came out and Miss Braithwaite arrived. She smelled of lavender and patience. She had endless patience. She smiled more than anyone I'd ever met. And it wasn't that fake kind, the sort that's pinned there like the tail on the donkey and you're just waiting for it to drop off. She just really seemed to care about you—not whether you got the answer right, but whether you were okay. Within a week of her existence I'd stopped worrying about helpless dogs and how much fruit everyone was getting. I felt somehow that she would look after them all for me, she had such a big heart, and in place of Tom or Mary I could just put a box with a number in it, and it felt great!

That's when I began to like numbers. As I calmed down the frozen cloud cleared and I saw patterns where before there was just a jumble of figures. I liked seeing the patterns, there was something so neat and tidy about them, like a well-planned city lifted straight from the map. If you followed the right method you'd arrive exactly where you were supposed to be. I looked forward to seeing Miss Braithwaite's neat red check next to my answers, and her comments of "*Excellent!!*" and "*Good work!!!*" Miss Braithwaite went in for lots of exclamation marks; she wasn't the kind to hold back. Sometimes after I'd finished my homework, I made up extra math questions and watched myself getting them right. I saw Miss Braithwaite smiling at my brilliance, and I felt powerful, like God or something (if I believed in Him). Numbers that were even seemed the most complete, and I started to make up math problems all the time, like some kids watch TV. When my answers involved eight I felt the best.

That was the hardest thing I ever had to do, leaving that school. But Miss Braithwaite told me that wherever I went, I could take those numbers with me. No one could take that away from me, she said. Just like the Africans and their music. And she was right.

What they *can* take away from you is your calm. Just like that. And then everything loses its shape. One comment from Badman and I'm a beanbag.

At lunch Asim sits down on the bench and silently passes me a bag of chips. He doesn't need to say anything. We munch away for a while and watch the pigeons pecking at our chip crumbs. There's this one kind of bird with a tall plume growing up from its head like an exclamation mark. As it bobs about it looks so enthusiastic. I'm really fond of that bird.

"This afternoon if you want to come over, we can finish putting the possum house together," Asim says after a while. "My father thought we did a good job with the sawing."

I smile and start on my apple. I remember the feel of the saw cutting into the wood. It was hard at first, working against the resistance of the pine, and then the blade cut through, sliding deeper and deeper, into the groove. I liked standing up all those pieces of wood we'd cut, one against the other, so they made a perfect straight line. I liked, too, working at the bench, surrounded by all the busy jars of nails and screws and the tools hanging neatly on their hooks, polished and ready to use. Thinking of this, my heart lifts a little.

"Dad has left us the brackets so we can put the sides together."

"They're those metal things you fix to the wood to make the corners?"

"Yes. They look like they'll be the right size. We'll need to trim the roof planks—"

"Ooh, you wanna be careful you don't *hurt* yourself with those dangerous *tools*." There's a loud guffaw behind us and we whip around to see Badman and Joe, breathing down our necks. How long have they been standing there?

Badman comes around and slumps down on the bench next to Asim. Joe slouches near me. We're sandwiched between them now like sardines. What do they want? I feel a cough coming on.

"You making a little home for the possie-wossies?" says Badman. He leans out over Asim. "Isn't that cute, Joe? And Daddy's lending them his little tools!"

Joe snorts, nodding like those toy dogs you see in the back windows of cars.

Anger is heating up my cheeks. I can feel my face starting to throb. "Haven't you got anything better to do than spy on us? What a pathetic life you must have."

Asim nudges me in the ribs. "Be quiet," he whispers. His breath is hot in my ear.

112

Badman stares at me. I watch his leg starting to twitch. Getting faster. I think of Mr. Kemp and his lit fuse. Something's building up in Badman.

Suddenly he leans over and grabs Asim's lunch box.

"No!" cries Asim before he can stop himself.

Badman laughs. He flicks up the lid. "What's this stuff?" He holds the box near his face and sniffs. "Phew, it stinks!" He doubles over, pretending to vomit.

"Yuck, I can smell it from here," says Joe, holding his nose.

"If it makes you spew, why don't you give it back," I snap.

But Badman is rooting around in the lunch box. "Oh, and look, there's a note!" he crows, waving the piece of paper in Asim's face. "It's all in foreign scribble but wait," he peers closer, "there's something at the end, *love from Dad* and how cute, there's a heart—"

Asim lunges at Badman, grabbing at his arm. "Give it back, you stupid!"

Badman gives a shout of laughter, holding the note higher. "*You stupid*," he mimics in a high voice.

Asim's eyes are filling. Hold it back, I'm willing him, just hold on.

Scrunching the note up in his fist, Badman shouts, "Ooh *Daddy*, where's your *daddy* to protect you? Why don't you go back to where you came from? No one wants you here, you stupid refugee."

Asim makes a terrible choking noise. Tears are spurting down his face. He's not even trying to wipe them away.

"Oh, look at him, the wuss. Cry about it!"

"Shut your mouth," I say. I say it quietly, almost in a whisper.

"What?"

"I said shut your mouth or I'll shut it for you."

"Oh, yeah, how will you do that, you wimp?"

Badman is leaning out over Asim. He shoves his face near mine and I can smell his stinking breath.

"What is it with you?" Anger is starting to cramp in my guts. "I bet you never got a note in your lunch box. Is that it? Who'd ever write *you* one, huh?" I'm trembling with rage. My head is going black, just this sea of hot burning darkness. "You're a pathetic bastard, Badman. You spit on everything good. That's why everyone hates you."

Badman lets out a roar, so deep, so loud, it's as if it's been growing in him since he was born. It cracks the air like one of his explosions, like the engine on a Mustang, full throttle. He springs up and comes at me, throwing his body right at my chest so that we thud to the ground. Pain bites into my spine. He's on top of me, and I can't breathe. All the air has been punched out of me. His hands are on my throat, his thumb pressing hard into my windpipe. He's swearing, purple in the face, but I can't make out what he's saying because there's such a red roaring in my head. I'm dying here on the ground with the stones and pigeon poop digging into my back and a panic grips me so hard that I shoot out my fist and smash it hard against his hateful jaw.

Badman sways above me. I feel something hot and slippery on my fingers. His cheek is bleeding. He's losing his hold and I heave myself sideways, trying to slide out. My shoulders are off the ground and I lift my head just as I see his white knuckles coming toward me. It happens in slow motion, like the car accident I was in once where there were only fractions of a second before the impact but it seemed to take forever. I unfreeze enough to turn my head before his fist slams into my ear.

The world explodes.

A rushing sound in my eardrum flows into the sea behind my eyes. It mixes with Joe's voice, urgent, scared. His arm is around Asim's neck in a headlock, and he's yelling something at Badman, warning him. I close my eyes and when I open them there's Mitch and Esmerelda grabbing Badman's shoulders and old Norton hurtling up the path behind him.

Asim and I catch the three-thirty bus home. We sit quietly on the bus, looking out the windows.

"Badman got detention," says Asim. "He saw the principal while you were in the nurse's office. His jaw is pretty bruised. You know he said you hit him first."

I shrug. "I did. We told them what happened."

"There's a note going home to his mother."

"I bet he's really broken up about that."

The rushing sound in my ear is still there, but fainter now. It's more like a distant surf breaking, right out the back.

I crack my knuckles four times. "Bastard," I mutter.

Asim nods.

"Moron," I go on, feeling the anger rise again, "dirty stinky-breath maggot."

Asim nods again.

"I'd like to stick a firecracker up *his* butt and light it."

Asim grins.

"I'd like to squash him like a fly and flick him into a spewing volcano—"

Asim holds up his hands. "You mustn't say these things. It solves nothing."

"But it makes you feel better, doesn't it?"

Asim smiles briefly. "For a minute, yes. I just hope Badman never rules this country."

We stare gloomily at the seat in front of us.

At Asim's house there's a new bag of chocolate chip cookies on the table and a bowl of green grapes in the fridge. We munch steadily and after a little while Asim says, "Come on, let's go out to the shed."

As we walk into the smell of clean wood and fresh paint, I take a deep breath. Asim goes over to the workbench and picks up the metal brackets, showing me how they work. We take two of the wooden walls of the house and angle them to form a corner. We measure them again from random spots, to make sure they're all even. Exactly twelve inches high. We take turns to hold the wood in place and hammer, and Asim starts to whistle. It must be a Kurdish tune, I'm thinking, strange and haunting, making you think of wild places you've never been to. His whistling winds like a thread around the shed, coloring everything.

We finish one corner, and stand back to examine it. The join is smooth, perfect! We give each other a high five. Now we get started on the next. As we work I'm thinking how good this feels, to make a real object with my own hands. It makes me wonder if this is what I'd like to do for a career—work with wood and build something beautiful that is also really useful. I can't wait to see if the possums like it enough to make it their home.

For the last couple of weeks I've been leaving pieces of apple and banana out on the porch. Sometimes, late at night, I see a flash of fur dash across the table. Once I beamed the flashlight right into a pair of black eyes. The possum had a bit of apple in its paws, and it just went on nibbling in the spotlight. As soon as I inched forward, it fled. Maybe one day they won't mind me sitting with them while they eat. In the morning, the fruit is all gone. It's such a good feeling, looking at that empty tin plate. When their house is built, we'll leave the food in there. Then they'll have full tummies and they can just sleep where they eat, like a real home.

"I'm sorry you got hurt today because of me," Asim says suddenly.

I take a moment to answer. I was far away. I sigh, because I don't really want to come back. "He didn't hit me because of you," I say. "I make him angry all by myself."

"Yes, but you didn't have to do anything when he called me a stupid refugee—"

"Listen, you should have seen him all through math. He couldn't wait to thump me. I think there's a lot of people he wants to thump. His rage seems sort of spread out, and if you're in the general direction, you take it." I sigh again. "I'm so sick of trying to get out of the way."

"Yes."

"And Esmerelda," I go on, "why does she even talk to him?" I feel angry again just thinking about it. "Just before lunch, on the way out of class, did you see her jabbering with him? And they were laughing together. When she talked, you could see him really listening. He was being *nice*. Well, nice for *him*. It made me want to puke."

Asim is quiet for a moment. Then he says, "They talk about music, I think."

"Yeah, whatever, but why would you want to talk about *any*thing with that maggot? I mean, say I met a person who shared the same interests as me, you know, maybe this person was an even-number freak or something, or they'd discovered that the answer to life was the number eight—well even so, I wouldn't spend time chatting and *laughing* with him if I found out he was a murderer, you know, or a racist or a phone stalker . . ."

"But it was Ez who ran to get Norton and Ez who pulled him off you. She went white, you know. I saw her. She was really worried." Asim puts down the hammer. "I wish it had been me who had stopped him."

"No, but Joe—he had you in that headlock, you couldn't—"

Asim shakes his head. "Not at first. We both were just standing there, staring. My legs wouldn't move. It was as if they were stuck to the ground."

"It's okay, don't—"

"No, I felt very bad and then I tried to run, to get help and that was when Joe grabbed me. But I was useless, like being stuck in a dream—"

"It's okay, Asim." I pick up the hammer. I want to go back to that soothing place I was in, with the wood and the possums. "Look, we just need another couple of nails in here and we'll have made another perfect corner!"

"While you were at the nurse, quite a few kids came up to see how you were. Lilly was one of them. She said you were very brave. 'I like that in a man,' she said."

I snort and we grin at each other.

"And what *about* Lilly," I say. "Do you think Badman likes her?"

Asim shrugs.

"Do *you*? Do you think she's hot, like everyone does?"

He shrugs again. "I suppose so."

"I don't, really. It was strange that day at the beach—for a minute she looked at me like I was special. But it's the same look she gives Mitch, you know, and then she just suddenly switches it off. Makes you feel you're not as good as her somehow, like you haven't found the right thing to keep her interest. Like you're some lowly evolved insect in the food chain."

Now Asim snorts. "Insects have amazing survival mechanisms."

"I know. Take the cockroach. Did you know it's the only living creature that could survive a nuclear blast?"

"That's right. Because it has no central nervous system."

"No kidding!" I stop and think about that for a while. "Anyway, the thing is, I think Lilly is an outside kind of person—you know, everything about her is on the outside, whereas Esmerelda is fuller, busier inside, and you're always wanting to know what she's thinking. To know the inside of her."

When it's my turn to hammer, I really whack in the nail. "But no matter what, I'm finished with Esmerelda if she's friends with Badman after this. Finished."

Asim grins. "Sure," he says, and we stand back to look at the house.

It's starting to get dark as we're trimming the roof planks. Through the windows I can see the streetlights coming on. I'm thinking I should get home and that Mom may be worried, when sure enough we hear the phone ringing from the house. Asim runs across the grass to get it.

"It was your mom," he pants as he comes back in. "She says we've got ten minutes. She invited me for dinner."

"Good. Listen, don't say anything about today to her, okay? She's cranky, and I don't want to make things worse.

She'd probably go and yell at Badman's mother or the principal or something."

"All right. We can leave the roof now, and tomorrow we can nail it on. Then we'll be ready to take it to your place and show the possums."

As we're packing up, I say, "You haven't had any weird calls have you? You know, when you pick it up, no one on the other end, just heavy breathing?"

"No. Do you mean like the other night?"

"Yeah, and there've been more. It's creepy. Do you think it's Badman?"

Asim shakes his head. "I don't know. He is not the type, I think. I don't know if he could keep a secret. He just seems to go off like one of his firecrackers. But then you cannot be sure."

The sun is setting behind the wires lacing the sky as we cross the road to my place. There are dinner smells in the air, and I wonder if the sausages are ours.

"But I did see something strange last night," Asim says as we open the gate. "I tried to tell you this morning before math, and then I forgot after the fight. I saw that blue Mustang again."

"The 777?"

"Yes. But this time it stopped a couple of times going down the street. It stopped at your place."

I freeze on the path, my hand holding the gate wide open.

"There were two men in the car. The passenger man got out and put something in your mailbox."

"When was this?"

"Last night, at about nine o'clock. I was coming to put the garbage out."

"Maybe it's still there!" I let the gate bang shut and lifted up the little door on the mailbox.

"No, I wouldn't think so, your mother went to the mailbox right away. She must have seen the car stopping from the gate. Maybe she was putting out the garbage, like me."

He's right. I find nothing but a shiny flyer for Dominoes Pizza.

"What did the man look like?"

Asim thought for a moment. "Tall, thin man in a dark suit. I could not see the driver."

"Strange, she didn't say anything about it to me this morning."

As we walk in the door and smell the sausages frying from the kitchen, I suddenly remember Mom swearing over her coffee this morning because she'd forgotten to put out the garbage can. "Don't even know what day it is anymore," she'd said, and her mouth had quivered as we stood looking at the mess of orange skins and milk cartons and cereal boxes still poking out of the plastic bags bulging from the wheelie can.

6. Esmerelda

"And now, give it up for . . . ES–MER–EL–DA!"

A hand at my back pushes me into the footlights. The shimmer is blinding, a wall of light. I know I'm here to sing, but my throat is blocked by a stone the size of an egg. Below me the audience swims in shadow. The neon sign, Blue Moon, blinks from the blur.

The hand pushes again and I'm falling, holding my head, waiting for the crash to Earth. But the dark just goes on and on. It's not dead space—there are folds and rustles, soft as a car's purr. A riff of guitar steals out, electric. The notes make me ache, rising so high and pure above the dark that they burn like stars and suddenly everything is clear.

The stone flies from my throat and drops like a dead thing. It smashes hard on something a world away. I'm so *GLAD* to hear the smash and my voice rips up through my throat and I'm singing.

Something clutches at my hand. The touch is gentle but in my hand the lightness becomes heavy, dragging me down. I'm not flying anymore—I'm sinking down to the bottom of the sea. I open my eyes and there's Lilly smiling and nodding, her hand clamped on mine like a vice. She's whispering something in my ear. *Oops*, she giggles and I'm wondering why her hair is all dry and golden when we are under the sea.

The weight of the water is crushing. It's pressing on all the bones in my head. I tell her we won't survive unless she lets go when suddenly, she does. She opens her hand and there, deadly as a cannonball, is the stone. She taps it against my head and the sound is like thunder, *boom!*

My heart goes wild with another crack of thunder and I'm dripping wet, tossing and turning but now there's something soft wrapped around my legs and I look down to see my own sheets with the little blue boats on them and the curtains blowing out toward me with a gust of wind. I lie still, waiting for my heart to slow, feeling the edge of the dream curl back. I listen for the rain that should go with the thunder. But there's only the low whine of wind and after a while, there's no sound at all.

"Hey, Esmerelda, wait!"

Jackson. Damn. I stop and turn around. "Hi—listen Jackson, sorry, but I'm in a bit of a hurry. I have to talk to Lilly about something before class. There she is over at the lunch tables with Catrina and Mitch. I won't have long."

"But did you hear about Asim?"

"What? Can't it wait?" I hear the impatience in my voice and bite the inside of my cheek.

"His mailbox was blown up last night." Jackson's lips go thin and angry.

Oh, not now!

"Can't imagine who would do something like *that*, can you?" he says slowly. Sounds like he's squeezing something nasty out of a tube.

No! I don't want to think about it. I haven't done my math homework, I don't get this new reciprocal fractions business, and I'm thinking out my speech to Lilly.

"Blown apart," Jackson goes on. "You know his dad made it himself? Looks like a little log cabin? Well the door was blown off. It's the sort of thing you could do with copper pipe and dynamite. Although maybe if you had a bunch of powerful firecrackers like Thunders or Three-Quarters, you could do that much damage."

I remember the soundtrack to my dream. "Where's Asim now?"

"He's coming later. Wants to help his dad fix the mailbox. He was too upset about it to come to school. He said he heard something in the night, but was too sleepy to get up and have a look. Did you hear anything?"

"Yes, but I was having this weird dream, and I thought it was thunder. Did it rain last night?"

"Ez, what are we gonna do about this? Badman—"

"Look, Jackson, that fight you had with him was terrible. I thought you were going to kill each other. He just goes crazy sometimes. But we don't know for sure he's responsible for this mailbox thing. It might've been one of those racist gangs that write on the store walls or maybe just . . . a bunch of idiots. You can't always blame . . . anyway, he just likes to show off about his fireworks, you know that. I think he's all talk."

"Oh, come *on*. Everyone knows he did old Mrs. Shore's mailbox down the road. Me and Asim saw him running away, the smoke practically hissing from his feet. You know his dad can get him those fancy fireworks—he buys them on the black market or something. You should see Asim, he's a mess."

Out of the corner of my eye, I watch Lilly stand and pick up her bag. I jiggle my own with frustration. For sure the bell will go and I'll lose the moment. There won't be another time, because I won't find the courage again. "Look,"

124

I burst out, "it's only a mailbox for God's sake. No one was hurt, were they?"

Jackson looks at me strangely. "No." He starts to speak again, very slowly, as if explaining something to a very dim and not very nice kindergartner. "Esmerelda, for you or me, having our mailbox blown up might be just annoying, but for him, well, you know what he's been through. I've told him we're going to get whoever did it, but all he says is forget it, don't make trouble, 'is nothing compared to what life was like before.' And then he goes on about all the 'wonderful' things there are in Australia, but he's bawling and his hands are all trembly. That bastard—I'm just not going to let him get away with it!"

A sinking feeling is spreading in my stomach like sour milk. "Yeah well, nothing we can do right now, anyway," I say briskly, not liking myself or him. "We'll talk about it at recess, okay?"

"Yeah, whatever."

Jackson turns on his heel and stalks off. I look at his hurt back and grind my teeth. Nothing I can do about *him* now, either. I walk quickly toward the lunch tables. As I wave at Lilly, she runs toward me.

"Hey, Ez, guess *what*! Double, triple guess what!"

The tone of her voice reminds me of her knock knock jokes in second grade. I had to say "who's there?" fifty times a day or she'd stop being my friend.

"Guess *what*, I said!"

"What?"

She takes my hands and flaps them up and down with excitement. "We were chosen for the concert!"

Lilly's face is almost fluorescent with triumph. The sour milk feeling clumps in my guts.

125

"Only three groups got in and we're going to be first. Imagine, I'll be so nervous!"

I look down at my hands in hers and remember the dead weight in my dream.

"Oh, don't be scared, Lilly, you'll be a star," says Catrina, coming up and patting her shoulder. "You could wear your new halter top."

"Well, actually my mom—"

"Lilly, could I talk to you a moment?" I try to pull her away.

She looks sideways at Catrina and rolls her eyes.

"It's okay," says Catrina, grinning. "You stars must have a lot to talk about."

We walk a little way along the path toward the classroom. I'm trying to begin but I feel like there's something stuck in my throat again.

"Well, what?" says Lilly. "Aren't you glad? You've got a face like Mom's when she's about to ground me. Geez you're weird, Marx. I'll never figure you out, as long as I live."

This wasn't a promising start. "Well, look," I began, "I really wanted to talk to you about this."

"This what?"

"You know, the concert. It's just, well, the thing is I don't think I'll be able to sing 'Oops! . . . I Did It Again.'"

"Are you kidding me? You do that song in your sleep. What are you talking about?"

I take a deep breath. Lilly's eyes are wide and innocent, like perfect blue plates before you put anything on them. "No, see, I really do find 'Oops' hard to sing. It's just that song, Lilly, I think it's kind of creepy—"

"Creepy?"

"Yeah."

Lilly hasn't taken another breath. She's going red in the face. I wonder if I should remind her to breathe. I start to babble.

"See, I go dead inside when that music starts. I don't know why. I guess I just don't like it—for me it's like eating too many doughnuts with fake cream, sort of makes me sick. It means so much to me to really like the song I'm singing. You know?"

She hasn't breathed yet. Then, with a clutch of horror, I see her eyes filling.

"Oh, I'm sorry, Lilly, look I'll do anything else, even another one of Britney's maybe. Something we both like. It's just, see, the sick business is getting worse. I'm even having nightmares about it. We could try harmonizing, like Valerie says."

"Oh, Valerie this, Valerie *that*. What's *she* got to do with this? It's her that changed your mind, I bet!"

"No, she's got nothing to do with it. She's just helped me see what I *do* like—"

"Ever since you met Jackson, you've been different. No one sees you anymore. *I* don't see you anymore. Girls should never drop their best friends just because they get a boy-friend. You should read what *YM* says about girls like that. You'll be very lonely one day."

A mass of protests crowd into my mind—isn't it all the other way around?—but a foggy heat is gathering behind my eyes. I stare, dumb, at my shoes.

"Never mind." She looks at me kindly now. "Everything will be all right. It's settled. We were chosen, *us*, and everyone thinks we're great!" She throws down her bag and lifts her arms in the air like a singer accepting applause. A shower of dust flies up into our faces. I rub my eyes and wish I could rub myself away, like the genie in Aladdin's lamp.

I mumble something and start to walk away but suddenly she grabs my arm. Her eyes are hard again. "I mean it, everything is *settled*. Say it is, and I'll forgive you."

I stare down at my shoes again. The hot, cloudy feeling in my head blurs the ground.

"Oh, Ez, why do you have to be so weird? Why do you always have to change things, upset everyone!" She lets go of my arm as if it burned her. "My mom has even made us costumes—we've got these pink skirts with black sequins and a pink bikini top, oh, you should see them. I was going to bring them to your house as a surprise!" She stamps her foot, kicking her bag so her math book falls out.

Oh no, math is first thing. My stomach drops like an elevator.

"Lilly, please let's forget this now, we better get to class."

"I'm not moving until you say sorry. Till you say you'll do it, just like we planned and re*hearsed* so many times. And that you'll wear the outfits."

I look at the set of her jaw, the pout of her lip. I've seen that expression so many times. It means *I won't be your friend if you do that, no one will like you anymore, you're so weird, Marx.* I think of all the things over the years that I've done because of that look.

A spark of pure rage clears my head for a moment, like clouds parting. "God almighty, Lilly, I've obeyed your orders since we were five. Have you ever thought maybe I don't *want* to do everything you do? Maybe I've got my *own* . . . things, like . . ."

"Like what?"

"Like . . . oh, I don't know." A fog seems to have taken over my brain, drowning my thoughts. I've gone blank, stupid as a stone. All I can think about is this video clip of Little Richard that Valerie showed me—his band was called The Upsetters and their hair was piled high as Marge Simpson's beehive.

"Well, what are you talking about then?"

I stare at Lilly's socks, pink instead of the regulation white. A thin gold anklet is looped around one ankle. "It's just . . ." I can feel her waiting. The words I'm looking for are nowhere under the fog.

"All right then, let's get to class. I'll just forget you ever said this, okay?" Lilly picks up her bag and gives a little skip. "Wait till you see the costumes. You'll *love* them."

Math is even worse than I'd imagined. And that's saying something. People always tell you the thing you're dreading "won't be as bad as you think." And they're usually right. But some days, the minutes keep on unraveling like a crazy ball of string until all you're left with is a tangled mess at your feet that you can never wind back.

First thing, Norton asks to see my homework. Why me? I'm starting to think he's afraid of my mother. As soon as he sees my blank page, before I can explain about my allergy to reciprocal fractions, Norton gives me detention and ten extra questions. And then he hovers behind my chair watching me do them. "Esmerelda, you should know that," he says every time I hesitate, "why DON'T you?"

The fog hasn't cleared from my head. I feel as if a wall of tears is banking up behind it. Norton is shouting now at someone else, throwing up his hands in despair like some doomed soul pleading for mercy. That's just how I feel. I'm dying to cry, let the tears come like a river flooding, washing away Lilly and that dream and evil Mr. Norton. But I can only cry like that on my bed, facedown, with the door closed. I'll just have to hang on till then.

Catrina stretches across the aisle and passes me a note. "From Lilly," she whispers. It's folded up in tight little squares. I open it under my exercise book. *See our costumes*, it says, and underneath is a drawing of a model as thin as a nail file wearing a short flared skirt and bikini top. There's an arrow pointing to the skirt saying *pink*. I loathe pink. It's my worst color. If Lilly had ever heard anything I'd ever said over the last seven years, she'd know that.

As we file out of class, I catch Jackson's arm. He's in the middle of a coughing fit. "Are you okay?" I ask him.

"Yeah," he chokes. "What about you?"

"Oh, great, couldn't be better." I shrug. "Norton really lost it today, didn't he?"

Jackson nods. "But you know what? Just five minutes of anger like that and your immune system is disabled for six hours."

"That'll teach him."

Jackson and I decide to walk around the track during recess. Both of us feel too restless to sit down, and I don't want to have another conversation with Lilly right now. We talk about Asim, and Jackson tells me the possum house is finished. I can see he's really excited about it and he waves his hands around as he describes how it looks and the tools they used to make it. He might be a carpenter one day, he thinks, maybe go into business with Asim. I guess they'd wear those leather belts around their hips with little pockets for nails and bolts and all. Daniel used to have a toy tool belt like that with a plastic hammer and wrench. He'd try to hammer the salt and pepper shakers into the table. It used to annoy the hell out of Dad. I'd like to see Jackson in a real tradesman's belt. He'd look so cool.

"Well, maybe I could be your secretary or something," I suggest. "I'm never going to be a singer at the rate I'm going."

"I don't think carpenters need secretaries. Anyway, if ever I saw a singer waiting to happen, it's you."

I shrug. "You have to be strong to make it out there. You need to have artistic integrity. That's what Valerie says. And I'm a wimp when it comes to standing up for myself."

"What are you talking about?"

So I tell him about my stupid conversation with Lilly. I bring out the drawing of the skinny model in the pink outfit.

Jackson looks at it and laughs. "Poor girl looks like a stick insect. Did you know some spiders are so thin they have to keep their organs in their legs?"

"It's not funny!"

"No, it's not. Imagine a bunch of huntsmen sitting around going, 'Hey, watch out, you hairy twit, you just stepped on my kidney!'"

I smile weakly.

"Look, I don't know Lilly anywhere near as well as you, but I do know one thing. No matter how loud you talk, Lilly won't hear you if it's something she doesn't like."

"Yeah, just like my mom."

"Sometimes you just have to go it alone. Trust your guts about what's right. That's what Mom says, especially about music. Because the songs you sing are like the guts of you—you can't do it well if you're faking it."

"Like the gospel truth, right?"

131

"Yeah. And she says you've really got it, girl. She thinks she hasn't seen so much talent in years."

A glow spreads out in my stomach. It warms the chill of the whole morning. "Really? She said that?"

"Yeah. She thinks you put your secret self into it, and that's what real artists do. Says you lean toward hard rock, though. Gritty music with strong base lines, that's your thing. Bit of a rebel you are, she says."

"That's me! A hard-rock tragic! She's right. I've been listening to a lot of the stuff she's given me—you know, there's this amazing singer, Patti Smith—"

"Oh God, not Patti Smith. Mom puts that on when she comes home mad from work. She dances around the living room and shakes her head so much I'm sure it's going to fall off."

I grin. "Patti Smith does that to you."

Jackson shrugs.

A small flame of excitement is fanning its way through my chest. "You know, Jackson, what my dream is? I want to sing with a live rock band, or just to start, with an electric guitar. You know, be a rock singer, let myself go. I know what you say about Badman, but if you could just hear him play 'Smoke on the Water,' or Led Zeppelin's 'Stairway,' imagine if we did *that* at the concert, it'd blow them out of the water—"

Jackson's face closes over. He looks as if he's tasting something bad at the back of his throat.

I feel hot all over, and not in a good way. How stupid can you get? I can't believe I told him that. He's gone down deep into that place where you can't get him. And we were so close; he gave me that comment of Valerie's like a present. And I just gave him a slap in the face. Oh, this is such a miserable damn day. It's an "eat crap and *die*" day, just like old Badman says.

"Listen, Jackson, I'm not saying I *like* him or anything," I begin, but my voice trails away like a tap when the main is turned off. I try again, searching for the right words. "I don't understand all this myself. But somehow I don't believe that the *real* Badman is the one everyone sees. He can't be, to play like that. His real song, you know, his true story is in his music. He just wears all that bad behavior like a coat. I wish he'd take it off."

Jackson makes a disgusted face. "A naked Badman is a frightening idea."

He puts his apple core in his paper bag and scrunches it up tight. "Listen, I don't even want to talk about that guy. Just thinking about him gives me a stomachache." And he starts to walk so quickly back to class that I give up trying to catch him. I sit down on the grass right where I am and put my head in my hands, just like old Norton.

After recess there's art; we lay down stripes of colored pastels on dark blue cardboard. It's like watching the sun come up; pale yellow dissolves into orange and red, deepening into the blue above. You rub the stripes into each other, smudging them so that lines disappear and there's just the soft, gradual colors of the sky. Everyone's drawings look beautiful—it's hard to make a mistake with this method, and we're feeling pretty pleased with ourselves. The colors glow like jewels against the dark. We're all instant artists.

As we're hanging the drawings up on the wire, I see Lilly's. It's pretty much total pink. "That's great," I say. But she just rolls her eyes and looks away. I suppose I should have come looking for her at recess. Groveled a bit more.

"The ice queen giving you a hard time?" says a voice at my back. I swing around to see Badman, standing there holding his drawing. His sky is very dark, with jagged black lightning raking through it. I've never seen black lightning. It looks like a CD cover for a heavy metal band.

"Just wanted to say congratulations for the concert tryouts." He's grinning and his voice doesn't sound sarcastic.

"Oh, thanks." I reach for the pegs and give him some. "I'm not sure about the song, though." I say it low, under my hair.

"Yeah. But you've got a great voice—you can go deep, loud. You ever tried rock?"

I glance in Lilly's direction, but she's busy admiring Mitch's drawing. My heart is starting to pound.

Badman sees me looking. "She wouldn't know a good rock song if it leaped up and bit her on the butt. But you, you could be really wild."

"I heard you playing the other day, Led Zeppelin. You were really something. Did your dad teach you to play?"

"Yeah." He rubs his forehead and the pastel on his fingers leaves a streak of black lightning across his eyebrows. He looks fierce, like a thunderstorm about to break.

"Is he still away?"

"Yeah, he's got gigs in New Zealand and some other place. Don't know for how long. You should hear *him* play."

"Your dad plays lead guitar?"

"Yeah, like heavy metal falling from the sky." Badman's face looks different. "That's what some guy wrote about Jimmy Page, the first time he heard Led Zeppelin."

"Jimmy Page?"

"The lead guitarist, dumb ass." Badman's eyes are full of light. "Led Zeppelin was the heaviest blues-rock band back

134

then. But Jimmy didn't want to be labeled, you know? He was really into Indian and Arabic music, too. Gave him ideas. He did the most amazing licks, sometimes his lead breaks would go for half an hour. But he always caught himself in time. He used to say, "That's what it's all about, catching yourself."

I stared at Badman. This was the longest conversation I'd ever had with him. Maybe the longest *anyone* had ever had with him.

"What did the singer do during these long lead breaks?"

Badman's eyes light up. "Robert Plant—that's the singer —he just got into it. See, his singing was real intense, he did the whole rock god thing, and he used his voice and his body like another instrument. The band all worked together, you know, like a single living thing, it was wild."

"How great would that be?" I was having trouble keeping the excitement out of my voice. "It's amazing, Valerie said something like that about soul music—you can use your voice like the chords of a guitar. You know Valerie? Jackson's mother? She's a singer. She's cool, sings soul, blues, she's a professional."

Badman turns away from me and throws his pegs hard into the basket. "Yeah, a professional working at the pub. What does she do, sing her way through sausages and mash, chicken and fries?" He wipes his hands on his pants.

Ruined it again. I just should never have gotten up this morning. Quickly I check Jackson's location. He's over at the other side of the room. At least that's something. If he'd heard Badman, he'd be over here as fast as that black lightning hanging on the wire.

Badman starts to say something. He's hesitating. Maybe he's sorry he said that. Maybe he doesn't want the conversation to end like this, either. Imagine, imagine if he said, *Hey,*

Ez, wanna work out a song together? A rock song? Perform it for the concert? We'll get around Mrs. Reilly somehow. You could sing something wild, Patti Smith, although I bet he doesn't go in for female rockers, he'd say they've got cooties . . .

"Hey, Ez," he says, and he looks at me, all intense. My heart is hammering.

"Yeah?"

"I've got something you've *never* heard before."

"What's that?

He leans in close, glancing around, not moving his head, just sliding his eyes to the corners to make sure no one is near. "Do you want to see something *really* wild?"

"Mm." A prickly feeling is starting to inch up my spine.

"Then come around to my place this afternoon."

"No, I can't, I've got detention and—" The chill up my back is growing icy.

"Forget that, you gotta break loose. If you come you'll see Golden Eagles spreading their wings."

"What are you talking about?"

"Explosions, color, and movement like you've never seen before. It's the sweetest music of all, Ez. 'TNT,' 'Highway to Hell.' You ever heard of AC/DC? I've got Thunders and Three-Quarters—firecrackers with power equal to three quarters of a stick of dynamite."

I shake my arms loose. A cold sweat has broken out on my face. I don't want to hear anymore. Maybe I'm just like Lilly. Or my mother—there's a line like that from Patti Smith. "When doves cry." I can hear it in my head, her voice deep like the bottom of a cave. Over and over, she's playing in my head, so loud I can't hear anything else.

Badman follows me back up the aisle. His breath is hot

on my neck. "You should experience that power, Ez. It'll really rock you."

"Go back to your seat," I hiss at him. "The teacher's looking at you. I'm not interested."

Badman is scowling now. His eyebrows meet in the middle in one long dark line. "I've got enough power stockpiled under my bed to blow up anything I want. A mailbox. A pretty possum house. Watch the fur fry!"

"No!" I put my fingers in my ears. I try to listen to Patti Smith.

"Yeah, so stick that up your snooty little skirt, you try-hard," and he storms back up the aisle and rips his painting from the wire, crumpling it to a black mess in his hand.

7. Jackson

5:55 A.M. Why aren't I surprised?

I stretch and turn over but my fingers nick the cord of the digital clock, bringing it down on the bed. The red numbers glare up at me. Devil eyes in the dark.

Every time I wake in the night that clock says 11:11 or 1:11 or 3:33. How creepy can you get? Odd numbers only. Does this happen to other people? Or is it just me? Maybe there's a pattern at work here, something bigger than me. I'm thinking: am I supposed to learn from this? If so, what? Maybe I should pray more but I'm not sure what to pray for, or who to. I used to do a lot of praying a few years ago, when I was going crazy in Kemp's class. I'd kneel down on the floor beside my bed with my hands together making a cathedral like I'd seen people do in movies. *Please give Mr. Kemp typhoid tomorrow.* When Mom caught me doing it, she just said whatever gets you through the night, but she told me to look out for my knees because she did a lot of kneeling when I was a baby—changing my diapers on the bed—and that's how her knees got all calloused and yucky-looking.

I turn on my back and think about Esmerelda's knees. And her thighs. The way they went up into her black bikini that stretched smooth and tight as licorice. Her cheek was

138

so soft, the day I kissed her after the beach. I wanted to keep feeling the softness against my lips. I could smell her breath, like apples, like the inside of her.

Then that bastard, Badman, outside the gate. *Bastard*.

A queasy feeling starts in my guts. Makes me think of skin congealing on hot milk. My chest is pounding away. I hate this feeling. Happens every time I think about Badman. I raise myself up on an elbow and shove the damn clock back on the shelf above my head.

5:57. The numbers are thin and jointed, like spiders' legs.

In my opinion, those red neon numbers could be sending out an evil signal. Like devil language in morse code. Like Badman putting a spell on Esmerelda. What other reason *can* there be why she can't see he's evil? I wish Mom would stop encouraging her to find her secret self. "Let yourself go," she urges Ez, "explore all kinds of music: go with the songs that thrill you. That's how you'll find your inner voice." Well, that "voice" seems to have something to do with Badman.

Right down inside, somewhere beneath my third rib, I have this nasty feeling that I'm like those white sixties parents in America, the ones who wanted to stop their kids dancing. If I could stop Esmerelda liking Badman's guitar, maybe I would. If I could change her taste in music, maybe I would. But I'd never admit it. Ever.

You've got to let people be free if you love them. Mom's always singing about that.

Whenever I think about Esmerelda, Badman drifts in. He's like some creeping strangler vine, or maybe one of those alien monsters in horror movies—they just move on in with their multiple tentacles and squeeze the life out of everything.

Even my dreams aren't safe from him anymore.

5:59 A.M. My chest feels like a rocket's going off inside it. I need to move. I leap out of bed and pull on my shorts. I have to be at the newsdealer's by six-thirty. I've got a paper route to do.

I make it in eight steps from the front door to the garage. The last two have to be gigantic steps and my legs stretch like scissors. This time of the morning is great, because no one ever interrupts my challenges. I hate being interrupted. You have to go back and start all over again. I arrive at the garage with two feet together and no wobbling. That's good. It's a positive sign, for sure. It might still be a good day.

Inside the garage there's tons of stuff left by the last tenant. Shelves of paint tins, boxes of old books and records, jars filled with nails. There are lots of rat droppings, too. Mom says one day we'll clear it all out so that when she gets a new car she can put it in here, like a real suburban family. Mom puts a lot of faith in family. Once, at Milson Elementary, a parent herding her children into some fancy car told my mother you couldn't call yourself a family unless you had the full house of cards—you know, mom, dad and 2.4 kids (and a fancy car). Mom just looked at her and said, "Congratulations, you're a miracle of evolution." Later, when I asked her what she meant, she said the woman was a throwback, a dinosaur stuck in the ice age. I still didn't really get it but I laughed when she said, "Didn't you notice how small her head was?"

Still, I'd really love it if Mom had a decent car. She's had her Ford Escort for nineteen years (which is a very bad number) so I guess it's only natural that the radiator is gone, the brake pads need replacing and yesterday she was given the news the automatic transmission is messed up. It's all going to cost a fortune. An explosion of cash even louder than

Badman. I told her she should just get rid of it. We live really close to everything now. But Mom's lip got trembly again. She's so loyal to that car. It's like a relative, and we don't have many. Dad bought it for her and later she called it *Sal*. When I asked her why, she said it had been the name of a great-aunt of hers who was bold and daring. Said she'd need a lot of that to get us through the tough times.

So I figure a paper route is the least I can do. Given that no one will offer a thirteen-year-old a job as a dealer in a casino, which is a pity because you can make real money that way.

I wheel my bike out of the garage, trying not to make much noise. Mom worked an extra dinner shift last night and arrived home when I was already dozing off.

Before I open the gate I go over to the maple tree and check my possums. If you stand on tiptoes you can see right into the little house. It nestles in the fork of the tree, comfy and solid just like we'd hoped. The house doesn't seem to be inhabited right now. The guys are still out foraging for their food, I figure. I've seen one bigger possum and a little one inside. I bet they're the family I saw that first night. Even the babies are what you'd call nocturnal. Mom says she knows a lot of singers like that.

Asim and I looked up possums in *Australian Wildlife* and found out about their habits. The day we went to the library it was stinking hot, and it was nice being in that quiet room. You could feel all these secrets lying curled up inside the books. In *Australian Wildlife* there was a photo of a flying fox and its penis was shaped just like a human's, only really little, like a toy. It said that bat poop, called guano, was mined from bat caves and sold for megabucks. Asim and I talked about that for ages—if bats have to go to the bathroom while

141

they're hanging upside down, do they poop all over their faces, or what?

That night I heard on the news that twenty thousand flying foxes dropped dead from the heat. Twenty thousand! I imagined their little feet loosening on the branch, and the thud as they hit the ground. Mom listened to the rest of the news (I got too upset) and she said the flying foxes dropped dead up north because it's even more stinking hot than down here, but still, I wondered how the heat affects possums. Anyway, I make sure now there's a bowl of water for them, even though Mom says there's a lot of moisture in fruit. Every day I leave chopped up banana or apple, just in case they didn't find anything nourishing on their hunt.

You know what? I'd almost put possums up there with even numbers. When I pass their house, even if they're not home, I get this glimmering of gladness like a chink of light when you open the curtains just a little way on winter mornings. It's like looking at the future. That's what the possums do for you.

I unlatch the gate and the morning breaks open above me. Sunrise is the best time of day. You feel as if you could start over, completely.

I put the bike into first gear to ride up the hill to the newsdealer's to pick up my route's newspapers. I could say a little prayer of thanks to Bev Halliday, but I'm not sure it counts properly if you're puffing up a hill and not kneeling next to your bed. Bev gave us the bike when we moved here—it's a brand-new mountain bike—plus she went looking and found us this house to rent, paying half the security deposit money up front. She said Mom could pay it back whenever, she was in no hurry. "Money is only a tool of trade," said Bev. "It's made to be passed around."

Bev doesn't believe in possessions. She told me once that even parents don't own their children. "They are the bows from which children shoot forth as living arrows." She said it was from some old Arabic poem. Bev's house was full of books, even in the kitchen. I used to love the smell of Bev's house. It smelled like spice and mystery, with her Indian incense and herbs boiling on the stove. She'd always cock her head on one side and look you straight in the eye before she smiled and said hello. It was as if she looked right inside you, clear as a TV screen, and whatever was on, it was okay with her. When I'd walk out the door after a visit I knew I'd learned something about the world, even if I couldn't exactly say what.

It was Bev who taught me how to ride this bike. I guess with all the moving, Mom and I had never got around to it. "A boy who's going places has gotta have a bike," Bev said. "Speed is freedom." Funny thing though, for a person who cares so little about money, she still works at the Blue Moon, and that's a place where money is everything.

At the newsdealer's, Bill gives me my box of *Homeland Dailies*. I stuff the rolled-up newspapers into my basket and take off. I head for Boundary Street, to start the two-block rectangle that is my route.

There's a downhill freedom ride before the first house and I pedal fast for a few seconds so I can enjoy the speed. I fling the newspapers at the concrete drives like a dart at a bullseye. I've got a good rhythm going and I think of Mom's pleased smile when I told her Bill had agreed to my delivery job. "You'll be a real suburban kid," she'd said, cuffing me on the shoulder. "Good exercise, good friends, good environment—see, it was all for the best, our move to the quiet shoals of Homeland." She says the last bit in her solemn politician's voice, placing her hand on her heart.

In some ways I agree—if I hadn't moved here, I'd never have met Esmerelda or Asim. But then I'd never have met Badman either, and he's hardly a plus in anyone's life. If I look at Mom's face for a fraction longer after she says the thing about "quiet shoals" and "air you could bottle," I see her smile fade like the sunrise and the clouds come into her eyes. I think she's glad for me, with my new friends and the bike and all, but sad for herself. Waitressing just can't be as much fun as singing.

I haven't told her I'm saving to help with the car. She'd just protest and grow sadder, worrying that *I'm* worrying she can't provide for us and she's a bad mother and all that kind of thing. No, I'm just going to present her with the money like a surprise.

She sure needs a surprise. A good one. In my opinion, Mom is someone who needs really good news right now.

Last night I heard her on the phone talking to Bev. I sat up in bed so I could hear with both ears. "You've got to know when to give up," Mom was saying. "It's one of those skills I never learned." There's silence and I guess Bev was protesting on the other end and Mom was shaking her head. "But, Bev, I've had this dream since I was sixteen," Mom went on. "I was going to write my own songs and be political, famous, make a difference in the world. Yeah, yeah, my voice is okay, but it's not really anything *unique*. I'm not Aretha damn Franklin, am I?" She's quiet again and I could hear her fingers tapping on the kitchen bench. (She doesn't have any nails to tap, what with the way she chews them down to the raw, I'm always telling her.) "Do you remember Band Aid?" Her tone was suddenly lighter. How can the thought of small surgical dressings make anyone happy? "It was 1985, and there was that terrible famine in Ethiopia? And Bob Geldof—remember the Boomtown Rats, 'I Don't Like Mondays'—well, he organized that amazing Band Aid concert to raise money. You watched it on TV? Did you call up and donate? Yeah? Well one-third of the world watched with you, Bev. China, everywhere. The Sheik of Arabia rang up with one million dollars! They made so much money, Ethiopia ate again. That's the power of music for you, huh? It's like magic, touches everyone's soul."

Bev must have told her she could still hang on to her dream, but maybe just lower her expectations a little because Mom got impatient and said, "Yeah, but how much lower do you have to go? I'm not even earning a cent singing anymore, let alone changing the world. But I'm good at taking orders for T-bone steaks." Then she said the thing with the sudden smile in her voice that made me lie back down and put the pillow over my head. "You're right, Bev," she said, "that's the most important thing. Jackson is happy and safe, not a care in the world. That makes it all worthwhile."

Well, that does it, I promised the pillow. She'll never hear any more about Badman from *me*. But if that maggot makes one more heavy breathing phone call, or blows up one more thing that doesn't belong to him, I'll go to the police.

As I work my way along St. Peter's Road, I wonder if all this money I'm earning should go instead toward singing lessons for Mom. I think she's a wonderful singer, just like Bev does, but she's always going on about her range and how it should be bigger. Maybe singing lessons would build her range. Maybe if she could get that low C she'd be happier. Esmerelda told me that before she met Valerie she thought a range was something you cook on. Her mom dreams of getting a new one, plus a dishwasher. There are actually sixteen different meanings of the noun "range." I looked them up that day in the library. The mathematical meaning really hooked me. It was about corresponding sets and numbers going together, tight as twins. You should look it up.

In just half an hour the day has arrived, hot and still. My face is wet as I turn into my street, chugging uphill. The sky is already a deep blue but I can see a last streak of gold cloud, drifting over Esmerelda's house. Even as I look it breaks up into fluffy strands like cotton wool when you pull it slowly apart.

Suddenly a shout trashes the stillness. Something smashes behind doors. I just about fall off my bike and dart a look in the direction of the voices. Badman's house on my left. Quickly I swerve off the sidewalk and into the road. A woman stalks out of the house, not glancing back. At the door, looking after her, stands Badman. He's still in his pajamas. Blue, with yellow bunny rabbits all over them! I start to smirk but the expression on his face stops me. He looks different somehow, and I realize it's as if his face is usually wearing clothes and now they've been ripped off. He looks like he's been crying. Suddenly he sees me and puts his mask back on.

"Take a picture, it lasts longer!" he shouts at me, and thrusts his rude finger up in my direction.

I put two fingers up and jerk them back at him a couple of times. Then I shake my head sadly as if he's the lowest mammal on the lowest rung of evolution and saunter away, if you can saunter on a bike. I go very slowly, to show I'm not scared of him or his rude finger but I'm finding it very hard to pedal uphill without wobbling.

When I've passed two more houses I stop. My heart is gunning and the sweat is pouring off me. Opposite now is Esmerelda's house, minus the gold streak. I stand a minute in the shade of a paperbark tree while my heart slows down. I take a good long look at Ez's house, and the shiny brass even numbers on her front wall.

Unfortunately, leaning on the wall is the woman I just saw stalking out of Badman's house: Mrs. Bradman, I presume. She's watching me and I can tell from the way none of her body parts move, she's concentrating. I bend down to look at the front wheel of my bike, shaking my head again as if there's something terribly wrong with it. When I look back, she's studying her watch. She peers up the road, and gives a little wriggle of irritation so that the cardigan slung round her shoulders falls off onto the wet grass.

The 141 bus into the city is practically always late. Mrs. Bradman probably works in some office in the city. I wonder if she's supposed to be at work by eight A.M. She's probably the sole breadwinner now that her husband's gone. I wonder if she has a bastard of a boss who gives her detention if she's late. Maybe he'll give her the sack.

The next minute I figure this must be it because she's suddenly down on the damp lawn in her stockings and good skirt and all, her head on her knees. She must be really worried. Gone crazy with worry. Her shoulders are shaking and I can hear a thin wailing like the kettle we used to have on Trenches Road before we got it fixed. Her poor cardigan is still lying on the grass. Her shoulders are so thin, like a child's.

Oh, what should I do? Should I run over and help her

up? I wheel my bike off the curb and head toward her. But what can I say? A storm of ideas rush through me. Oh, hi, Mrs. Bradman, can I help, I'm the one who smashed your son's nose? Or maybe I could just warn her about possible knee problems if she makes a habit of collapsing like this? I could bring her over to Mom. Maybe Mom could take her into the city. But no, then Mom would be late.

While I'm thinking all this the 141 bus blunders around the corner. I wave at it and point to Mrs. Bradman. But then I realize she's seen it and in a flash she's picked up her cardigan and brushed down her skirt, standing on tiptoes at the sidewalk. Her stockings have big wet patches at the knees. She disappears into the dark of the bus like a small animal into the stomach of a whale. I watch as the bus swims off. There she is at the window. She looks at me and gives a small shrug. A smile so quick you'd miss it as soon as you caught it.

I watch the bus go all the way down the street and turn left onto Halliwell Road, until it's out of sight. I think of praying again, praying that Mrs. Bradman and her bus don't hit the usual peak hour traffic and that she doesn't get fired.

I realize I'm standing with my bike in the middle of the road, but I've only just begun a challenge and I need to finish it. I'm blinking my eyes in sets of eight, thinking about Mrs. Bradman's shoulders shaking. It's hard to believe someone as tiny as her gave birth to Badman. He must take after his father. But hey, wouldn't it be good if he left home like his father, too?

Then I think of Mrs. Bradman stalking out of the house and the sound of the smashed thing, and I imagine it must be pretty hard to be suddenly left alone with Badman. Damn it to hell, why do I always have to feel *sorry* for someone just when I'm busy being angry? I'm standing here looking at the spot where the bus stopped, feeling so sorry for this stranger Mrs. Bradman that my guts ache. But I just keep seeing her poor cardigan lying on the lawn like one of those horrible chalk drawings police make around a dead body.

Suddenly, in between blinks, I catch sight of something blue moving at the top of the hill. At the same moment the low purring noise that seems to have been throbbing in the background builds to a roar and a blue Mustang turns into the street. I finish on sixty-four and grab the handlebars of my bike, pulling it out of the way. It twists around and I almost drop it. Surely the driver's seen me by now? But the Mustang's not slowing down. He's heading straight for me! He's accelerating—his foot must be flat to the floor!

In the count of one I realize I haven't got time to save the bike and I make a flying leap for the curb. My feet hit the concrete and I tumble headfirst into the neighbor's garden as the sound of tearing steel cracks the air. I lift my head to see my bike shoot up in the sky like a pinwheel. It smashes down on the sidewalk, an inch away from my foot.

As the car squeals around the corner onto Halliwell, I try to make out the license plate. I can only see the first two letters—RO, I think. I don't bother with the numbers. I know them too well.

I sit on the curb, my heart pounding. My whole body is flushed hot. The world seems to be sliding downhill into a tiny black pinhole. A heave like a wave flipping over wrenches my guts and I vomit all over my shoes. When I'm finished I sit with my head in my knees, just like Mrs. Bradman. I remember Mom saying once you should keep your head at the same level as your feet when you feel sick. But all I can smell is the vomit on my shoes.

Mom—what am I going to tell her? The good news? This is just what she needs. I lift up my head and look around. The morning is as silent as if it's holding its breath. The neat lawns, the concrete drives. You could blink and imagine none of this happened. Badman in his bunny pajamas, Mrs. Bradman and her cardigan, the blue Mustang. I am the only witness. If I dropped dead like a flying fox, maybe you'd have to say none of this was real. Mrs. Bradman sure as hell won't admit to it. And her stockings would have dried by now.

Then I remember the bike. That, for sure, is real. I stand up to take a look. My legs are shaking. I don't really want to see the damage.

The back wheel must have taken most of the impact. It's twisted around at an angle, and there's a long dent in the steel. It could be fixable, but how much would that cost? Sure as anything I can't ride it like this. I wonder how I'll be able to do the paper route on foot. I mean, I can do it all right, but I wouldn't bet I could do it as quickly, in time for school.

I haul up the bike and start to drag it home. It's hard with these jelly legs. I brush some hair out of my eyes and feel something sticky. When I look at my hand, there's blood. Now I realize my head is aching like crazy in a place just above my ear and I want to be sick again.

I open the gate and wheel the bike in. I'm going to have to lock the bike away and sneak into the bathroom to wash my face before Mom sees me. I creep up the path and see something dark flash up the trunk of the maple tree. Quietly I lay the bike down and sort of stretch myself around the tree. I hold my breath. There, now, is a curl of tail. Above it, a glint of eye. I stand beside the tree for a moment, letting myself know that whatever happens out there beyond the gate, my possums are safe in bed.

I lock the garage and creep in the back door. In the bathroom I twist my head to the side and swivel my eyes to study the sore place. There's dried blood around a long gash and underneath the skin is already bluish and dead looking. Just bruising, I tell myself, but the sight of it makes me want to heave again. Maybe I've got a concussion, I whisper at the mirror, panic rising. Maybe I've got brain damage and I won't even know the difference between equivalent and improper fractions. What *is* an improper fraction? I look into my own eyes. They're full of fear like that chimpanzee I saw once at the zoo. An improper fraction is when the numerator is larger than the denominator. Quickly I look away and get busy with the soap and water.

It's hard to wipe away the encrusted blood without wanting to scream. The warm water is making the wound bleed again and now I'm really wondering if I should tell Mom. I mean, this must be quite bad as far as bike accidents go. Particularly when it didn't look like an accident at all. That Mustang didn't slow down when it saw me. It didn't swerve. It accelerated, and came straight for me. On a scale of one to ten, this accident could definitely be a seven.

As I hold the warm washcloth to my head, a total baby moment sweeps over me and all I want is my mom's arms around me.

I go into the kitchen. Mom must still be in bed. The kettle is cold and empty. I fill it and wait for it to boil. I take deep breaths in sets of four. I count them at the back of my mind while I rehearse what I'm going to say to Mom. The counting is soothing, like a lullaby.

English Breakfast tea, lots of milk, no sugar. I put a cookie on the saucer.

Mom's room is dim, with the curtains still pulled. I can see a round boulder shape under the Indian comforter. As I gently put the cup down on her bedside table, Mom stirs and pops her head over the sheets. She looks like a sleepy panda.

"I was too tired to take off my mascara last night." She grins and spits on her finger, rubbing at the black crusts under her eyes. I think I might be sick again.

"That's such an icky habit," I say, looking carefully at the cup instead of her. "I made English Breakfast."

"Oh, thanks, honey," she says, sitting up with excitement. "Aren't I the luckiest mom in the world?" She takes a long noisy slurp and pats the bed. "So, did you do your paper route this morning?"

I sort of collapse onto the spot she's patted. "Yes and well, see—"

"That's great, Jackson." She leans forward and Frank, my old teddy, falls off the bed. "Pick him up will you, darling, I'd hate him to think I don't care about him just because now I've got real company."

I bend down to haul up Frank, who's been sleeping with Mom ever since I gave him up at eight. No wonder *I'm* weird, I think wearily. Let alone poor Frank.

"Jackson, are you ready? Frank, are you listening? I've got some wonderful news!"

I look at her face and see the black has made its way into her eye wrinkles, which are deep with smiling. She looks strangely, crazily happy!

"What?" I say cautiously.

"Well, I nearly told you last night but you were so sleepy and I wanted you to enjoy the full glory of this moment—"

"What?"

"I'm singing tomorrow night!"

"Where? Not at the casino!"

She shudders, and her smile tightens for a moment. "No, Jackson, my boss asked me to perform at the pub—how about that?" She does a whooping kind of laugh and squeezes Frank. "The jazz band booked for Thursday called to cancel because their singer has the flu, so Bradley, the boss, asked me to audition. The band came over and do you know what, the boss *loved* it. You should have seen him, foot tapping away. The band was great and then, as if he didn't want it to finish, Bradley asked me to do another number just for fun. He grabbed poor old Polly, you know the one with the dodgy knees, and whisked her around the dance floor. I saw a whole other side to him. After that he bought me a drink and told me his entire life story. Hey, Jackson, what's that on the side of your head?"

I ducked and turned away. 7:57 said Mom's digital clock. As the last number clicked over to eight, I made up my mind.

"I fell off the bike—wasn't looking where I was going."

"Let me have a look, have you washed it—"

"Yeah, yeah, it's okay. You know, it's getting late and I haven't taken a shower yet." I get up and start backing away. "But listen, Mom, I'm really pleased about your gig."

Mom almost claps her hands. She looks so happy sitting up there in bed that even the black smears under her eyes don't make her look old. She makes me think of the sunrise this morning, like she's starting over.

How can you take that away from someone?

"So wait, Jackson, do you want to ask Ez to come? I know it's not her kind of music, but she might be interested.

You two could have dinner together first. Maybe she could even do a number with me."

"Yeah, I'm sure she'd want to come." The thought of going out to dinner with Esmerelda, even if it was somewhere with my mother, nearly made me forget the pain in my head.

"And Asim—do you think he would want to?"

"Yeah, sure. I'll ask them both today."

"Okay." Mom picks up her cup again and dunks her cookie into it. "This is the best tea I've ever tasted. See, Jackson, isn't it like I always said? Love the universe and it will love you back." She sits smiling in this dazed way while her cookie breaks off and goes floating soggily around her cup.

I suppose she'll go on sitting there, being happy, until all of the cookie gets waterlogged and sinks like a submarine.

8. Esmerelda

I wonder what Valerie is singing right now. Maybe it's Patti Smith's rendition of Prince's "When Doves Cry." Doves make you think of peace, of soft gray winter mornings. There's none of that in this song. There's sweat, heat, blood, and guts. Patti Smith feels things "in her bowels." Valerie says Patti is electrifying. She says you ache with her. It's true, too. You wouldn't classify Patti Smith as soul—she's more punk rock—so I think Valerie might be exaggerating when she says Patti is a favorite of hers. But for sure Valerie thinks Patti Smith is a legend, a real artist. Who wouldn't, if she can make you ache?

Valerie *could* be singing that song right now.

Maybe I could leap out this window right now. Maybe I could smash the glass and leave home. Then I'd be on the missing persons list at the Homeland Police Station. Mom would have to go there every day after the bank, sobbing into her handkerchief. She'd hang onto the detective's sleeve. *If I could just have that day again, I'd let her go,* she'd sob, *if I could just have my daughter back, I'd let her fly . . .*

Yeah, if I ran away, then she'd be sorry. Maybe I could write a song about it. I could call it "Let Me Go to the Pub!" Well, maybe I should cut out the pub bit. What rhymes with "go"? Sew, low, show . . .

Patti Smith says people screaming at each other sounds like doves crying. That line makes *me* cry.

Valerie burned that CD for me. But I could never play it at home because one of the songs is called "Pissing in the River" and the f-word is all over the place. Mom would have a fit.

I guess it doesn't matter anymore what Mom thinks because I'll probably never talk to her again. She sure doesn't want to talk to *me*. She called me a "mindless airhead," which is actually a tautology, the English teacher said. A tautology is when two things are saying the same thing, so that makes one of them repetitive and useless. Like most of the things my mother says. I tried to tell her this, about the tautology business I mean, because I wanted her to notice that I've actually been paying attention in English, which is a subject that some people think is just as important as banking but she just went on screaming at me. We really screamed at each other. It's never been quite like that before. Daniel went and hid behind the sofa. Dad went for his two mile jog. Tonight was just about the worst night of my life.

She was really, really mean. Called me names like a little kid. She called me a "singing canary" as well as a "mindless airhead." I told her the singing canary bit couldn't be true because that was the term used to describe Kylie Minogue and I don't even *like* Kylie Minogue. Patti Smith to Kylie is like red meat to fake cream. But Mom couldn't care less what kind of music I like. She has no idea. She just looked at me with that horrible sneer on her face. You could tell my words weren't going in, in between her ears. Her face was so hard, it looked like it was made of concrete.

But her words went into me. They're still in here, pricking just under my skin. They're like little arrowheads. I

wouldn't tell her, but they really hurt. I can feel them starting to sink into the deeper part of me. Maybe they'll bury
themselves in my *bowels*. I hope not, I don't want those
mean little arrows to become part of me. Why do parents
only love you when you do what they want? When you act
like little models of them? And then you're supposed to be
grateful for all the time they put into helping you grow into
a banker.

I knew it wasn't going to be easy. I'm not allowed out
on a week night anymore because there's always extra math
to finish. So I planned it all really thoroughly. I decided to
tackle Mom on her own. Parents together are like a brick
wall—there are no footholds or ways through.

So I picked five o'clock when Dad was getting ready for
his run and Mom was in the kitchen about to start dinner.
I planned to have dinner out at the pub. After dinner (fish and
chips or maybe that new special, curried lamb chops), I was
going to hear "When Doves Cry," "Respect," "A Natural
Woman," "Say a Little Prayer for Me," "I Feel Good," "River
Deep Mountain High," "Send Me," oh, anything Valerie
chose to sing in her black sparkly dress. She even said I
might do a song with her. Imagine *that* . . .

"No," said Mom, and started peeling the potatoes.

"What?"

"I beg your pardon."

"For what?"

"Say, I beg your pardon. 'What' is rude."

"Well, I beg your pardon then." See I didn't answer back
even though I wanted to run that potato peeler over her
fingers.

"I said no. It's midweek and you have to catch that early
bus tomorrow for your exam."

"I'll put my alarm on. So what if for one day I don't have the required nine hours sleep or whatever."

"Have you forgotten what day tomorrow is?"

"Friday. It will be the day after Valerie Ford sang at the pub to a standing ovation. The day after her young friend, Esmerelda Marx sang—"

"No, it is the day you have a second chance at the scholarship exam for Hammond House."

"So what? We're talking about tonight, not tomorrow. I won't be at the pub to*morrow* for Christ's sake."

"Don't swear or you can go to your room. And don't take that know-it-all tone with me, thank you. You've got all your life to sit around in some pub listening to amateurs—"

"Valerie Ford is not an amateur! She's sung in—"

"But only one day to take an exam that could decide your whole future. Do you want to be tired and not thinking clearly on that very important day?"

"I don't even want to go to that pushy private school, I told you that. And as *if*. As if I'd get in with *my* math. You're just kidding yourself. I'll just have to sit there in some freak-out cold hall for four hours staring at questions that make me feel stupid. I'm only doing the exam because you want me to. I don't want to change schools. But what *I* want doesn't count. It's only *my* life, I suppose."

"Bye!" called Dad from the porch. "Be back in forty-five!"

"Do you know how much all this tutoring is costing your father and me?" Mom goes on. "A fortune, that's what. And all the thanks we get is you swanning around singing low-life songs and trying to get away with as little work as possible. What I want to know is, what's in your head, Esmerelda? *Air?*"

That's when I got really angry and told her *she* should go to the private school if she was so crazy about it and she said the thing about mindless airhead. I said, well I'm your daughter, so what does that make you? She ended up throwing the potato peeler at me and bursting into tears. Her face went all scrunched and collapsed like the wet dishcloth I had in my hand. I threw it on the floor at her feet and she just about went crazy. Her eyes went all wide as if she couldn't believe what was happening and she actually screamed, like some wounded jungle animal.

I ran out of the kitchen but she came after me.

"Go away!" I yelled, slamming the door against her.

"Don't you shut me out, young lady. I'm your mother. When you're eighteen you can do what you like but while you're in this house you'll do as I say. I'm only doing what's best, you're just too young to understand it now. One day you'll know all about it!"

I opened the door wide and yelled at her angry back disappearing up the corridor. "One day I'll leave this house and you'll never hear me sing again. I'll be *out* of here!"

Mom came flying back down the hall then with her mashed potato thingy in her hand so I shut the door quick as lightning. She banged on the door, telling me she didn't know how she'd got a daughter like me and I said well there must have been a mistake at the hospital and she said she would never have dared to speak to her mother like that, so I said maybe her mother was much nicer than her and that really got her because she kicked the door with her foot, it was a low savage *futt* sound and then she started going on about her mother and how much she missed her and *she* would have known what to do. I was starting to melt a little hearing the break in her voice and all this stuff about her childhood but then she said the thing about mindless airhead again so I yelled, "Leave me alone!" and pushed over the chair at my desk and it made a great crack as it fell against the bookcase. A chunk of wood fell out of the leg.

I didn't have any dinner. I stayed in my room, watching the light dying outside. Asim would have gone to the pub with Jackson. He said he was going to ask his father. *His* dad would have let him go, for sure. Asim says his dad just wants him to be happy. But then Asim gets good grades in math without even trying. I guess when your kid is really smart it must be easier to let them be happy.

I hate it when they say, "We're so disappointed in you." That's worse than anger. Mom gets this sorrowful tone in her voice as if she's at a funeral; you can see all her hopes for her daughter's bright future flashing before her eyes, R.I.P.

I creep out of the room about nine o'clock to pee. I tip-toe into the kitchen to get a glass of water. The television in the living room is blaring away and the Treasurer is talking about interest rates going up. Is that all anyone talks about in this country? Dad is shaking his head, groaning, and Mom is holding his hand. You'd think war had just been declared on Australia, the kind of grief they're in.

On the way back to my room, Daniel bumps into me coming out of his room. He's carrying a plate.

"We had hamburgers. I said I wanted two but I only ate one. Here," and he shoved the plate into my hands. "I can't sleep when I'm hungry, can you?"

Daniel's always the one that tips me over the edge. Little kids, they've got such big hearts. If grown-ups only knew it, they could learn so much from them. Little kids only want the people they love to be happy. You don't have to be rich or smart or anything for Daniel. Just happy.

He starts to pat my shoulder, which is a bit awkward seeing he's so much smaller than me. We stand there in the hall with the hamburger balanced between us, and he's making this kind of cooing sound he's heard Marge do for little Maggie on the Simpsons. "Don't cry," he mumbles.

"Go on, you get back to bed," I say softly. "I'm all right. I'll go to sleep now. Thanks for the hamburger."

Sleep. As *if*. Hunger isn't good for getting to sleep, but anger is worse. There was this boy from France in our class last year and he used to get "unger" mixed up with anger. He had trouble with his "H's," never putting them where they should be. "Et ez almost ze time for lernch?" he'd ask. "I ham very angry." Everyone laughed but I remember thinking that maybe the two things *are* connected. When you're really, really angry, there's a kind of emptiness in your stomach, a hole that feels as if it will never be filled.

After I ate the hamburger (*it's your own fault it's cold, if you'd come to the table when you were supposed to it would have been much nicer*), I tried getting into bed and closing my eyes. But behind my lids there was Valerie at the mike in her black dress. The drummer sitting behind her, the electric guitarist on her left. There'd be a sax, too, and a keyboard. By now Valerie would be really loose, she'd be getting wild. There'd be sweat running down her neck and dark patches under her arms. She said she always bought dresses for performing that wouldn't stain under the arms because if you didn't get hot on stage, then you weren't really singing. Once, in America, when she went to a Tina Turner concert she got front row tickets and got hit by flying sweat when Tina did a shimmy way down low like a wet dog shaking.

It's no use, this sleeping business. I'm not hungry anymore but I'm angry. Will I be angry all my life? I won't live very long in that case because Jackson said just six minutes of anger and your immune system is disabled for five hours. Or was it the other way around? Numbers just don't stick in my no-brain. Why doesn't my mother get that? Why doesn't she know her own daughter? Hi, I'm Esmerelda Marx, I've lived here for thirteen years and I like hard rock, soul, a bit of jazz, some heavy metal, fish and chips, my brother, catching waves. I hate math and tautologies. How do you do?

Sometimes when you can't sleep you get so hot under the covers you feel like you might start melting into the bed. I'm sure sticking to the sheets. So I give up for a bit and trudge over to the window. I open the window wider and lean on the sill, my face in the breeze. Except there is no breeze. It's a hot, still night, like a pot of glue. Everything looks stuck on out there, even the white circle of light beneath the street lamp. It lies on the road like a big paper moon some kindergartner might have cut out and pasted on.

I look across at number seventy-three. You can't see the number very clearly, not like our sixty-eight that Mom polishes with Brasso. Valerie has let Chinese jasmine grow all over it. There's no outside light on. The house is so deserted it looks as if no one's lived there for the last century practically. They're all out far away, dancing in the light. I'm stuck here in the dark looking at the last signs of life like some usherette after a movie.

I pinch my arm to make sure I still feel. How does that song by The Rasmus go? It's from their album *Dead Letters*. Something about watching and waiting in the shadows, waiting for the right time . . .

There are snatches of song, melodies in my head all the time. Sometimes I wonder if I've ever had an original thought (as my mother suggests) or if everything I think is some line from a song. It's a frightening idea. But music takes you over, takes you somewhere else. It's like Valerie said that day after the beach—about kids dancing to rock 'n' roll. Listening to a good song is a bit like going into a trance: you forget the outside rules and go inside, into this space of your own. How good will it be one day when I have a boyfriend? We'll dance with our arms around each other, in that space together. My head will be on his shoulder and we'll feel so close. We'll listen to our favorite songs, over and over. I can't wait to be older.

Valerie showed us a video of those Motown singers, Diana Ross, Marvin Gaye. They practiced their hip wiggles and grapevine dances six hours a day. Marvin Gaye did this song, "Sexual Healing." That's a bit gross but he just wanted people to love each other. Jackson rolled his eyes when his mother put on the song. Make love not war, Marvin Gaye said.

My dad thinks Frank Sinatra was the best singer in the world. Well, you know what old Frank said about rock 'n' roll? He said it would be the end of civilization.

What are they all so afraid of, I want to know?

All the lights are off across the road. It must be really late. I check the clock—11:41. Geez, and on a school night. Jackson and Asim are so lucky. Valerie must be doing about a hundred encores.

Suddenly, in the light from the street lamp, I see something move. A shadow creeps across the pool of bright asphalt. It freezes for a moment in the middle of the road. I can see a solid shape, bulky but not tall. He's twisting around, looking straight at this window. Quickly I snap off the bedside lamp and duck down, so that only the top of my head peeps over the windowsill. But I can make out a baseball cap and a bomber jacket. The light is glinting off the metal buttons. He raises an arm. Is he pointing at me? Waving? No, he's picking his nose. He's doing a real excavation. It's Badman!

I almost laugh out loud but then I see he's turned and is crossing the road. He's careful to go slow, his boots making no noise on the road. He steps up onto the sidewalk, across the grass. He's heading toward Jackson's house. Oh, no, what's he planning to do?

Just before he opens the gate he fumbles in his jacket pocket. He brings something out and looks at it.

I'm not waiting to find out what he's got. I yank my bathrobe off the bed and run down the hall. He's going to blow up their mailbox, I know it. *Idiot,* he's everything Jackson said he was. I can't believe it. I make myself slow down at the front door and carefully twist the knob so it doesn't squeak. I leave the latch thingy pressed in so it's unlocked and I can get back in. I won't be long, I tell myself, unless Badman kills me.

My heart is pounding away as I spring out onto our lawn. *Ow*, those damn thorns! I wish I'd put on slippers. No time, for sure he's heading toward the mailbox. What nerve—Valerie could be home any minute. But wait, he's not stopping at the mailbox. He's disappearing inside the gate . . . Oh, no, the possum house!

I run at the gate and push it open. There, right under the maple tree, a small plume of flame floating in the dark. I make out Badman, leaning against the tree. He swings round to face me. There's a lighter in his hand. In the light of the flame I see his eyes go wide and a surprised smile flits across his face. Everything's happening together, fast like a speeding train, but it's so weird because I'm picking out each detail in the dark as if it's a list I'll need to remember. I watch him open his other hand, and see the long thin cylinder that fits neatly in his palm. He grins at me and his fingers close around it. I'm stuck here, glued. It's like watching a bus coming at you and not getting out of the way.

The wick catching alight does it. As he reaches up toward the little house I leap across the path and lunge at him, my head barrelling into his stomach. He topples and we both crash to the ground, football style. Out of the corner of my eye I see the firework still in his hand. The wick has almost burned away. It'll blow any minute. "*Throw* it!" I yell.

"Get your shoulder off me!"

I lift up and he throws the thing way down the lawn. Just a heartbeat later there's the loudest explosion I've ever heard. My ears are singing in top C. The sound keeps going, *eee eeeee*, like ripples around a stone after you hurl it in a river.

"You *moron*!" I pant.

"That was my best Thunder!"

"Cretin!"

"Hey, you like this position? I do."

I look at him and realize I'm still lying on top of him with his great mug leering up at me.

I jump off and pull my bathrobe around me. I'm shaking like a leaf. "Why do you *do* this stuff? You're such a fool, I just don't get it, hurting people, hurting yourself."

"You're the one who goes jumping on me like Bruce friggin' Lee! My back's just about split down the middle!"

"You could have blown off your hand, or my head!"

"No, see, I made the wick extra long. You just add string to the real wick and dip it in a bit of kero and that way there's time to put it where you—"

"But why? What's Jackson ever done to you?"

165

"Friggin' almost broke my nose—"

"Only when you insulted him nearly to death. And all those phone calls, what a cowardly bloody thing to do, just breathing away like some shabby porn star."

"What phone calls? I didn't do any phone calls. I just like burning stuff." He bends down and starts hunting around for his lighter. "Where is it? Now look what you've done."

"What *I've* done? God almighty."

"That lighter is my dad's, from his Queensland tour. Everyone in the band got this special Zippo each. It's a world famous windproof lighter with a lifetime guarantee. My dad gave me his."

"Oh, boo hoo."

He finds it halfway down the lawn near the mango tree. I hear his grunt of relief and he comes back, trying to walk casual, with his old swagger.

"You ever try this again, and I'll tell the world," I say.

"Yeah? Why don't you tell them now?"

We're standing there, glaring at each other, when we hear a car door slam.

"They're home!" I whisper. I don't know why I'm whispering. But I feel guilty standing here in my pajamas, as if it was me who was trying to blow up the possum house.

"Ah crap!" hisses Badman. "What'll we do now?"

"We?"

"You messed this up, I'd have been outta here so fast—"

Another door slams.

"Come on. We can go that way, climb over the side fence."

I'm standing there wondering what I should do when the gate opens.

We freeze.

It's not Valerie. It's not Jackson.

It's a man built like a mansion with extra guest rooms attached to his shoulders. The muscles in his legs are so big they seem to prevent him from walking. He's moving toward us, lumbering from side to side like a doll that can't bend at the knees. It's like watching King Kong coming at you.

I want to scream but there's a stone in my throat.

"What are you two kids doing?" His voice is low like a double bass. I bet he could get the bottom C on the piano.

"Nothing," mumbles Badman. He's staring like a maniac.

The man raises his hand to smooth back his hair. His coat swings open and I see SECURITY written on his black T-shirt.

"You make that explosion?" asks the man. His voice doesn't go up at the end. It isn't a question.

We just go on looking at him.

"Are you Neighborhood Security?" asks Badman. "Like Neighborhood Watch or something?" There's relief in his voice. I know how he feels. Even if we do get into trouble, a neighborhood kind doesn't seem so bad. There'd probably be a lot of sitting around and talking about anger management. Maybe some community service. This guy probably lifts weights because he's got low self-esteem. Maybe he's a banker.

But the man just raises an eyebrow. "Something like that. Do you live here?"

"Yes, sure do," says Badman quickly.

The man nods. "Your mom out, huh?"

"Yeah, we just had some friends over," Badman goes on. "A party." He points at me and grins. "She's my sister. She's thirteen today. We just had a little firework or two, you know, to make it special. We're sorry," Badman adds with an oily smile, "we didn't know it would be so loud. We won't do it again, sir, promise."

Fool. He's thinks he's being so clever.

A cold feeling like iced water is spreading along my neck. If this guy belonged to Neighborhood Watch he'd be part of the neighborhood. He'd know who lived here, wouldn't he? And *we'd* sure have spotted this King Kong on the street before now.

I kick Badman but he ignores me.

The man is frowning at Badman. Then he glances at me. "Didn't tell me he had a sister," he mutters to himself.

"What?" says Badman.

The man is looking around, over our heads. "Seventy-three all right," he says, nodding his head. Then he does something that makes my heart just about leap through my chest. He starts humming the theme to *Rocky*.

"Listen," I burst out. My voice is a squeak. "Listen," I say, a bit louder, "we don't live here at all, he's just making up stories—"

"Why are you here in the dead of night in your pajamas then, girlie?"

I look at Badman. But he's standing there like a tree. I open my mouth to explain about Badman's firework fixation when the man reaches into his jacket, pulling it to one side. We both see the gun sticking out of his belt.

"Hey, you're no Neighborhood Watch!" bursts out Badman.

"No kidding," says the man. He pulls out a pack of cigarettes and a box of matches. He takes his time lighting a cigarette. I grab Badman's hand and tug it. But he's still doing the tree thing, rooted to the ground. The man slides his pack of cigarettes back into his inner pocket.

The repeat glimpse of that belt must have unfrozen Badman because suddenly I feel his hand tugging mine and he starts to yell. "*HEL*—" he screams but the man whips out his gun so quick that his hand blurs. He drops the matches.

"Shut up," hisses the man.

The sound is sliced off. It falls dead into the silence.

Badman starts to whimper.

"Now you're irritating me," the man says. He leans close to us so that the gun just brushes Badman's bomber jacket. "And I don't like to be irr-it-a-ted." The man looks at us and smiles slightly. He looks pleased with himself, as if he's proud that he knows such a big word.

Four syllables. Jackson would notice that. Oh, Jackson, why don't you come home?

"The people who live here aren't home," I try again. "See there was no party—"

"Yes, there was," Badman cuts in, staring hard at me, "and our mom and dad are right there in the house."

"Thought you said your mom was out," the man says.

"No, she went out before, I forgot, but she came home. And my dad will come out here any minute with his hunting gun . . ."

Rocky looks at the dark house that was supposed to have just finished a party.

"Yeah, sure, and I'm a gorilla."

"*Well*," I say before I can stop myself.

"Shut your gob," the man barks at me. Then he takes a step toward Badman and leans close. "You don't have a father, little boy. I know that. You live here with your mother. That's the sad story. That's what I've been told. And your mother has to work nights. So no more fairy

169

tales or I'll get agitated again. Ag-it-a-ted, see? I might even get *incendiary*."

Badman looks like he's been hit.

"You kids know what *in-cen-di-ary* means?"

"No," I say quickly. I try to make my voice interested. Maybe if we can spin this out Jackson and Valerie will get home. "What does it mean?"

The man starts to hum. *Rocky*. His face looks smug, like a kid with a secret. *I know something you don't know!*

But then Badman makes this sound. It's low, coming from deep in his throat, and suddenly he charges at Rocky, his fists slamming into the guy's stomach.

Rocky must do a lot of sit-ups because he doesn't even flinch. His stomach is probably like a brick wall. Badman staggers back and Rocky doesn't sway even one inch. But his face has lost that pleased look. He looks angry now and very *irr-it-a-ted*.

Suddenly he reaches out and grabs us both under the arms, lifting us up. He has us dangling there like rag dolls, one in each hand. We both start to kick but he just lumbers straight to the gate and kicks it open.

"Get in the car," he barks, putting me down first.

"Damn, this is a Ford Mustang," says Badman. "What model is it?"

"Eighty-nine. Two door coupe, turbocharged, massaged from head to toe—"

But Badman isn't listening. He gives a mighty lunge and breaks free of Rocky's grip. With Badman grabbing my arm we take just one running step before we feel the man's hands like iron clamps on our necks.

"Where are you taking us?" says Badman in a high voice I've never heard before.

Rocky doesn't answer.

I glance quickly down the street. Rocky sees me and reaches into his jacket.

"Get in the car or you'll be a *dead* girlie," he snaps, showing me his gun.

He opens the door of the Mustang. I stand there, not breathing. My heart is thumping painfully. I won't be able to stay upright much longer—the bones in my knees have dissolved into something floppy. Couldn't some miracle happen now? Couldn't Badman turn into Superman and flatten the guy?

Suddenly I feel something hard in my back. It grinds into the knob of my spine. Rocky gives an extra twist of the gun and pushes me forward. He lifts up the passenger seat and I fall into the back, my knees hitting the floor.

Before I have time to crawl up onto the seat I feel Badman dropping on top of me, his chin hitting hard against my spine. This is the smallest backseat I've ever seen. It's like being thrown in the trunk. Or a coffin. Rocky gets in behind the wheel and I hear the key click in the ignition.

We're both still half on the floor when the engine starts up. Rocky revs the Mustang to a roar and swings out from the curb, sending us sliding against the doors. My face slams against the door handle. It stings like hell. I hold my face and look up to see Valerie Avenue disappearing out the window.

9. Jackson

"Do you want sausages and mash, too?" the waitress behind the counter asks.

"Excuse me?" says Asim.

"Sausages," I tell him.

"I'll have whatever he's having, please," Asim tells the waitress. "It looks very delicious, thank you."

The waitress smiles and gives him an extra sausage.

We take our meal over to the table. The football is on the big plasma screen right in front of us: highlights from last season. There's a replay of the Bulldogs versus the Roosters. The man at the next table sits with a forkful of steak poised halfway to his mouth while we unload our tray and get silverware and stuff. He doesn't move until a whooping cry goes up around the pub—the Bulldogs scored a goal.

"See that?" The man winks at me. He swallows his steak. "Perfect shot. Damn beauty!"

"That was El Masri kicking, wasn't it?" Asim leans over to the man. "He hardly ever misses, does he?"

"No, that's right, son," nods the man. "You watch, he gets another before half time. He's amazing."

Asim nods happily and starts on his sausage.

I'm starving and I've devoured half the plate before I look up.

"Okay, boys?" It's Mom leaning over us in her bright red dress. She kisses us on the top of our heads and I just about keel over and die. I hope the man next to us isn't watching. When she leans down like that you can see this long line of her cleavage. I should have told her before we left home to keep her back straight.

"Hello, Valerie," says Asim. "These are very tasty sausages. Thank you for inviting me."

"I'm so glad you're here, sweetheart. When you finish you can come into the other room where I'll be performing. You know, next door? With the dance floor and tables with the lamps? Normally kids aren't allowed in there but because you're with me, Barry says it's okay. Just mention that if anyone asks." She straightens up, to my relief, and stands there beaming at us. Her flowery perfume drifts over our sausages. She's jiggling away, sending out waves of excitement and nerves.

"Make sure you visit the bathroom before you go on stage," I remind her.

She bursts out laughing and kisses me again. My ears are burning. She's so over the top she's like a weather pattern out of control, the scary results of global warming. I hope she sings okay. I hope *she's* happy with it. Her eyelashes are about twice as long as usual. They must be false. I hope they don't fall off in the middle of everything.

When she's gone El Masri kicks another goal just like the man said he would. Asim raises his glass of ginger ale at the man and they smile at each other.

"This is a beautiful place, Jackson," he says, and swigs down his soda.

I look around the room, at the glary yellow walls and pink carpet and the steaming roasts and lasagnas, salads and pastas lying stacked in their silver trays behind the glass counter. We can hear the *doiing doiing* of the slot machines coming from the room at the end of the hall, with the bright lights flashing like Las Vegas. Soon the chicken raffle will be called over the loudspeaker, and then it'll be time to go in and hear Mom sing.

I suppose it *is* nice here. It's so friendly with its fresh paint and clean surfaces it almost makes you forget about the bad things that can happen. Things like nearly getting killed on your own street in broad daylight. Well, sunrise.

All day I've been burning to tell Asim about the bike and the Mustang, but somehow it never seemed like the right time. He was so excited about tonight. He was like Mom, a bit out of control. And now he's so damn happy and all, with his sausages and El Masri or whoever it is, I don't want to spoil it. Seems like I'm always the one about to spoil things. But if you can't tell your best friend, then who can you tell?

"Listen," I say, trying to smile, as if I'm just a bit puzzled and sort of amused, "something happened this morning. I saw that blue Mustang again. It was early, and this time it wasn't going slow."

Asim puts his knife and fork together dead parallel on the plate. He wipes his mouth with his napkin and puts it back on the table. Then he looks at me. That's one of the things I really like about Asim. He knows when something's important. He cuts through all the crap and gives you his total attention. He's a serious person.

"Tell me," he says quietly.

So I tell the whole story, about Mrs. Bradman waiting for the bus and Badman's bunny pajamas and me doing my challenges in the middle of the road. When I finish he doesn't say anything. But his face has gone pale.

"You know what?" I say quickly. "When you look at it, it's probably all my fault because what kind of lunatic stands in the middle of the street counting in sets of eight? I mean, the guy couldn't have been expecting a person to be rooted there like some basketcase who's escaped from the hospital. He might have been bending down fiddling with his stereo or something. You know, not looking at the road."

Asim still says nothing.

"I mean, like, there are probably eight million different reasons why he didn't stop."

"You said he *accelerated*."

"Well, maybe it just seemed like that."

"He smashed your bike." Asim takes a deep breath. "It was deliberate, I think. And that car drives down our street too often for it to be just a . . . what is the word?"

"Coincidence," I suggest reluctantly.

"Yes, that one." He sips the last of his ginger ale. "This happened to me and my family back in Iraq. It feels the same. Saddam, when he was suspicious that you were not being loyal to him, he sent his spies to look at you."

"Like stalking you?"

"Yes. Many people disappeared."

"But this is Australia, it couldn't be anything like that—"

"No, I know." But Asim was staring at his plate. His eyes had gone inward. I knew he was looking at something I would never see.

"Number 33! 33 is the winner, ladies and gentlemen! Come and collect your top class chicken from Chunky's!"

175

I tap Asim on the hand. "Let's go and get a good table. Don't think about it now."

Asim swims up out of his thoughts. He tries a smile. "Yes."

I nod and we walk up the pink carpet, past the yellow walls to the concert room.

A guy with an electric guitar is introducing the band as we find a table near the front. "We're the Shining Souls," he announces quietly. He's got dreadlocks folded into a knitted beanie sort of hat. The beanie is all red and yellow stripes. He looks shy.

"Cool hat," I say to Asim.

The guy introduces Mom and then he does a riff right up the scale. He doesn't look shy anymore and Mom launches into "Try a Little Tenderness." It's a song by Otis Redding off *The Otis Redding Dictionary of Soul*. I know it by heart. It has a great horn solo to it. I wonder if she had to bribe the Shining Souls on the choice of music? The guitarist looks more like a reggae fan to me.

Mom never starts off slow. By the end of the song her face is glowing with sweat. She gives it everything she's got. She never holds back. When I used to watch her at the casino I thought she was a bit like the kids running in marathons at school carnivals. The teachers are always telling them to take it easy at first and save their energy for the last laps. Otherwise they'll run out of breath. Still, I've never seen Mom tired at the end of a good show. She's always buzzing and she can never sleep right after a performance.

The shining soul on the guitar is really getting into it now and they go onto a medley of songs that just seem to flow into one another. There are lots of *nah-nah-nahs* and *gotta-gotta-gottas* and Mom is doing this thing where she's no longer singing words, but keeping the rhythm with her voice, as if she's a piece of percussion. She and the guy on the bongo drums are sort of working together, and then Mom takes the melody suddenly into a whole new direction and I recognize "In the Midnight Hour." She starts to shimmy her shoulders and shake down low and I'm sure her cleavage is showing. I look around to see if anyone is staring but people are smiling and nodding their heads in time and a few jump up and start dancing on the polished wooden floor.

I catch Asim's eye and he gives the biggest smile I've ever seen on him. His mouth is wide open as if he's drinking in the sound and his hands are working steadily on the table like it's a bongo drum. I think he's forgotten about the other stuff. I think he's enjoying the night.

After about an hour Mom announces they'll have a short break and she'll be right back. We're watching her hanging up her mike, talking with the bongo player when a man looms up behind us and claps a hand on both our backs.

I nearly fall out of my chair. We whip around to see Asim's dad, Mehmet, smiling down at us.

When I can breathe again I say, "hi." Mehmet grins and ducks his head and gives Asim a big loud kiss on the cheek. Asim throws his arm around him—he never seems embarrassed by his relatives like I do—and starts telling him about the music. He's talking at about eight million miles an hour and his dad is laughing.

Asim's dad has big strong white teeth and a silky dark mustache. His hair is quite long and wavy, and he's wearing his work shirt with a blue jacket. When Asim told me that his dad might come after work, because he really likes music, I made sure to tell Asim that he'd need to bring a jacket.

There are these weird dress rules at the pub. *Don't* Wear This and *Do* Wear That, *No* T-shirts, *No* Flip-Flops, *No* Shorts (even in summer). So Mehmet's sitting there, dressed like everyone else in his jacket and shirt, but he looks like he should be right up there on stage. I guess he's quite good-looking. Drop-dead exotic, Mom would say.

Mehmet goes to get a couple of ginger ales (Muslims don't drink alcohol) and Mom comes over and collapses on the chair Asim pulls up for her. Oh, what a sight. She looks like she's just stepped out of the shower with her clothes on. What will Mehmet think? He's threading his way back now, juggling the drinks and a bowl of nuts. He looks so neat and elegant, like a parcel that's been carefully wrapped. I can see a stream of sweat making its way toward Mom's top lip. She sucks it up with her bottom lip. Then she gets my napkin and wipes her chest.

"*Mom*," I hiss at her.

Mehmet puts the glasses and nuts on the table and pushes a glass toward Mom. "Would you like a drink? You look very thirsty to me!"

Mom goes red. She dabs at her face in a ladylike way.

Mehmet puts out his hand. "We have not met properly. I am Mehmet. I always seem to be at the store when my son is at your home. I am very grateful for the friendship, and all the dinners you have cooked for my son!"

"Oh, it's a pleasure, he's a lovely boy. I am grateful, too!" Mom sits there beaming at Mehmet, her glass in her hand.

"Mom, don't you think you ought to go to the bathroom? You don't have long."

Her mascara has started to run and it's smeared down one cheek where she's rubbed her face. Soon she'll be doing her panda look-alike routine.

Mom laughs. "It's okay, Jackson. There are longer breaks here." She leans forward confidentially toward Mehmet. "When I worked at the casino, the manager, Tony, only gave me six minutes between sets. Can you believe it? I learned to pee very fast, I can tell you."

Mehmet looks puzzled as Asim whispers in his ear.

"You don't have to translate every stupid thing my mother says," I tell him.

Mehmet laughs out loud. He's got a nice laugh, the deep kind from the belly that shows the person isn't keeping anything back for himself. Mom grins at him and gulps down her drink.

Mehmet asks Mom about her singing and they talk music for a while. Her neck is less red now. Then Mom asks if there's any news about renewing their temporary protection visa. Oh, why does she have to bring that up? No one wants to think about that here! She never knows how to put parentheses around things, or periods.

Mehmet sighs. "No news. But we're hoping. Now that many children have been released from detention—"

"Oh, yes, what a sudden decision that was! It only happened because there was an election looming, you know. The government were told by the United Nations to release all children from detention back in May! But they just ignored them. The United *Nations*."

Mom bangs her glass down on the table so that ginger ale slops over the side. Asim looks around furtively to see if anyone's heard.

"Well—" Mehmet spreads his hands. "At least many refugee children are out in the community now. This is a good thing."

"Yes, it is, it is," agrees Mom and she raises her glass

to Mehmet. "And here's to your happy settlement in Australia."

Mehmet raises his glass and clinks his against hers. "And here's to new friends," he smiles.

At eleven P.M., just before the band is due to finish for the night, Mom does a strange thing. She turns and whispers something to the bongo drummer who smiles and nods his head. Then she says into the mike, "And now we will invite a special guest to come up and play with us . . . Mr. Mehmet Guler!"

What? I glance at Mehmet and he looks shocked. But Asim is saying, "Go on, go *on*!" and then suddenly Mehmet laughs that deep laugh again and sort of springs up out of his chair. He skirts the tables like a dancer and almost leaps onto the stage. He must not have seen the stairs.

And for once Mom isn't embarrassing or excessive. She's done the right thing, I think. Mehmet is awesome. He sits down next to the bongo drummer and when they launch into this kind of African jazz number, Mehmet goes wild. His hands fly over the drums, faster and faster, so that one minute it sounds like rain on a tin roof, *pat*ter patter *pat*ter patter, light, constant, and another it's thunder and storms and rushing rivers. He does this solo that makes my skin shiver.

"So that's where you get your skill with the drums," I whisper to Asim. "You never told me."

He just grins, but I bet his chest has swollen to twice the size with pride. He doesn't take his eyes off his dad for a moment.

Everyone else in the audience must be thinking Mehmet is awesome, too, because they clap like crazy and won't let the band go. The shy guy with the electric guitar tears off his beanie hat and shakes out his dreadlocks. Then he does a solo that would have left Led Zeppelin gasping. And Mom is great. She's *great*. She knows just when to hold back and let the others star and when to come in. And when she does ride in with the melody, it's like all the lights in the world switching on.

The only bad thing about the entire night is that Esmerelda isn't here to see it. If she had been allowed to come, I think this night would have been better than any Christmas present, ever.

Asim and I watch our parents together up there on stage. We watch, too, the way they take such a long time to come back to our table after it's all over. They have their heads together, too busy talking.

We don't look at each other. We don't say anything about it. Because sometimes, if you tell a wish, it doesn't come true. But if you say it to yourself eight times in your head, and then another eight times until you make sixty-four, you never know, it just might.

10. Esmerelda

I give up hunting for a seatbelt. I can smell spearmint and Rocky's pine forest aftershave. It would be a nice smell if it weren't Rocky's. I try not to breathe it in. There's not a speck of sand or a smear of muddy shoe or one candy wrapper to be seen. Mom would love the way this car is kept. The thought of Mom makes tears spring up. I swallow and press my nose against the window, trying to make out where we're going.

Trees, houses, shops flash past like familiar faces in a dream. We're going so fast the world is drowning in a river of light and dark. I can feel Badman's fear blowing in hot waves against my arm. We're crammed like sardines in this backseat. It isn't meant for two. As we take another corner I smash my funny bone against the window ledge. I've never felt less like laughing.

I close my eyes. I don't know which is better—looking or not looking. I dig my nails into my palm to make sure I'm awake, that this is really happening. There's a growing thickness like fog working its way up around my ears. It's quite calming in a numb kind of way, like falling asleep when you're freezing to death. Everything just melting away. Suddenly I want to laugh and laugh and never stop.

"What the hell are you doing?" There's a sharp nudge in my ribs.

I stare back at Badman. I realize my face is wet with tears. The laughing dies as Rocky turns up his Prince CD. He's tapping out the rhythm with one hand on the dashboard, weaving in and out of traffic like a bumper car. We overtake a souped-up Mazda on the inside and nearly hit a parked car at the curb. Badman gasps as Rocky swings out and crosses lanes with a squeal of rubber.

I clear my throat. "You'll get booked for speeding if you keep driving like this." I hear my voice as if I'm outside myself, looking on. I sound just like my mother. "There's a speed camera up here."

Badman looks hopeful. But I'm thinking, if Rocky slows down, maybe we can jump out. Then I remember about the child locks. Anyway, you can get killed that way. But if Rocky doesn't slow down, we'll get killed by that truck we're about to overtake in the next lane.

Rocky doesn't reply. Prince is pretty noisy.

"That camera will zap you," I say a bit louder. "We must be going 75 in a 35 mile zone." We screech around a corner overtaking the truck, and the car slides out before gunning straight ahead.

Rocky gives a grunt and opens the glove compartment. I can see a stash of envelopes sliding around in there.

"I got hundreds of fines," he laughs, flicking the glove compartment closed before all the letters tumble out with the next screaming corner. "My boss, Tony, he just says, 'give 'em to me, I'll handle 'em.' So every few months, I dump 'em all on his desk." Rocky lights another cigarette using a lighter in the dashboard. He steers with his knees. Oh, when will this nightmare end?

"See, there's a lotta driving in my job. Lotta urgent matters, if you know what I mean." He turns down the stereo and gives a meaty chuckle. "You should hear my boss, he's crazy for speed. He insisted, *in-sis-ted* on adding the turbo. Sometimes I need to get to places yesterday, you read me? Deliver stuff fast."

"What *is* your job—*kid*napper?" Badman has found his voice again. I wish he hadn't.

"No, smart ass, it's security. My boss, he says I've got the most responsible job in the casino. *Fun-da-men-tal*, he says."

"Casino?" screeches Badman. His voice sounds like Rocky's tires.

"Ssh!" I mouth at him, my finger on his lips. When Rocky's turned up the stereo again, I whisper into Badman's ear, "We're not who Rocky thinks we are."

"Rocky? You *know* this guy?"

"I think so. Well, I don't know him, but I've heard of him. It's all starting to fit."

"*What?*"

And so I tell him the story Jackson told me, about the Blue Moon casino and the mean manager named Tony, and the stuff Valerie shouldn't have seen that night.

"But what's that got to do with us?"

I sigh. I forgot things take time with Badman. "We were at Jackson's place in the middle of the night, remember? And you told him we lived there, right?"

"Yeah, so?" Then his frown clears. "Oh, I get it, Rocky thinks I'm Jackson! Oh, great, the number freak!"

"That's right. Rocky was probably meant to deliver Jackson to Tony. I guess they think that's the best way to scare Valerie—make sure she stays quiet."

"Like a ransom type thing. Like that Mel Gibson movie, where his kid—"

"Only," I bite my lip, "we're not the right kids, are we?"

184

"No," says Badman, brightening, "so this Tony will probably just let us go, right?"

I look at him. "Yeah, Tony'll probably just say, "Oh, sorry kids, our mistake, this will just be our little secret, okay? Off you run then, have a nice day!"" The weird laughter is bubbling up again.

Badman pales. I can see him swallow. I wish I'd shut up.

"Okay, I'll try to tell him again who we are," I say. In a loud voice I call, "Rocky!"

"Yeah?"

"We're not who you think we are. This is NOT Jackson Ford next to—"

Rocky swings around, taking his eyes right off the road. "I've had enough of you little smart asses. Don't think you can fool me. *I'm* not stupid!" He glares at us, then his eyes suddenly narrow. "And how do you know my name then? Ho *ho*! I wasn't born yesterday! Just sit back, shut up, and enjoy the ride."

Sometimes it's better not to wonder, not to think. Just let that foggy feeling creep back.

Out the window the night is pitch black. We're on a long wide stretch of empty road. The freeway.

Rocky turns down the music. "Listen to the power in this beast. Did I tell you it's turbocharged? Now we can really gun it."

I strain to see the dashboard. The needle on the speedometer is climbing. 75, 80, 95 . . .

"She's a monster, isn't she?" crows Rocky. "T67 turbo kit, full suspension upgrade, 18 inch Ford racing wheels . . . Hope you kids wiped your feet before you got in."

Badman and I look at each other. "How stupid can you get?" he whispers to me.

"I vacuum every day you know," Rocky goes on. "Wipe over the seats with Wet Ones. I get all types in here. Italian leather shoes, sneakers, rubber soles, doesn't matter which class of shoe, they're full of bacteria. *Bac-ter-ia*, little one-cell creeps. Parasites. Honestly, if you believed what you read in the dictionary, you'd never be without a can of antiseptic in your hand. Nasty crawling bugs."

"You have a very good vocabulary, sir," I say. An idea is slowly forming, trying to break through the fog.

Badman stares at me.

"Your boss must really appreciate having such a smart right-hand man," I go on.

Rocky makes a low grunting noise. I think it's a sign of pleasure. "Well, yeah," he says uncertainly. There's a pause and then he says more confidently, "You know, Tony really does appreciate me. He knows I can have conversations with any of your rich dudes that come to the casino. Your Egyptians, your French fries, your Eye-tyes, your tourists from Mont-y Carlo. They're all impressed by my English."

"Oh, is English your second language?"

"What?"

Badman snorts.

"Every week I learn twenty-one new words," Rocky leans around the front seat to tell me. "I go through the dictionary, see. My sister gave me one last Christmas. She says just because you're grown-up, you should never stop learnin'. I like in the dictionary how there's those little pictures next to the hard words, like arm-a-dill-o. I was lucky because I knew a lot of 'A' words from the Mustang. You know, like aeromotive fuel regulator, and autometer electronic boost."

The lights of the city are appearing on the horizon. If Rocky's taking us where I think, we don't have much time.

I want information, anything that might help us. And if we could get on Rocky's good side, maybe . . .

"Why twenty-one?" Badman pipes up, glancing at me.

"Twenty-one?" Rocky bangs the steering wheel with enthusiasm. "Twenty-one's my boss's fave game. It's the only game he'll play at the casino! He told me once, anything good ever happened to him, happened when he was 21. See," Rocky reaches for another cigarette, "Tony respects me, I know that. But, like, he could respect me *more*. I mean, us security guys, everyone thinks, they ass–*ume*, we're all brawn and no brain. 'Course Tony doesn't think like that, oh, no, but we can all improve, right? I just want to show what a big brain I *do* have, see? I want them all to know that *my* bit of the central nervous system is very large."

I give Badman the thumbs-up sign.

"I could give you a word we learned in English," I offer. "Tautology—it means—"

"I'm not *up* to 'T' yet," Rocky says grumpily.

There's silence as the road narrows and the traffic thickens. Neon signs wink past like strobe lights. Cars toot and Rocky winds down his window to swear at the drivers.

"Are we nearly there yet?" I ask.

"Where?" asks Badman.

"Don't give me that," snaps Rocky. "You know exactly where we're going."

We zoom through the middle of the city, streaming in and out of narrow roads. Rocky's about as moody as a rattlesnake. I wish I hadn't said "tautology."

Office blocks crowd around us, tall and spiky like Daniel's Lego buildings. Lights are shining in some of the windows. Are people still working in there? How can life go on, people strolling the streets, drinking in bars, eating in restaurants as if everything is normal and we're not trapped in some gangster's turbocharged car equipped with an aeromotive fuel regulator?

The roads start to widen and the lights are thinning as we head over a small bridge. When we pass the last pylon I see a steep hill stretching ahead to the right. And on top of the hill, like a glittering palace, sits the Blue Moon.

I hear Badman suck in his breath. As we drive up the hill we see the huge sign pulsing on and off. The letters look like jewels, sapphires maybe, glinting against a white fluorescent circle. It hurts your eyes to look at it for more than a second, like the sun. But you can't help glancing back.

A stab of dread starts in my chest. It spreads out through my arms and neck, making me shiver.

Rocky parks the car near a long white flight of steps. Like a waterfall it flows down from the casino, lined on either side by small fountains spraying arcs of glinting blue water.

"Get out," says Rocky. He lifts up the front passenger seat for us to squeeze through. It takes a few minutes because the space is so tight.

"Come on, shake a leg," he barks.

Once we're out I look down at my bathrobe and bare feet. A group of men in suits stand near a red Porsche. Strolling down the stairs toward them are two women in long shiny dresses.

"Kids aren't allowed in casinos," I remind Rocky. "Specially dressed like this."

"Yeah," says Badman weakly, looking around.

"It's okay," Rocky grins, "you're the boss's precious offspring." I see for the first time a gold tooth gleaming in his mouth. It's right where the vampire tooth should be—

a canine. He runs his tongue over it. "You see a policeman around? No? What a pity. Now you kids are gonna walk up those steps ahead of me. You'll walk slowly but without stopping. I'm gonna be right behind you."

Rocky reaches into his inner pocket to get his cigarettes. He takes his time fumbling around in there, making sure we see the gun at his belt. "Damn, musta left the matches in the car." He puts back the cigarettes. "Trying to cut down, anyway. Not good for training."

I look at the people getting into the red Porsche. One of the women glances back at me.

"Move," hisses Rocky. His hand glides to his belt and stays there. "Remember, me and my gun are right behind you. One word, even just one look that's outta place, and you'll feel the steel. Now go."

We start walking. It seems to take a year to cross the asphalt. We walk past the expensive cars all polished and lined up like kids at assembly. My legs feel so strange, heavy. But I keep walking. It makes me think of actors in a film, just doing what they're told. I want to scream, call out my own words, but I can't find them under all this strangeness. I still remember the feel of that gun at my back.

I peep at Badman walking beside me. He looks stunned, too, as if he can't believe anything he's seeing.

"Should we make a run for it?" he whispers to me.

Suddenly he falls forward and nearly trips up the step.

"I said not one word, bug brain." Rocky's breath comes in gusts against the back of our necks. I can smell spearmint.

We continue up the steps like sleepwalkers. At the top we stop. We can see our reflections for a moment in the big glass doors. Rocky looms behind us like a well kept gorilla. He runs a hand through his short hair.

"Good," says Rocky. "Now turn to your right and walk until you come to some escalators. Turn the corner and you'll see a bar with fake palm trees. Pass that and stop at the elevators."

We do as he says. First we pass a room that seems to go on forever, divided by row upon row of poker machines. Along the aisles men and women sit alone at the machines, cranking those handle things back and forth. The straight rows and repetitive movements remind me of a factory I saw once where they make car parts. If there wasn't that pop music blaring, you get the feeling there'd be total silence.

"Keep walking," Rocky grunts behind us.

If ever I get out of this place alive, I'll never go gambling. Up close, this place is not nearly as glamorous as people make out. Jackson was right. It's spooky. Lonely as hell.

At the bar the leaves of the palm trees sway in a tropical breeze from the air conditioner. You can even smell coconut suntan oil. I wonder if they pump it out with the air.

"Can I have a drink?" asks Badman.

"Smart ass, aren't ya?"

"No," stammers Badman, "I mean I'm really thirsty. Just water or something."

"Suffer," says Rocky.

We keep going until we see the elevators. When the doors open Rocky pushes us in. He presses B2. We're going down to the basement. As I watch the doors slide shut the reality of where we are crashes down on me. This is no nightmare. I'm not going to wake up. We'll never get out. We're trapped, at the mercy of these thugs like bugs in a jar.

Rocky leads us up a narrow corridor. There are no windows. But there is a red carpet, thick and soft under my feet. He stops at a door with a gold plaque. Engraved deep into the gold is the name: TONY SERENO.

My heart starts to thud so hard it hurts.

Rocky knocks on the door. "It's me, boss."

"Come in."

I feel sudden pressure closing around my fingers. Badman is hanging on to me. I squeeze back. Right now, it's better to be with anyone than to be on my own.

Inside the room it is dim and shadowy. Only a desk lamp spreads a pool of yellow light across a stack of papers, a whiskey bottle and a couple of glasses. I'm rubbing my eyes, trying to adjust to the gloom when Rocky gives us a prod. We stumble in, nearly bumping into the large square desk. The wood gleams, dark and expensive-looking. My eyes are smarting and I see, in the oval of lamp light, a plume of smoke curling up from a nearly dead cigar. The ashtray is an overflowing cemetery of wet, chewed butts.

Then something flickers at the back of the room. The shadows are thick but a sudden flame from a match highlights a man sitting in an armchair. The flame shows a hairy, ringed hand with a gold bracelet.

"Who are these children, Rocky?" The voice is light and almost welcoming as if he's asking after a friend's family. But in the silence that follows you can hear how thin the tone is, the warmth barely a smear over something cold and hard.

Suddenly the man flicks on another switch and the room bursts into light. The man gets up and strides toward us, Tony, the manager of the Blue Moon. He's tall and powerful-looking, his chest swelling out of his crisp blue shirt.

He stares down at us. He takes Badman's chin in his hand and thrusts it from side to side, studying his face. Then he looks at me. I try to look back but he's got the scariest eyes I've ever seen. They're so black, you can't see where the pupil starts and finishes. They're so focused you feel like you'll burst into flame if he stares any longer. His dark brows draw together to make one angry line.

"I'll repeat the question for you, Rocky, and I'll go slow. WHO ARE THESE CHILDREN?"

Rocky starts to fidget with his collar. "I don't get what you mean, boss. This is what you asked me to do. Bring Val's kids here to you."

"Kid, singular, means just *one*, Rocky. What we have here is a plural situation. I suppose we can be grateful you didn't look 'kid' up in the dictionary and bring me a baby goat."

Rocky looks puzzled as well as worried. Then his face clears and he shouts, "Ha ha! I get it! That's a good joke, boss."

"Where did you find these children?" Tony's voice has the thin friendly tone again.

"Well they were in the yard, see, at the address you told me. Number seventy-three, right?"

"That's correct, Rocky. You got that bit right. But did I tell you the boy had a sister?"

"No."

"Then why did you think he had?"

"Because he said so. Why would he say that if he didn't? And anyway, why else would she be there in her PJs?" Rocky is starting to sweat. His shirt collar is wilting.

"Hmm," says Tony mildly. "And didn't you get a look at Valerie's son when you gave him that little fright the other morning?"

"Well, like, it all happened so quick and the sun was coming up, right in my eyes. All I saw was the bike—it was in the middle of the road! I wasn't expecting it."

Tony examines the lapel of his suit and flicks off an invisible speck of dust. "All right, now if you can, Rocky, reach back into the vastness of your mind. Didn't I tell you the boy was skinny and wears his hair long?"

"Well, yeah, but I figured anyone can put on weight. Take my own case, for instance, if I don't work out every day, swim eighty laps, and lift—"

"I'm not interested in your case, Rocky. The amount of interest I have in your case would fill one side of a twenty-cent piece. No, what I'm interested in is what we are going to do now that you have gone and kidnapped the wrong children."

"Wrong children?"

"Yes."

"What's your name, boy?" Tony suddenly barks at Badman.

"Bruce Bradman."

"And you?" He flicks his gaze at me as if I'm an insect on his lapel.

"Esmerelda Marx."

Rocky's jaw drops open. "But they were at the right address! I figured, this girl here, well, maybe Val had another kid, see, one she might not have told you about. Val was scared of you all right. I thought you'd be pleased I found 'em both—"

Tony steps right up to Rocky then and I see with horror that his face is slowly turning crimson. "Valerie has been very stubborn. You know that. She refuses to do that one little thing we asked her, to show, how shall I put it, her continuing good faith. She might be scared, Rocky, but not terrified. We need her terrified."

"Yeah, so I figured—"

"I DON'T PAY YOU TO *FIGURE*, ROCKY. I DON'T PAY YOU TO *THINK*!"

The cold threat at the bottom of his voice cracks like thunder. He's thumping one fist into the other, shouting right into Rocky's face. "You've got a brain the size of an *AMOEBA*. Do you know what an *amoeba* is, Rocky?"

Rocky takes a step back. Sweat is bubbling on his forehead. He clears his throat. "I do, Tony. And I'll have you know I take offense at that. An amoeba is one of the most primitive forms of life, a single-celled protozoa, a *parasite*. Well, I'm not like that, I *work* for my living—"

"Well, now you'll have to work very hard because you're going to have to find a way to correct your mistake."

Badman and I look at each other. Badman is sweating almost as much as Rocky.

"How you do you mean?"

"I don't want these kids, you see, Rocky. These kids spell trouble. Big trouble." He's talking to Rocky as if he's a mentally challenged four-year-old. "Their parents will call the police. The police will be out searching as soon as morning comes. They won't be like Valerie. They won't stay silent with a little pressure from us. It's not the same, Rocky."

"Yeah, but, but," Rocky is scratching his head, "but these parents, they won't think to come to the casino! Kids aren't even allowed in here! They'll just think their kids have run away or something."

"Eventually Valerie will talk. That was the whole point of getting *her* kid. The whole point of those phone calls. To make sure she didn't. Do you understand that, Rocky?"

"Yes," says Rocky slowly, "but I've got an idea. We could get rid of them piece by piece. That way there'll be no bodies to find. I saw it in a movie once. The murderer chopped up his victims like cold cuts at the butcher's, and he buried all the bits in different places. No one ever found them."

Something hot and wet is seeping under my foot. I curl my toes back and see a stain spreading down Badman's jean leg. The puddle is growing on the floor, the red swirling pattern of the rug darkening into a muddy mess.

"Oh, Christ, the boy's pissed himself!" Tony's staring in disbelief. "That's my Persian rug!" He turns to Rocky. "*Do* something, you big oaf! Get him off my rug!"

Badman's eyes are closed and he's swaying slightly. His face is white.

Rocky picks him up at arm's length and folds him away in a corner on the polished floorboards.

"Put your head between your knees," I call over to him.

"You shut up," snaps Rocky. "Go and sit over there with your wimpy friend." He's lifting up the sopping rug, peeling it back from the wet spot. But I can't stop looking at the floor underneath. There's an indented line cut into the wood, and the grain of the wood inside the line is different. It's a kind of door, an opening.

I look up to see Tony staring at me and then back at the floor.

"That's it," he says softly. "At least for now." He bends down and mutters something to Rocky.

"How long for?" asks Rocky.

"Until we can figure out what to do. Maybe your cold cuts idea isn't so bad."

Rocky grins with pride. "You can count on me, boss." He peels back another foot of rug and lays bare a big lock. He starts to fiddle with it then suddenly stops, twisting around to me. "I said go and stand over there with leaky legs."

I inch away, over to the corner. From here I can't see much. But then I hear something click over and Rocky pulls back the door in the floor. He disappears down into the hole.

A minute later Rocky's head and shoulders pop up again. "Come on, you two," he calls to us. He sounds cheerful, like we're going on a picnic. "You're coming down here."

Badman looks up. "For how long?" he says softly.

Rocky shrugs.

I can hardly breathe. The unreal laughter is edging back up my throat. "Is there a night light down there? I don't like the dark. What about a bathroom? Or should I go on the rug too?"

"Witty girl, aren't you?" Tony marches up to us. He leans down and puts his face right in front of mine. His black eyes nail me to the floor. He's so close, but he gives nothing away.

"There's everything you could wish for in the cellar," he tells me in that fake friendly voice. His face doesn't move as he speaks. It's like a mask—plastic. But you know something is boiling behind it. "Nice soundproof room, excellent Picasso on the wall, a luxury bathroom." He turns to grin nastily at Badman's wet jeans. "*You* might need the bathroom, boy. It can get quite cold down there. Affects the bladder, you know." And he stands up and goes to select a fresh cigar from a box on his desk.

I start to shake and I can't stop.

11. Jackson

Mom and Mehmet are standing outside the glass doors of the pub.

Asim and I are already across the other side of the parking lot, leaning against Mom's Ford Escort. We're having a yawning competition. Mine goes for about nine seconds. I leave my mouth open for just a second longer to make it an even number.

"That was a huge yawn," says Asim. "I even saw your uvula."

"My what?"

"Uvula. The fleshy part that hangs down at the back of the throat."

"Oh." It's amazing how often Asim teaches me words in my own language.

I'm so tired I could fall asleep standing up. Asim is sneaking a look at his watch. It was a great night, but now, I want to tell Mom, it's over. I can see her leaning slightly forward as if she's hard of hearing, laughing too much and throwing her arms around. She looks like a little kid who's overexcited. I remember her telling me when I was little, "The game's finished now, Jackson. Jackson? Just calm down and get ready for bed." Well, someone needs to tell her that. Valerie? Valerie!

197

But neither of us wants to call them. They probably wouldn't listen to us anyway. It's sort of nice watching them together, and painful. Maybe I could go to sleep standing up. But I think only horses can do that.

"Did you know that pythons can dislocate their jaws?" I say to pass the time.

"What, when they yawn?"

"No, so they can swallow their food. Like maybe when they've strangled a cow or something. Mom told me once she was scared I'd dislocate my jaw when I yawned."

"You'll probably be good at kissing then."

"Why?"

"Well, I saw a movie once where the boy did not know how to open his mouth when he kissed. The girl told him he had to open wide."

"Yeah, well I'm sure you have to go easy at first. It's not like being at the dentist."

"No."

We stand there watching our parents. They're standing very close. But I don't think they're going to dislocate their jaws or anything. They're just getting to know each other.

Finally, after we've had a holding our breath competition (I won), a finding 2% of $12.56 competition (Asim won), and who could name the capitals of Uzbekistan, Libya, and Norway in four seconds (Asim got that, too), Mom and Mehmet wander over.

"Come, Asim, it is late," says Mehmet.

Asim grins at me, rolling his eyes. Mom and I watch them as they walk across the parking lot to their car.

When we climb into our car, Mom points to the gas gauge.

"Damn," she says.

The little green arrow is pointing to empty. In fact, it's pointing below the red danger zone of empty.

"Maybe we'll get away with it," she says hopefully. "Home is only five minutes away."

"No," I say firmly. "Tomorrow you'll forget to look and be on your way to work and suddenly there'll be that coughing, choking noise of the engine and the car will stop. You might be doing a right-hand turn in the middle of traffic. The service station is on the way home. Let's go."

"You're right," says Mom. "It's a bad habit of yours."

She starts the car and switches on the radio. The baby boomers' station, 101.7. That's specifically for people in the middle-aged bracket like my mom. Sometimes the disc jockeys try to pretend that young people listen to it, but everyone knows who the real audience is. Van Morrison is singing "Brown-Eyed Girl" so Mom sings along, getting so carried away that she nearly forgets to stop at the gas station.

"Turn here!" I yell and she brakes suddenly with fright so that the car behind nearly crashes into us.

At the gas station I go into the little shop while she fills up the car. I wander along the aisles, looking at all the candies and mints and cereal boxes. I get absorbed in reading the marketing stuff on the back of the boxes. The cereals are all full of iron and vitamin B and folate, whatever that is. But it makes you feel healthy just reading it.

Then I hear Mom telling the service station attendant all about her night. Her voice is loud and I see another young guy look up toward the counter. My ears start to go red and I decide to stay down here among the breakfast stuff. Maybe no one will ever know I am related to her.

"Jackson? Jackson, where are you?"

Mom's voice is frantic. The whole shop stops and looks around.

I rush up the aisle toward her.

The man at the counter grins. "Do you want that?"

I realize I'm still holding the Wheaties.

Mom grabs me so hard in a bear hug I can hardly breathe.

"Oh, Jackson, I thought some horrible man had kidnapped you!"

"It's okay, Mom, calm down."

She smiles. "It's just—I guess it was such a wonderful night, I can't believe I can really have it. You know, without something awful happening to punish me." She smiles at the attendant. "Do you know what I mean?"

"Not really, lady. But are you going to take the Wheaties?"

When we get outside and no one can see, I take Mom's arm. "You really were wonderful tonight. I was so proud of you."

Mom throws her arms around me again and I can feel the Wheaties box suspended between us.

"I was so scared in the store," her voice is loud in my ear. "It came over me like a tidal wave. I saw it all—all my past horrors grabbing you, taking you away from me."

I think of the smashed bike in the garage and the blue Mustang and decide not to tell her that the Wheaties box is crushed to smithereens against my chest. "Remember Miss Braithwaite?" I say instead. "How she told me that no matter what happened, I could take the good numbers with me? Well, same for you. You'll always have tonight. Nothing will ever change that."

The clock in the car says 12:37 when we turn into our street. Mehmet's car is already parked outside their house. Their porch light is on, the only one in the street. I turn to Mom and see she is looking at number sixty-four as well. She smiles as we clamber out of the car.

Before I go in, I glance up at Esmerelda's window. Her bedroom faces onto the street and sometimes when I've woken at 1:11 or 3:33, I've wondered if she is lying there sleepless, too. But no light is shining from her room. I stare up at the dark window and imagine what it would be like to tiptoe in there and sit on the bed and gently wake her up with a story about tonight. I could tell her about the guitarist's dreadlocks and Mehmet's surprise performance and how mom shimmied and sweated like Tina Turner. We could whisper about it all until the sun came up and then I could kiss her on the cheek or maybe the lips and she'd be all warm and soft in her nightgown.

Mom is standing at the gate, smiling at me. "Do you remember Rapunzel, that fairy tale I used to tell you? Rapunzel, Rapunzel, let down your hair . . ."

I make it to the gate in two lots of eight steps. "Yes. She was kidnapped by a witch when she was just a baby, wasn't she? And imprisoned in a tall tower?"

"Mm. And the witch used to climb up the rope of her golden hair to reach her. But one day a prince heard Rapunzel singing, and her voice was so beautiful he fell instantly in love with her. He came back every day to hear her and one day he saw the witch come and call, 'Let down your hair!'

"So the next day when he came he called out 'Rapunzel, Rapunzel, let down your hair!' and she did and instead of the nasty old witch climbing up to her window, it was the

201

handsome prince!" Mom grins. "Do you remember how you'd always clap your hands over your ears then? You never wanted to hear what happened after. How the witch found them and turned the prince blind and abandoned the girl in the forest—"

I clap my hands over my ears. "I still don't want to know—"

"Love really hurts without you," sings Mom. "Billy Ocean, d'you know it? Great dance song. But listen, Rapunzel and her prince did find each other, and Rapunzel's tears of love healed the prince's poor eyes and they lived happily ever after."

We open the gate and walk down the path together. Mom takes a deep breath. "Summer nights are magical, aren't they?" She does a shimmy with her shoulders and breaks into an old dance routine, the Swim. She even holds her nose as she does the dive part. Just as well it's dark and no one else can see her.

I can't help laughing.

"When I was a girl, I always used to think there was a lesson in Rapunzel for me," she says as she puts the key in the lock. "You know, that you've got to let your hair down, take a risk, or you'll never live."

"And if you're a boy?"

She stops for a moment to think. "I don't know, maybe you've just got to climb up and find out."

12. Esmerelda

Badman goes first down the concrete stairs. He takes one careful step after another like an old man. I suppose we're thinking the same thing. This cellar might be the last place we'll ever see.

The room is bare except for rows of filing cabinets and a square table. Rocky is leaning against a cabinet, his arms folded. He points to two chairs lined up at the table. We sit down and watch Rocky take a couple of cans of tonic water from a small fridge.

"There's your drink," he says to Badman. "Enjoy it."

Badman suddenly leaps up, knocking over the chair. He starts to say something but Rocky slaps a heavy hand on his head, rights the chair, and pushes him back down on it.

"You be quiet and don't make no trouble. You've already caused me enough pain tonight." He runs a hand through his hair. "*Amoeba*," he mutters. "Honestly, I'll never get over it." Then he bends down and glares into Badman's face. "You and your damn stories."

"I'm sorry for your trouble," I say to Rocky. "But was it you who made those phone calls to Valerie's house? You know, with all the heavy breathing?"

"Who else do ya think, the Holy Spirit?" Rocky thumps the table, making the cans jump.

"But how did you find them? Jackson told me they even rented their house under a different name."

"You can't fool Tony—no one can. And, 'course, *I* helped track her down." He thrusts out his chest. "I'm good at undercover work, always have been. Even Tony says that." He frowns suddenly. "If only she'd behaved herself and made the payments, we wouldn't be in this mess now."

"So the phone calls weren't just silent. You were threatening her, *black*mailing her!"

"Uh yeah, numb brain. After she said that about going to the police, what do you expect? I heard her myself."

"But that wasn't *Valerie*! I know, I was there that day. Didn't you hear the change in pitch?"

"In what?"

"In tone—*voice*, whatever. It was a kid who said that—Mitchell, from school. Valerie tried to snatch the phone away from him. Now I understand why."

"Well, how was I supposed to know that? Anyway, soon as the cops get a mention, we make a move. That's just the way it goes. Tony's a professional. Got a business to run. And he don't believe in a promise unless he sees some dough."

"But Valerie doesn't have any money!"

Badman kicks me under the table. *Enough*, he mouths at me.

"Of course she doesn't." Now it's Rocky's turn to treat me like a moron. "Tony just *re-quest-ed* a small percentage of her wages each week. As an act of goodwill. He wanted her to do a little trans-ac-tion for him—just once or twice. Is that too much to ask? He told her he'd invest her money in his other sideline interests. She might have gotten a good return on it, if she'd taken a gamble. But no, stupid bitch refuses and she talks about the police and now look where we are!"

He takes another can from the fridge for himself. Rum and Bacardi. But I'm thinking, here are those percentages again, multiplying like germs until there's a full-blown crisis. I see Mom and Dad sitting at the kitchen table, adding up the percentage of their salary each week that goes to the mortgage and food and electricity . . . Imagine if you had to budget for Tony money, too—*oh yes, and here's the money for keeping my son and me safe.* It'd make you want to go to sleep and never wake up. No wonder Valerie's been looking so ill. And we all thought it was Badman.

Rocky pulls the ring open and sips, then without another glance at us he pounds heavily up the stairs. The clang of the trapdoor closing over our heads is loud and final.

We both sit for a moment listening to the silence. I hear Jackson's voice telling me how happy Valerie was about the chance to sing again. He said she woke up like a different person. It was only this morning—heavens, by now it's *yesterday* morning. I wonder if she thought Tony would just give up after a while? Like, if he saw she was making a new life, keeping quiet, he'd leave her alone. Maybe she thought if she made a life in the suburbs, the memory of the casino would disappear like a bad dream. And singing would keep her safe. Sometimes you can hope so much for a thing, you almost believe it.

The walls are cushioned in a squashy kind of leather and lined with filing cabinets. On the one bare wall hangs the Picasso—a woman with an eye coming out of her forehead. She looks all broken up like pieces of glass. It's not a comforting picture.

Badman has gotten up and is examining one of the filing

cabinets. There's a round dial on each of them, like the one I saw on the trapdoor. He fiddles with them for a while but nothing happens. I watch him give up and trudge back over, slumping into his seat. He looks all around, at the windowless walls, the concrete ceiling, the sea grass matting on the floor. He looks at anything but me.

I guess he feels embarrassed as well as everything else. His leg must be cold and wet. I'm chilly already in this cotton bathrobe.

"In second grade, you know what happened to me?" I wait for a moment. He says nothing, but he stops playing with his glass. "I was in the front of the class, getting in trouble with Mrs. Hatfield, and I had this sudden urge to pee. I couldn't cross my legs or hold my breath or anything because I was in full view. Anyway, there I was struggling, trying to think what to do when suddenly, the dam burst. I peed right there in front of everyone. They could see it all gushing down my leg, everything. It's amazing really that I ever recovered."

His eyes are wide, staring at me. Then he looks away. "I don't remember that."

"No, you were doing detention in the principal's office. So," I go on, "if you happen to take a leak when some gangster is threatening to make us into cold cuts, it's hardly worth mentioning."

He goes on looking at me. "So you're not going to blab about me?"

I think that we'll both be very lucky if I have another chance to blab about anything, but I say, "We'll have much more interesting things to tell."

Badman frowns. "Right." He starts to drum his fingers on the table. I recognize the beat. He's jiggling his leg under the table. "Feels like a coffin in here, huh? You wouldn't want to be clostro—whatever that word is."

"*Claus-tro-pho-bic*," I say. "Fear of *en-closed* spaces."

Badman grins for a moment. "Is that guy for real?"

"I wish he wasn't. It's so strange but I've had a feeling all night that none of this is really happening. It's like a bad dream. Makes me want to laugh—or scream."

"Same." He stares at the Picasso. "I think we just don't want to believe it."

"Yeah."

Badman gets up and starts to pace. I notice he's not trying to hide his wet jeans anymore. "So, what are we going to do? This is some strange kind of cellar. Aren't there supposed to be stacks of wine bottles growing old in here? I can't see any, can you?

"No. I think it's more like a safe room. I remember Jackson talking about a trapdoor, and a small basement like this where they keep all their money—and other things."

Like what?

"Oh, drugs, maybe, guns, Scrabble." I can feel the fog rising again. I don't like the look of that woman all broken up on the wall. I look away. But the laugh bubble is trapped in my throat. It's getting hard to breathe again. "I bet they shoot people in here, that's why it's soundproof. Or maybe this is where Rocky plays Scrabble." I'm not thinking anymore, just dreaming aloud. "They should have Scrabble in the casino. Rocky would be a winner. Why wouldn't they have Scrabble?" I can hear my voice ending on a screech. It's almost a high C. I sound like an ostrich. I start to laugh at the idea of an ostrich and Rocky playing Scrabble and I have such an urge to strut around the room like those bizarre birds. I remember Jackson telling me that the male ostriches (or was it emus?) sit on the eggs for weeks until they're hatched. The males are very protective, he said.

Badman is staring at me. Then he comes over and puts his hands on my shoulders. He grips me hard. He doesn't shake me, just goes on standing still and holding me.

"I'm really sorry that I got you into this, Ez. You gotta calm down now. You're a really good person. I'm just an—"

"Ostrich?"

"Yeah. Always got my head in the sand. But we gotta get out of here—"

I sing a couple of lines from a song, something about getting out, finding a better life . . . I belt it out really loud, as if I know what I'm doing.

"That's The Animals isn't it?"

"I don't know. I heard it at Jackson's place."

"My dad used to play that. He played that fifty times a day before he left."

I watch him go and sit down. He puts his head in his hands. The need to laugh dies. Somehow Badman sitting there thinking about his dad seems much more sad and real than this weird cellar where we're going to die.

He looks up. "Are you okay? It's all my fault, isn't it? When they shoot me and make me into cold cuts I'll go straight to hell."

"It's okay, Bruce," I say softly.

"No, it isn't. And now I haven't even got the guts or wits to get you out of here." He looks surprised that he said that. He looks around as if someone else did.

"Yeah well, it was a pretty crappy thing to do, the possum house and all. Sometimes you act really, really stupid. People think you're stupid but I think you just don't think things through. You act on your feelings all the time. I guess you didn't know we'd get killed for it. You know, you were pretty brave back there in the garden."

"What? When I said all that stupid stuff about being Jackson? Yeah, that was so helpful." He shoves his hands in his pockets.

"No. When you went for Rocky. You did that head butt, straight for the guts. Anybody else, they would have keeled over. You're not light you know. Harry Houdini died from a punch like that. And he was one of the fittest guys ever in the world. I read this book about him. A college student took him unawares and punched him—just for a joke. Busted his intestine I think, or his appendix. Something like that. But Rocky's got a stomach like one of these walls here. I guess he's always flexing, even when he's asleep."

"Yeah well, it didn't do us any good. Just got him mad." Badman takes his hands out of his pockets and cracks his knuckles.

"Hey, something fell out."

Badman bends down and searches the floor. He picks up a string of small firecrackers. His face is red when he stands up. He's looking at the firecrackers in his hand. "My mom, maybe she's right. She's always saying I'm just like my dad—good at making messes, bad at cleaning them up."

"Have you still got your lighter? The world famous windproof whatever?"

"Yeah."

"Show me." I'm staring at the firecrackers, wondering what damage they could do. If one firecracker can blow up a mailbox, what about a whole bunch of them? Or was that a different kind of firecracker?

He takes out the lighter and flicks it open, then strikes it against his leg. He does this a couple of times but there's no flame. He grunts with frustration. "It's a *Zippo*—it's supposed to light like that. The Americans used them during the war." He tries another time, striking it with his finger, then throws it down on the table. "Must be outta lighter fluid."

"Figures."

Badman stuffs the firecrackers and the lighter back in his pocket. "What, did you think we could blow our way out of here? Through concrete? These firecrackers might be loud, but they're not strong. Just make a big noise. Like me."

"I wasn't thinking straight, I guess."

We look gloomily for a while at the cushioned walls.

"They probably just said that cold cuts thing to scare us, I think. Don't you?" Badman looks at me hopefully. He suddenly reminds me of Daniel, and I feel so old. "Rocky wouldn't go through with it, would he? I mean, they're criminals but who'd kill kids?"

"I don't know. But I'm sure when Jackson knows we're missing, he'll put two and two together."

"Yeah. Then he'll go and do something useless like find the square root or something."

"Two doesn't have a square root."

"Oh. Well, anyway."

"The thing is, Jackson or anyone won't know till morning—"

"And then it might be too late. And the police, will they believe some weirdo kid? And what about the others, they might say we've eloped."

"Ha!"

Silence. Doesn't feel like there's enough air. When Jackson first told me about Tony he was so sure they'd left the casino behind forever. They'd moved fast, right across the city, to the suburbs. Jackson thought Homeland was secure, like heaven, like some place baddies could never reach. Badman is starting to pace again. He's grinding his teeth, you can see his jaw moving. I don't think I can deal with his freak-out. It's strange how we seem to take turns in freaking out. But for the first time I get the feeling Badman might be someone you could rely on. That he has a good heart. I'm glad I'm here with him and not on my own.

"Funny how everything that used to annoy you before looks so good now," I say into the silence. "I mean, I've been thinking if I could just have my life back, I'd appreciate everything."

"That's because you've got it all good. A mom and dad that are always there—"

"Yeah, too much! They don't let me do anything I want. Sometimes I don't think they hear what I say at all. You know, we used to have this dog, Rex. It had selective hearing, Dad always said. Rex only heard the words "walk," "dinner," "good dog." Everything else it ignored. Rex was a bit like my parents. If it's not about math or banking, they don't hear it."

"But you just said how much you'd appreciate them if you had them back."

"Yeah. Well, just thinking about it makes me mad again. I wouldn't even *be* here if they'd let me go to the pub."

"Ooh, the pub!" He mimics in this silly high voice. "Sausages and mash, it's enough to make you wet your pants with excitement." He goes red suddenly and looks down at his damp leg.

"Valerie was *singing* there. You know that. You gave Jackson a hard time about it all day."

"And you ran around like a stupid groupie. Oh, Valerie *this* and Valerie *that*," Badman mocks.

"You sound just like my mother." I sing a couple of bars of Patti Smith when she's complaining about her parents.

"Hey, that's from 'Doves Cry.'"

"Yeah, you like Patti Smith?"

He shrugs. "She's okay, for a woman."

"Oh, man, what a Neanderthal you are!"

"My dad really likes her. He saw her in concert in the seventies. Said she was amazing."

"Did he teach you how to play it?"

"He tried. But I didn't want to. I wish now I had. There are a lot of things I wish I'd done when he was here."

"Ssh." There's a loud creak of the floorboards above. It's right overhead. Are they coming to get us? Then we hear more footsteps. They sound as if they're moving away.

"I know what you mean," I say when it's quiet again. "I had a really bad argument with my mom, just before all this happened. I keep thinking, those things I said, maybe they'll be my last words to her."

"Yeah. You think a lot about the last things a person says. The words sort of hang in the air like ghosts. Every morning, I sit down to breakfast with my mom and dad's last argument. Mom said he'd better grow up or he'll never be any good to anyone. She said he talks like a rock song. He just got up and went to get his bag then. And as he was walking out the door, he recited this whole song by Black Sabbath at her, as if it was Shakespeare or something. It was about freedom and love and death and all." He grins for a moment. "So I suppose he got her back, you know, with the rock song. But he still left, anyway."

I'm sitting there with my mouth open. This is the most personal stuff I've ever heard straight from Bruce Bradman's mouth. "Will your dad be coming back?"

Badman shrugs. "Said for Christmas. Said if the tour goes well, he'll bring me back a new guitar. But I told him I don't care about that."

"Really?" I can't help looking surprised.

"Well, see, I already got his old one. He says it's falling apart, but there's nothing wrong with it, I think. And I figure if he doesn't get paid too well and he can't afford some fancy guitar, what if he felt so bad about it, he doesn't come back at all? Mom's always going on about how he doesn't make enough money to provide for us. That he's selfish and all. But he's a musician. That's how life is."

I think of Dad and his line about tragic musicians. I can hear his voice in my head, *Your mother and I just want you to be secure, have a good life, safe*. I think of the way he kisses the top of my head and gets my ear. It's like an explosion in your eardrum. Daniel and I are always telling him.

"But me, I just want him back. And even though Mom gets so mad, she wants him back, too, I know it. She's a lot happier when he's around. The slightest sound at night, she runs into my room. 'Just wanted to see if you're all right,' she says. But she's shaking. It's started giving me the shivers, too. Can you imagine what she'll do when she finds me gone as well?"

We sit for a while in silence. It's eerie. Every now and then we hear footsteps overhead, the floorboards creaking. Especially the trapdoor. What are they doing up there? What are they planning? I don't want to think about that. Talking is better. About anything.

"Why do you like Jackson?" asks Badman suddenly.

I jump.

"What's that got to do with anything?"

Badman shrugs. "I dunno. Just wondered. Seems such a

nerd to me with his number crap. How could anyone be that interested in numbers? Or his friend, either."

"Why are you so horrible to them?"

Badman spreads his fingers out on the table.

"You know Jackson lost his dad when he was two."

"Yeah, well, he's over it now isn't he? Seems pretty friggin' confident to me."

"You think you're the only one with feelings? Everyone else has it easy? How do you think Asim copes with everything that's happened to him? You have your guitar. Jackson and Asim, they have their number . . . thing."

Badman looks at me. "Jackson knows a lot of stuff. Is that why you like him?"

"He's interesting, sure. If you got to know him, you might find that out."

Badman grins. "He told the science teacher that fruit bats' poop is worth megabucks. Is that the kind of stuff you need to know?"

We laugh. It feels good.

Badman starts drumming the table again. I recognize the rhythm quick as blinking.

"That's 'Smoke on the Water,' isn't it?"

"Yeah. See if you can get this . . ."

"'Thunderstruck,' AC/DC."

He drums some more.

"'TNT.'"

"You're amazing!"

"I heard you singing it under your breath."

"You're a real rocker then, huh?"

"Yeah, I'd like to be."

"So why do you sing that crap with Lilly?"

I shrug. "I guess because she wants me to."

"You're stronger than that!"

I shake my head.

"Well well, you really get to know a person when you're trapped in a cellar with them."

I smile.

"You know what, if we ever get out of here, we should do a number together."

"Yeah? Would you? Even though I'm a *woman*?"

He goes red. "Yeah, it'd be all right."

"Why don't we write a song then? We could write it about being in here. We could do it for the end-of-year concert." I figure we have to believe we're going to get out of here, otherwise there'll be no chance of it happening at all.

"We was sittin' in the cellar," raps Badman, "waiting for the end . . . When she said be my fella—"

I hold up my hands. "Just the music though, okay? We're just friends, all right?"

Badman sighs. "Yeah, okay. Rock is dead, long live rock!"

"That doesn't make sense. Who said that?"

"The Who."

"Who?"

"The band called 'The Who.' Pete Townsend."

We start laughing, I don't know why. Badman is really shaking and I'm wondering if he's caught my unreal fog thing when suddenly I look up and see the trapdoor opening. We didn't hear a sound. The first thing we know is that Rocky is lumbering down the stairs like a grizzly bear.

"Glad to see you're making the most of your last night here," he says. But he doesn't smile. He goes over to the filing cabinet behind us. We swivel around to see. He pulls out a drawer and inside, perfectly laid out on a white cloth like a dentist's instruments are all kinds of guns. He stands surveying them like a kid in a candy store.

"Beretta, 9 mm, parabellum," he says, pulling out a gun. He aims it at Badman and purses his lips, miming "*pow pow.*" He pretends to pull the trigger.

Badman freezes. I can hear his breathing stop. His face loses color so quickly, it's as if the blood has been sucked right out of him.

There's not a sound in the room. We've both got our eyes locked on Rocky. He blows on the end of his gun as if he's just nailed someone, and gives a low false baddy's laugh. What does he think he is, a cowboy in some Western cartoon?

We watch as he wipes the gun with his sleeve, giving it an affectionate last pat. "You can't beat the Eye-tyes for style and efficiency, now can you?" Swinging around, he pushes the drawer shut and locks it.

As he turns he waves the gun at us. "Berettas always get top dollars on the market. Semiautomatic. They're handy for the mugs that don't cooperate. Remember that."

He shoves the gun in his belt and heads up the stairs.

13. Jackson

It's still dark when I tiptoe out of the house. The sun is a golden line at the top of the hill. I glance at my watch. 5:33 A.M. Now that I have no bike I'll need an extra half hour to complete the route.

Walking up the hill, I try to think positively about the morning. You know, the fresh air and the . . . But I keep counting my steps. I'm counting in twos and whenever I'm not counting I see the Mustang coming down this same road and the spot where my bike was smashed. 14, 16, 18, 20 . . . Up ahead, there are two dark skid lines wrapping around the corner. Were they there yesterday?

I used to enjoy my challenges. You know, I'd get a kick out of seeing how many breaths I could take by the time the bus turned into St. Peter's Road or winking twice at a red light (four for green). But sometimes, like right now, I don't want my mind to do that. I want to think about something else. Something positive.

The newsdealer's is probably only about one hundred and forty-eight steps from here.

I look straight into the sun. It's popped out over the horizon like a seed. I remember a story Miss Braithwaite told us about a giant who blew up a yellow balloon and set it off with a giant pat to float up into the sky. But one morning a blue Mustang crashed into the yellow balloon and burst it, bringing eternal darkness to the world . . .

No, that wasn't how the story finished but now I'm at the newsdealer's and I'm standing in the doorway. One hundred and forty-*nine* steps to the line. I can't pretend any different, it's just not right. Bummer.

Bill looks weary and I can see a crust of sleep in the corner of his eye. He's grumpy, too. "A bit early, aren't you?"

I tell him about having an accident with the bike and that I'm on foot. He grunts and gives me a half load of *Homeland Dailies*. "You'll have to come back for the rest. Do it in two lots. I don't want your mother coming here and suing me for your crooked back." He sighs. "Kids are so careless these days. You won't last long at this job without a bike. You'll be late for school, get sick of it. Kids, they just want the big excitement and then they get bored. You can't depend on them anymore."

I open my mouth to point out that in fact I'm early because I *want* to get the job done in time and anyway you can't just lump all kids together like that—you wouldn't say "adults, they're all the same," would you? But he doesn't want to listen and anyway I wouldn't have the guts to say it. I must have fifty-seven weeks worth of speeches in my head that I'll never deliver.

"So much delinquency around here," he goes on, shaking his head. "No respect for other people's rights. Something will have to be done. Take this noise pollution—what is it, cars backfiring, firecrackers, seems these young hoods will do anything for excitement. You hear that one last night? I nearly fell out of bed. Sounded like someone being shot. Then such a squeal of tires around that corner—thought they'd ram into my garden wall."

"I was out last night—"

"Always racing each other up and down this street. Souped-up cars—revving their engines. There's no peace anymore around here."

"What kind of cars have you—"

"Well, young fella, can't stand around jabbering all day. You'd better be on your way then, quick. Off you go!"

I turn on my heel with my bundle of papers and head off. Why don't people just talk to the wallpaper if they don't want to even hear what anyone else has to say?

I do the block in a jog. As I throw the papers I think about Bill and what a cranky old fart he is. I wonder why. Maybe he's a bit deaf. You'd go right inside yourself if you had that affliction. The whole world would seem far away, scary maybe, as if it didn't have anything much to do with you. Still, as I throw my eighteenth newspaper (house number thirty-six, perfect multiple, deserves four winks) I wonder if I should tell him about the Mustang. I keep feeling guilty about it, this dirty secret smashed up in our garage. Underneath, I think it's really my fault, because I was standing in the road doing a stupid challenge. No one would expect to see a lump of a boy in the middle of the road. By the time I finish the block I'm thinking maybe the driver was one of these young "delinquents"; he might even live around here. Maybe that Neighborhood Watch group might be interested. I've seen their posters up near the bakery.

Bill is busy unpacking stationery when I walk in. He just grunts and loads me up. Doesn't even look up. I stand there for a bit with my arms full. I can't help winking at the stack of red pens on the counter.

"What's wrong with you, kid, got a squint?" he says.

219

"No, I was just thinking—"

His brow clears. "Ah, you want your week's pay," and he hands me the small yellow envelope and turns his back on me.

On the second run the morning is already warmer and the air is heavier, almost sweet. Dew hangs from the leaves like those little crystal tears Esmerelda wears on her necklace.

I'm on my way home, back down my street when I see a police car. It's parked outside Esmerelda's house. Alarm pings in my chest. How strange, at eight in the *morning*? I'm crossing the road when I remember her telling me her uncle is a policeman. He lives in another state, I think she said. Uncle Bob. So probably he's just come for a visit. As I open our gate I imagine telling him all about the blue Mustang and the bike and asking him to promise not to tell Mom. It's a good fantasy and I stretch it out to last past the garbage cans and the maple tree. I imagine drinking a Coke with Uncle Bob and suggesting maybe he could do some investigating on the quiet. Then I remember he's here on vacation and why would he want to take on some strange kid and his problems, and anyway, Mom is so phobic about the police she probably wouldn't even let me finish the Coke . . .

I go the long way down the garden to the porch and the back door so I don't wake her. And I'm kind of interested anyway to see how many steps it will take if I go around the azalea bush, even though I'm tired and hot and know that I should just race in and take a shower and get ready for school and totally forget about the azalea bush. I'm up to twenty-three when I see something bright red on the path beside the grass.

I pick it up. Blood pounds in my head. A Thunder, it's a firecracker—*used*. I remember Bill's words: *These explosions in the middle of the night* . . . The possum house—I didn't check it this morning.

I run back up to the maple tree in twelve steps and peer into it. No sign of damage. But how do I know they're okay? I can't see any possums inside. I glance at the mailbox. Everything as usual.

Badman. The *bastard*. Inside my garden. What the hell is he playing at?

I go inside and take a shower. When I come out Mom is making tea in the kitchen. She's doing everything by feel with her eyes closed. When she hears me behind her she opens her eyes. "I'm pretending to be Ray Charles," she grins sleepily.

I don't say anything. I don't feel like joking around and anyway I'm hunting for my English book.

"You know, Ray Charles, the blind piano player?"

I'm still hunting for my English book. There are bills and shopping lists and stuff all over the kitchen table.

"Was that in bad taste? I'm sorry," says Mom. I can feel her eyes open now, considering my back.

"I've gotta go to school," I tell her, turning around. "You can go back to bed with your tea."

She smiles and pats my face. "That bruise still looks nasty. Does it hurt much?"

"No, I don't think about it."

She catches sight of the clock above the fridge. "Oh, gosh, I'll have to rush, too. I said I'd take Polly to have an X-ray for her knee. I'm picking her up at her place. All that peak hour traffic. I better fly. Have a good day, sweetheart!"

My English book has disappeared. And we're having a test today. Our homework was to give the Latin origins of ten words, like balance and benefit. What about the word *bastard*? "Badman is a bastard." Bastard means someone whose parents aren't married, so it's actually not such a bad word or even an insult because who cares if your parents were married or not when they had you? And it's hardly the fault of their kid anyway. But I just like saying bastard. The "b" is really explosive. Like you've got a bomb in your mouth. Mom says bastard may be my favorite word because I have abandonment issues. You know, with Dad dying and all. So every now and then she sits me down and shows me her marriage certificate and tells me again I *did* have a father and little stories about him. I don't protest because I quite like the stories and anyway she seems to enjoy telling them. Her voice sounds younger and softer when she talks about him.

The English book is not under all the stuff on the table or on the floor or hidden by the TV guide. I give up and fling out the door but as I march out into the street the bus drives off.

I throw my bag down on the curb and sit on it. I take out the Thunder from my pocket and look at it. Then I think of Mrs. Bradman and her cardigan. I wonder if she knows how evil her son is. Maybe she doesn't care. I remember a program I saw once on TV where they were interviewing a mother about her son. He had murdered some guy. He was on death row, about to be executed by the state. The interviewer kept asking her different questions but the mother just kept saying, "He's my son, he's my *son*." It was just about the saddest thing I'd ever seen.

The police car outside Esmerelda's house has gone. That

was a short visit—you'd think an uncle would stay for breakfast when he hasn't seen his family for a couple of years. When the next bus comes I head right down the back so I don't have to talk to anyone. I want to plan what I'm going to do to Badman when I see him.

Outside the school gates there are two police cars. They're parked in the bus stop zone. Has Badman gone and blown up something really important? Or maybe he's hurt someone, or himself? I feel a kind of sweet relief, like tasting chocolate on my tongue. I know it's bad, but if Badman's discovered to be a real criminal he'll be stopped, won't he? It'll all be taken out of my hands. I won't have to deal with him anymore. (And maybe I won't wake up at 3:33 A.M.)

I go up the steps to the administration block to get a late note. But the staff room next to it is filled with kids spilling into the hallway and as I look along the line to the end of the room I see two tall uniformed men. Police.

Asim spots me as he's coming out.

"Jackson, where have you been?"

"I missed the bus and—"

"Something terrible has happened. The police are interviewing everyone about Esmerelda—"

"Esmerelda?" A spurt of fear shoots into my throat.

"Yes. Ez and Badman are missing."

"*What*?" My throat is seizing up. I start to cough.

"Come on," says Asim, leading me back down the steps, "you can see the police later, they've got tons of kids to get through first."

We go to sit on a bench. "It's not true," I try to say through the coughing. "It can't be, I saw her uncle outside . . ." My heart is beating like a jackhammer. Not Esmerelda, no, please! Nothing's allowed to happen to Esmerelda.

Asim touches my arm. "When both Ez and Badman's parents went to wake them this morning they weren't there. It sounds so strange, there was no sign of forced entry, except Mrs. Marx cannot understand how she came to leave the front door unlocked. She and her husband were sure they had checked the door before they went to bed—"

"She's missing, with *him*. Missing." I'm repeating everything like a parrot. I want to say it all a hundred times so I can believe it. I wish it was printed out in a book so I could read it. Because just words in the air like this—I can't believe it.

Asim looks down at the ground. "Joe told the police this stupid thing."

"What?"

"That Ez and Badman eloped—"

"That stupid idiot. As if Esmerelda—and anyway, eloped means running away to get married and they're too young. We had it in our novel study. What an idiot—"

Asim squeezes my arm. "Of course no one believes him." Asim pauses a moment. "When the police talked to me I did say that I knew she was very angry with her parents for not letting her go out last night. You know, to hear Valerie."

I look at Asim. A kind of buzzing is starting in my head like wires suddenly connecting and making sparks. "She told me on the phone she was so mad she wanted to run away."

Asim nods. "She told me that, too."

We sit and stare at the ground. Nothing is making any sense at all. I think of that expression, "the rug was pulled out from under me." Mom says that a lot, particularly on the phone to Bev. She says, "Well, I felt like the rug was pulled out from under me!" That's what this feels like. As if the ground I've always known has suddenly shifted, cracked into tiny pieces.

"She wouldn't, would she? She wouldn't do a thing like that! And not with Badman!"

Asim grabs both my shoulders and holds me still. I realize I'm shaking.

"Ooooh, who's in love now?" Joe walks by doing a stupid wriggle of his hips.

"Shut up, you idiot. Why aren't you worrying about your friend instead of making dumb jokes?"

Joe laughs. "Old Badman? He can take care of himself. *And* his girlfriend."

I jump up but Asim is still holding my shoulders.

"Don't think about him now. He knows nothing." Asim pulls me back down on the bench. "Ez was angry but she wouldn't do anything as . . . what is the word? Well, as silly as that. You know it. She would not run away, I am sure. But maybe, if she was so angry, she couldn't sleep? She may have gone out for a walk?"

A clutch of cold grips my stomach. "I found something in my garden this morning." I feel in my pocket and realize it's still there. "This firecracker," I say, showing Asim. "See, it's been exploded."

"You found it this morning? It wasn't there yesterday?"

"No, I don't think so."

"Is there any damage at your home?"

"No, it's okay."

We look at each other. The firecracker is shaking in my hand. I make a big effort to hold it still.

"So, maybe," Asim says slowly, "maybe while we were out

Badman entered your garden. What was he going to do? The mailbox—"

"He could blow that up from outside the house."

"The possum house instead—"

"Is *in*side . . . Remember how nasty he was about it, how he said, 'don't hurt yourselves,' and 'the little possies?' And then we had that fight." I crack each knuckle twice. It helps me to think. "You know what, I think he came to blow it up. Otherwise, why come right inside the gate? And he knew Mom and I would be out. All day Ez made such a big fuss about how great the night was going to be. Remember the way she was raving about Valerie, how this was going to be her big break, how she'd be famous? Practically everyone in the school knew my mom was going to be out singing at the pub."

Asim is watching the kids trickling out of the office. They're sort of tiptoeing down the stairs as if they're part of a secret.

"And you know what? He couldn't stand it," I say suddenly. "The idea of everyone talking about my mother, that she might be famous. Mostly, he couldn't stand Esmerelda talking about it. Remember how he kept saying to me, 'Mommy's boy.' It was the only thing he could find to try to take me down. 'Aren't you a little mommy's boy?'"

Asim is nodding furiously. "So maybe," he hesitates, "maybe if Ez was out walking, or even just up late, she might have seen him. Seen him opening your gate . . ."

A red rage is burning in my head. It's hard to think clearly above the crackling noise. But I'm seeing something. It's like groping for a hand rail in the dark. "So why didn't he blow up the possum house? He certainly got to it."

"He must have been stopped before he could—"

"Esmerelda." A clammy sweat prickles all over me. I clutch Asim. "She stopped him somehow, I'm sure of it. But the firecracker did explode. Jesus, if she was hurt I'm gonna kill him. Do you think she was hurt?"

"I don't know. But it still doesn't explain why they're missing. I mean, Badman is bad, but he couldn't force her to run away with him, take her hostage or anything . . ."

We keep sitting on the bench. Kids file past, birds peck at the grass, Mrs. Reilly yells at her class in the distance. A feeling is growing in me, a kind of dread, but there's no shape or face to it. There's something missing here, some clue I'm not seeing. I know with this deep knowing that the thing is staring me in the face. I feel like Mom's Ray Charles—I'm hearing the music but I can't see it.

"The last place we can trace Badman to is your garden," says Asim. "He must have arrived late, but before you got home. Esmerelda may have been with him." Asim wipes his face. He looks very pale.

"Are you okay? What is it, what are you thinking?"

Asim looks down at his hands. "I'm thinking that there is just one thing to do. We must search this last place where Badman was. We should look it over very carefully. Maybe there is some clue you have not seen."

The cold feeling in my stomach is spreading. I stand up. "Okay. Let's go."

Asim stands, too, but he grabs my arm. "First, we should tell the police about this. They have not interviewed you yet. We should tell them too about your . . . accident. The Mustang."

"No! Mom would have a fit. I couldn't do it. Anyway it's over now. I haven't seen the car again. Look, I just want to go home, I've got to get home and check things out for myself. I promise, if I find anything I'll tell the police. Are you coming with me?"

Asim is biting the inside of his cheek. I can see one side is all sucked in. He's hovering there, standing on one foot then the other. "I don't know, I don't know," he whispers.

"Come on. If we just keep to the fence and walk behind those trees we can get out the school gates without anyone knowing."

"But that's against the law!" he bursts out. "It's called truancy! What if the principal finds out?"

I turn around to face him. "Look, it's just one day. No one can put you in jail for that! Kids do it all the time." I look at my watch. "There's a bus that goes back our way in five minutes. They go every half hour."

Asim's face looks all crumpled like a paper bag. He's sucking his cheek so badly I'm scared he'll bite right through it. A pang of sadness goes through me. He's panicking. Mom had a panic attack once and she looked just like that. White as a sheet. Sometimes I forget. It's too much for him.

"Listen, you're right," I say quickly. "It's best if you stay here. Probably better if I just go myself. It won't look so obvious, no teacher's even seen me. It's true you don't want to attract any attention like this. I understand, it's okay." I pick up my bag. "I'll let you know if I find anything."

I'm heading toward the trees, crouching down low when I feel a hand pulling my shirt. I whip around. Asim's white face is close to mine.

"I'm coming, too," he whispers.

"Are you sure?"

Asim draws his lips in tight. "Positive."

We squat down and inch forward with our knees bent like commando raiders. Asim doesn't make a sound.

On the bus we're both quiet. I wink twice at the red light. I wonder what Asim is thinking. I sneak a glance at him. He's still pale and he's hunched down in his seat with his shirt collar pulled up as far up as it can go. I feel pretty tense myself. My heart is still going at about 60 miles an hour. Hasn't slowed since I first heard Esmerelda's name an hour ago. I wonder if you can have a heart attack at thirteen.

As soon as we reach my place, Asim walks in the gate and drops his bag near the garbage cans. He starts at the maple tree. He peers at the trunk of the tree, rubbing his hands all over it, then up into the little house. I decide to check out the other end of the garden.

"Can you see anything?" I call after a while.

He puts his finger to his lips.

"A couple of round furry shapes," he says walking toward me. "And a pair of eyes, blinking. They must really like it in there, do you think?"

We smile at each other. It feels good to smile.

Then Asim drops to his knees again and starts looking at the grass. He runs his hand over the ground and points to an area shaped like a bean bag where the grass is flattened and a bit mashed. Patches of dirt show through. "This makes me think a scuffle took place," says Asim. "Like a body or two might have struggled on the ground."

"What? Esmerelda with *him*? Ugh!"

"So where did you say you found the Thunder?"

"Around here, more or less. On the path there beside the lawn."

Asim works his way along the path, clearing leaves away with his hands.

"Oh, look, here are the scorch marks! Was this the spot exactly?"

"Yes! The Thunder was lying on the concrete. That's why I saw it. If it'd been buried in the grass here I might not have noticed it."

But Asim is moving off now, scuttling across the garden like a beetle. His face is close to the ground. All he needs is a pair of feelers coming out of his head.

I watch him work his way up the garden. I'm checking out the area, too, but I'm a bit in awe of his methodical approach. It's as if he was born to it—this detective work.

"What are you looking for now?"

He doesn't answer for a moment. Then he goes to the gate and opens it. I find him on the other side, down on his knees. I crouch down too.

"See this dirt here, in the dip where the grass does not grow?"

"Yeah. Too many feet tramping on it. It fills up with mud when it rains. Mom's talked about putting paving stones there—"

"Look closely."

I look. "There's some shoe prints. A big one."

"Yes."

"Badman's got pretty big feet."

"Yes, but are they that big?"

I nod. "I think so. His fists are big, too, I remember the feel of them on my ear."

"Hmm." Asim is digging into the longer grass near the retaining wall. He's so focused, his fingers parting the thick tall weeds, his face disappearing into the green. He moves a few inches along the wall every few seconds. He's working with the concentration of those forensic detectives on TV.

I'm thinking how different he looks, right now. How

230

different everything seems. I'm used to him falling apart, of having to be so careful of his feelings. It's like trying not to joggle a valuable package marked "fragile." I guess I've been thinking I have to look after him. But now, well, it seems like he's in charge. He knows what he's doing. Even if we find nothing, it's so good to be here together.

"Jackson."

Asim stands up. He's holding something in his hand but I can't see because his fingers are closed tightly around it. I know from his face that the world is about to change. He looks so calm. Pale, but calm.

Slowly he unfurls his fingers. The cold dammed up dread inside me opens like a sea.

"The Blue M," says Asim. He's reading the logo on the book of matches lying in his palm. There is a smudge of dirt over the last word but when he wets his finger and wipes it, everything is perfectly clear.

"The Blue Moon," Asim says quietly. "That's the casino where your mother worked, isn't it? The place you told me about, with the bad men?"

All I can do is nod. The dread is like ice water gushing through my head. Numbing my brain.

"Someone from the Blue Moon was here, Jackson." Asim speaks slowly. It's as if he's dealing with a person who's been in an accident and he's being very kind. Somewhere at the bottom of all the cold I feel grateful.

"Why do you think that is?"

I shake my head. I try to clear it, to climb my way out of this dark, drowning feeling.

"You better sit down," says Asim suddenly. "You look like you might faint."

We sit on the grass.

"I have to tell you this, Jackson, but I have been worried about that Mustang ever since we first saw it. I know you do not want to hear this. But now, when it has hit you—"

"What's that got to do with it?" I feel angry suddenly, trapped, as if I can't breathe. "I was in the wrong place, I *told* you, standing there like some idiot in the middle of the road and anyway even old Bill said there are delinquents everywhere around here."

Asim takes my hand. A part of me is thinking we must look so weird sitting here on the lawn at ten o'clock in the morning holding hands. But mostly I just feel like I'm drowning.

Asim goes on patting my hand. "It's called surveillance, Jackson. I have seen it before. In Iraq, if Saddam Hussein suspected you of plotting against him, or even just being disloyal, he sent his men to watch you. They followed you in cars, or on foot, always waiting there like your shadow, watching. This is supposed to scare you, warn you, make so you can't think straight anymore. Then they start to threaten you. They hurt you, hurt your family." Asim takes a deep breath. His hand is trembling now. "Many, many people just disappeared in my country. Went missing."

I drop his hand as if it's burning. "This isn't Iraq! You're crazy, that doesn't happen here. Your trouble is you just can't forget what happened to you!"

Asim sighs. He suddenly looks so old, as if he's seen everything before and he knows exactly what I'm going to say and how this will all finish. I sit there watching him sighing sadly, looking so wise, and it seems as if he's done all the steps of this dance before and he's just waiting for me to catch up.

Well, I don't want to. I don't *want* to.

"Look at it this way," he says patiently. "It's like adding up fractions. You have to find a common denominator before you can see the whole picture."

"I know that."

"Well, what are our fractions? What are the pieces? What do they have in common?"

He waits for a moment, then puts the Blue Moon matches in the space between us.

"The casino is our common denominator," he says. "The Mustang is one piece, the phone calls are another—"

"The phone calls were from *Bad*man. Everyone knows that!"

Asim shakes his head. "Not me. I know Badman does bad things, but he does not like silence. It is not his style. He puts his name to things. He is very loud and very angry. He is not, what is the word? Subtle."

There's a pause between us.

"Did you get a better look at the license plate of the Mustang?" Asim keeps on. "I know we saw the 777, but what about the letters?"

I stare out at the street. "I was too busy jumping out of the *way*," I mumble.

Asim waits.

"I remember RO, is all."

"What was the manager's name? The one who threatened Valerie?"

"Tony."

"Oh."

I feel almost glad he's disappointed. What did he expect, another perfect piece of evidence? But those letters flash up again behind my eyes. It's like a scene from a dream, a memory you keep carefully trying to bury under real life.

"Tony employed a security guard." I give this to him with an effort. "He was there the night Valerie discovered the drug money."

"What was his name?"

"Rocky. Sometimes they called him The Rock."

"R-O-C," he spells out. "Do you think it could be that? Could it be a C?"

A wave of sickness floods me. "Or a K."

"I think it is this Rocky who drives the Mustang." Asim sits up on his haunches. "Rocky has been watching you and Valerie, showing you his boss has not forgotten. Valerie must not have given them what they wanted. So they hurt the thing most close to her. *You.* Maybe he came here to . . . to take you away."

I stare at Asim. There is a sinking feeling in my chest, as I swallow something I can't digest. Slowly, as if wading through wet sand, I see that if this is true, they will have known all our habits. That Mom works nights.

"They came when they thought I would be home alone."

"But Badman was here—"

"And Esmerelda. Remember we said—"

"Yes, I remember. And that's the whole picture."

We're both standing at the gate, looking at all the different pieces in our minds. I don't like this common denominator. I realize I've been trying *not* to find it for weeks. I remember Mom's strained face, her weariness, the look of fear every time the phone rings. The way she bear-hugged me last night because she couldn't find me for three seconds. She's been living with this common denominator ever since we moved here. She's been hoping it would go away.

"We have to tell the police," Asim says. "We can go back

234

to school. I bet they are still interviewing. We can show them the matches."

"No!" My voice comes out in a shout. Asim jumps. "You don't understand. Mom has a *phobia* about the police. She'd die if we did that. You don't know what it's like. See, her friend Bev went through this last year. Tony blackmailed her, threatened he'd hurt her mother—she's old and sick. So Bev gave in and did what they told her. I think she took part in some deal at the casino, and they gave her a 'bonus' as a reward, to pay for a nursing home for her mother. So then they could say she was involved in their dirty work, see?"

"But the police could fix that! Here it is different from my country—"

"No, Mom *did* go to the police to help Bev. Well, the guy she saw was an ex-cop. He used to visit the casino. He acted like her friend and so she asked him for help but all he did was rat her out to Tony!"

"But that was only one cop. Not all police are like that."

"You try telling Mom that. She thinks the Blue Moon has an advance warning system about police raids. She could be right. If we tell the cops and Tony hears about it, he might—he might get rid of them."

We sit in silence. Asim starts zipping and unzipping his jacket. It makes a horrible grating noise.

Suddenly I know exactly what I have to do. The dread is still pounding through me but with every second I feel more sure. It's as if I've been trying to hold back the sea. We've been running, Mom and I, running like people trying to outrun a tidal wave or an avalanche. You keep pretending you can't hear it behind you, see it. But some things are so big you can't escape. Sometimes you just have to turn around and face them. Maybe you'll get swallowed up, but at least you'll see what you're afraid of. The shape of it. The truth. And just maybe, even if the odd numbers are against you, you might strike lucky and come out even.

I'm suddenly dying to tell Mom this, make her see it's the only thing to do.

I can't now, but I'm going to do the next best thing.

"We're going to the casino," I tell Asim. "I know exactly where Tony will be hiding Esmerelda. We're going to rescue them."

Asim does this weird thing. He laughs out loud. It's the loudest laugh I've ever heard him give. "Now *you* are the one who is crazy," he says. "Even if we do find them, how are we supposed to fight off Rocky the strong man? Or Tony?"

"Well, it's like this. We'll get Mom's cell phone, it's probably still on the kitchen table with the shopping list she always forgets to take. We'll bring it with us and call the police on 911 just as we get there. We'll tell them it's an emergency. That way they'll come right away, no delay, no advance warning, and I can take them to Esmerelda."

"How are we going to get there? By bus? It'll take forever!"

"I have my month's paper route money. We'll get a cab. We'll travel in style."

Asim has turned as pale as his shirt.

I cuff him on the shoulder like some cowboy in a movie. Maybe I have gone crazy. But I'm so full of energy I feel like I'm hooked up to a power plant and electricity is running through my veins. "I'm going to bust that casino wide open," I yell, "and save Esmerelda. Are you coming?"

Asim picks up his bag and sighs. "I cannot let you go alone."

14. Esmerelda

Daniel waves at me through the window. He's holding something in his hand. It's a teddy bear, with only one eye.

I try to lift up the glass but the window is locked. Now Jackson appears behind Daniel. He's waving a teddy, too.

I fiddle with the lock, trying to heave up the glass but it's stuck fast. Panic is rising in me. I press my hands against the glass. I'm shouting, telling them I can't get out but they just keep smiling and waving their teddies. I start to bash the window with my fists, and suddenly there is a loud crack . . .

My eyes snap open. I look around the room at the filing cabinets and the woman with the eye in her forehead. There's no window. No Jackson. Then I see Badman in the corner. He's just smashed his fist against the drawer of guns.

"Do you think it's morning yet?" I ask.

He whips around. "Yep. You've been asleep." He walks over to the table. "Must be daylight out there, but we can't see with these damn fluorescents. You know, sometimes in casinos there's no natural light at all because they don't want people to know how long they've been playing."

I shudder. The memory of a window, a way out, is shrinking fast. "Did you sleep?"

He shrugs. "Probably a few minutes." He sits down. "I've been trying to *think*, think how to get out of here. I can't believe we're still trapped, like . . ."

"Bugs in a jar."

"Yeah."

"Well, everyone must know we're missing by now. And Jackson'll be racking his brains—"

"That'll take a while—he's got so many. Pity you're not in here with *him*."

I ignore that. "Look, there's nothing we can do here. But I know Jackson will figure it out. He's probably telling the police right now. He'll work out exactly where we are—he told *me* all about this place: the office, the trapdoor . . . As long as Tony keeps us here, I figure we're safe. Jackson will find us and bring the cops."

"Your faith is very touching, Ez." He doesn't look "touched." He looks scared. "Never thought I'd be pleased to see the cops," he adds, getting up.

I watch him pacing the length of the room. It doesn't take long. The cellar seems even smaller when he does that. "Can you *stop* it?" I ask.

"I gotta keep moving."

"We just have to wait it out," I say. "Try to distract ourselves . . . Are there any more drinks?"

"No. I tried to open the fridge door but that's locked, too. Stingy as well."

"I'm so thirsty."

"Same. There's a tap in the bathroom but the water tastes strange. It's sort of brown."

"At least it's water."

When I come back I ask Badman if he's thought anymore about our song.

"No." He clicks his tongue with annoyance. "How can you think about that now?"

"Well, I think it's what we need to do. Valerie says when she's in a bad situation it helps her to write about it. Songs are mostly about bad situations aren't they? The blues and all."

Badman shakes his head. "You're crazy. The tragedy stuff in music is about love, not being trapped in a gangster's cellar."

"It can be about anything you want it to be."

Badman stands with his hands in his pockets. He's fidgeting with his lighter and firecrackers. I know he's dying to pace.

"What's your favorite song ever?" I say to take his mind off things.

Badman clicks his tongue again. "Don't know, got too many." He smiles for a nanosecond. "My dad's is probably a song by Jimi Hendrix. 'Purple Haze,' you know it? It's about a dream he had, that he was walking under the sea. How cool would that be, to put a dream to music?"

"I had a dream like that once. Only I wasn't walking under the sea, I was drowning."

"I have a lot of dreams about falling off cliffs. Sometimes I wake up before I die, and sometimes I don't."

He looks as if he's falling now, into a dark and gloomy pit. I try to steer the conversation out of the dark. "Have you ever really listened to Patti Smith's lyrics? She's dreamlike too, a bit surreal. She makes you see strange pictures in your mind—like those paintings where ordinary things look weird because they turn up in unusual places. Like that painting at Jackson's house—"

"Haven't seen it. I've never been invited, in case you hadn't noticed."

"Well, there's a painting of a boat in the sky. It's a normal fishing boat but you notice every detail about it because it looks so foreign up there in the sky."

Badman comes and sits down. "Music does that. Makes you look at things differently. When you get into a song, *really* into it, it's like a way out."

"Yes!"

"If Mom's been yelling at me or shouting down the phone at Dad or something, I just go and plug in. About four bars, it takes, and I'm away."

"'Smoke on the Water?'"

"And 'Highway to Hell' ain't bad." He grins.

I'm smiling, too. My head feels light, as if I could float away, away out of this cellar. "It's the best escape from real life— but don't you think it helps you find your way back in, too? Through a different door. You know, back into yourself."

Badman is staring at me. "When I'm playing, that's the only time I'm, you know, happy. I don't think about anything else. There's just me and the music." He looks at his hands. "I like that part of myself. Just that part."

I nod.

Badman taps out a rhythm on the table. "That different door thing. Is that a line from a song?"

"I don't think so. But it's hard to tell sometimes—"

"You walked in through a different door," he raps under his breath, "one I'd never seen before . . ."

"Open the door, let me out, I wanna feel the fire . . ."

" . . . of your desire . . ."

"Hah! That's not bad!" Then, over our table rapping, I hear something else. "Ssh!" I hiss. "What was that?"

We sit stone still, holding our breaths. Voices, deep male voices. They're right overhead. We can hear their feet as someone tramps across the trapdoor and back again, making it creak.

A new light floods in from above as the trapdoor is flung open. A pair of shoes, then trouser legs appear. Rocky peers down at us.

"You gotta come up now," he says. "We're going on a journey."

"Where?" says Badman.

"Just do what I say, *now*."

We look at each other. I glance around the room for the hundredth time. The cellar looks almost cozy. At least it's familiar. And isn't it the only place Jackson knows where to find us?

"Move!"

Rocky's voice is so loud we both jump up and scramble up the stairs. My heart is thudding in my ears.

Tony is standing at the top, sipping a glass of whiskey. He smiles at us. The corners of his mouth turn up, but his eyes don't move at all. "I don't usually start so early," he says, pointing to the whiskey. "But these are, how shall I put it, trying circumstances."

He yawns, and walks over to the dark red table. "I trust you slept well," he continues in that fake friendly voice.

"Where are you taking us?" I ask. "What time is it?"

"Such big questions for such a little girl," says Tony shaking his head. "You're going on a vacation, to the seaside."

"It's Tony's secret beach house," Rocky puts in. "You should see it, swimming pool, spa, all set in rainforest country. You're so lucky, *I've* never been invited."

"Shut up," says Tony. "Why don't you keep your trap shut? The whole point of the exercise is that this place is supposed to be anonymous."

241

"A-non-y-mouse," repeats Rocky. "Having an unknown name or withheld authorship."

Tony gulps the last of his whiskey. "Idiot," he mutters into his glass. Pouring himself another he turns to Rocky. "Well, now you're invited. You'll look after these two charming children until the heat dies down. Then we'll think what to do. If the police trace them here, they'll come to a dead end." He grins nastily at Rocky. "Just like you, if you mess this up."

A loud knock at the door wipes the smile from his face.

"Quick, get those two back downstairs," he hisses at Rocky.

But before any of us can move, the door opens. A man with a chest like a beer keg strides into the room. "Sorry to interrupt you, Mr. Sereno," he says in a low voice, "but there's been some trouble upstairs at the blackjack table."

"What trouble?"

The man hesitates, looking at us.

Tony waves his hand as if swiping at a fly. "Don't worry about them—where they're going no one will hear."

"Well, there's this smart ass upstairs counting cards. Goes by the name of Facetti. Vince Facetti. He's gotta be stopped. He's been winning for the last hour and a half. Has some kind of system. Seems he brought his whole family with him. They're standing behind him like a football team. Big guys."

"Can't you deal with it?"

"Thing is, I recognize one of the guys. Remember that guy last year made trouble over the gun deal? Franco or Federico or something. Said we didn't pay him enough? Well, he's there tonight, eyeing me. I think this Vince Facetti is just a stooge for him. Because whenever I make a move to interrupt him, he's right at my elbow. 'We're just getting what we're owed,' he says. 'You shut up, and no one will get hurt.'"

Tony sighs. "Bad things come in threes." He points at us. "One, two," and he looks at the stocky man, "three."

"I'm just the messenger, Mr. Sereno," the man says nervously. "I just thought, like, you should be informed."

"It's all right, Sam, you did the right thing." Tony turns to Rocky. "This will only take a few minutes. You go and get the Mustang and park it around the back."

Rocky cracks his knuckles. "Are you sure, boss? I remember that guy from last year, too. He's a nasty piece o' work. And if his gang is here with him, you might need a bit of extra muscle, if you know what I mean."

Tony looks at him, considering. "All right. A show of force might be a good idea." He bites his lip, glancing at the whiskey bottle. "What have I done to deserve this?" He pours another shot and swallows it.

"Will I put them back down in the cellar?"

"Yes, for now."

"Okay, boss, you can count on me." Rocky pulls up the rug and opens the trapdoor. "You heard what he said," he grunts at us. "Down you go."

Sam nods at Tony and leaves. But we don't move. I'm frozen to the floor. All I can hear is my heart pounding loudly in my ears. We're both looking at the door. Sam has left it slightly ajar and a thin margin of orangey light steals through the gap.

Tony is explaining something quietly to Rocky. "So you come upstairs with me, just to show yourself. Give it five minutes, mingle with them, let them feel the weight of you. And then, act like you're just popping out for a minute, you know, to take a leak or something. But you go and get the car like I told you."

Badman has inched so close to me, his fingers are brushing

mine. I know what he wants to do. We're standing behind the table and we'd have to negotiate the corner and make it to the door in a fraction of a second. But I'm willing to follow him. My heart is pounding so hard I can't think. We keep our eyes focused on Tony.

"I want these kids gone in the next ten minutes," he's saying. "I have a feeling we don't have time to waste."

Suddenly Badman yanks my hand and he's past the table, a few feet from the door. My knee catches the corner and a knife of pain jabs through me. I try to let go of my hand but Badman pulls me forward. In just one beat I know that Badman could make it out the door if I let go. I try to loosen my hand, wring it away from him but Rocky swings around and plants himself between us.

With an arm each around our necks, he holds us in a headlock. It feels like a vice squeezing down. My throat is on fire. The weight of his arm is cutting off my air pipe. Out of the corner of my eye I see Badman's lips are turning blue. He can't make a sound.

"Are you ready, Mr. Sereno?" Sam reappears at the door. "I think you'd better come fast."

"Let's go, Rocky," Tony says sharply. "Throw them down there and come with me. You can give them what they deserve when you get back. You won't be long."

Rocky picks us up by the necks like chickens about to be slaughtered. His thumb digs deep into my throat. I start to cough and the pain burns everything black behind my eyes.

I must have fainted because I remember being at the top of the stairs and now I'm at the bottom. It hurts to breathe. But something else hurts even more. I look at my arm and it's sticking out at a strange angle under my head. It reminds me of the woman with the eye in her forehead, of the boat in the sky. It doesn't look right. And then a deep throbbing, like a drumbeat from far away, starts to work its way up my elbow. I gasp. It feels like my whole body is on fire.

"Ez, Ez! Are you all right?"

Badman is reaching over me. He moves my arm, his fingers gentle as a breeze, but the pain gashes me and I'm flying, falling into a long dark pit.

15. Jackson

"Where you boys going?" asks the cab driver.

At least I think that's what he said. The plastic screen wrapping around the driver's seat separates him so well from the passengers that his voice is muffled. He has to lean across the other side of the car practically to see us through the gap.

"To the city," I say.

"To the casino," Asim chimes in at the same time.

I give Asim a look.

"Where you say?" asks the driver, twisting around.

"To the city, please, just south of the Central Business District. You can drop us just before the Brighton Bridge."

Asim gives me a sharp nudge in the ribs. "Why aren't we going straight there? Don't we want to arrive as soon as we can?"

"Yes, but he'll get suspicious if we get dropped off at the casino. Kids aren't allowed there unaccompanied by an adult. And anyway, we don't want to be noticed. If we go in by foot, we can find some camouflage, choose our moment."

"Okay. Will it take long to walk across the bridge?"

"No, only ten minutes."

Asim hangs on to his seat belt. He's still pale, but his jaw looks set.

I study the screen in front of me. It's a thick transparent plastic, with deep scratches along the bottom. I remember Mom telling me it was introduced because cabbies wanted protection from violent passengers. Last year a cabbie was killed.

I wonder what it's like, driving inside this screen. Maybe you'd feel like you were in a bubble all on your own, with everything on the outside kept at a distance. That's how I've been feeling ever since I came to Homeland. I've been living inside this protected bubble, not wanting to hear or see what's going on in the real world. And now it's exploded in my face. But in a strange way I'm glad I've found my way out.

"I'm going to tell him to step on it," I whisper to Asim. "I've always wanted to do that."

"I am worried for your mental health, Jackson," he says. "I think you have gone crazy."

I shrug. Maybe it's true. I feel terrified or excited, I'm not sure which. But it's strangely electrifying. I've never felt so sure of anything in my whole life. Never like this—so sure I'm doing the right thing, that everything will be all right. How crazy is that, when we are on our way to confront a gang of killers? But this buzz of power is fantastic. It feels sparky and quick on top but deep down below, right in the center of my guts there is this calm kind of confidence, like an anchor on a ship.

"Could you step on it?" I say to the driver. "We're in a hurry. It's a matter of life and death."

Asim rolls his eyes. "He can't hear you. And didn't you just tell me we should not make him suspicious?"

"You're right." I look out the window, at the signs pointing to the freeway. We stop at a red light. It's only after we've moved off again that I realize I've forgotten to wink.

"Why you boys not at school?" the driver shouts through the screen.

We look at each other.

"We're going to meet my mom," I shout back. "She works in the city."

"What is her work?"

"Um, she's a waitress, we're going to see her for lunch. She's been away."

"It is early for lunch."

"Yes, yes," I agree, a bit desperately. "She gets hungry any old time, even in the middle of the night."

Asim jabs me in the ribs. "Her break time is early because she does shift work."

"Ah, yes," says the driver. "I am doing shift work at the hospital in Kabul. In my first year of being doctor I start work at dawn. Now in Australia I still start at dawn, but I am driving cabs."

Asim asks why can't he be a doctor here and is he on a protection visa, too? Asim leans forward, straining at his seat belt and they talk all the way along the freeway. Somehow they don't let the screen get in the way.

We go under a tunnel and when we come out we are in the city. Downtown. It's so much busier here, with people hurrying along the sidewalks, and the cars slowing right down to a crawl.

"Now would be a good time to use the phone," Asim whispers to me. "Is it in your pocket?"

"Yes."

"Well, we are almost there, right?" Asim starts chewing his thumbnail.

"Yes, but look at this traffic. We could get stuck here for half an hour. I don't want to ring emergency and the police get there first. Tony will hide . . . everything."

Asim starts on his index finger.

"Timing is everything," I say. "Trust me, it will be okay."

Our cab is jammed in a long line of cars a block away from Brighton Bridge. Now I'm chewing my nails. Apart from time, I'm worried about money. I keep trying to sneak a look at the driver's meter. I don't think I have that much. Paper routes are not incredibly well paid. Not like casino dealers.

"We could jump out here," I say to Asim. "It's not far to the bridge anyway."

"What do you mean, without paying? No way! This man has been working since three A.M., he has a family to provide for—"

"No, no, that's not what I mean." Asim's face has turned red. "It's just I don't know if I'll have enough, for sure if we sit here for another twenty minutes racking up the fare. Let's just pay and get out."

When we tell the driver we want to get out, we apologize about leaving him in the traffic. I hand over all the money I have, but it is seven dollars fifty short. Typical.

"We are very sorry," says Asim wringing his hands. He looks like he's just murdered someone. His thumb is practically bleeding. "If you give us your address, we can send it to you or—"

The driver takes off his seat belt and twists right around. His face is stern and he's not smiling. "In this world I believe we are here to help each other. I think you are good boys." He looks hard at Asim. "Do not worry about this small matter; it seems you have bigger troubles. You do need help?"

I see Asim take a breath. His eyes are moistening, his lips working.

"No, no," I say quickly. "But thank you so much. Look here, we can hop out now at this red light. Thanks very much!"

Quickly, I open the door. As I'm climbing out, I see the driver hand something to Asim. We make our way to the curb.

We don't talk as we start across the bridge. We're practically running now and I can feel the phone jabbing against my leg. "We'll call at the tenth pylon," I puff to Asim. "That's the last one. Nine to go."

He nods, staring up ahead. The Blue Moon. The sun is glinting off the white tiles, dazzling our eyes. It's so bright it looks like a mirage, something that will be whisked away when you blink.

When we reach the end we lean for a moment against the rails. I get out the phone and turn it on. Nothing. I try again, digging my nail into the little cavity at the top. Still there's no signal. I look at Asim. "I, um, think the battery is low. Dead, in fact. I guess Mom forgot to recharge it."

"Oh, Jackson, what'll we do now?"

I try to smile at him. I'm trying to give him some of my confidence. I'm thinking, this is a sign. A piece of luck. Maybe there's no battery because we're not meant to tell the police now. Just like I thought all along.

"We'll ring when we're inside. There'll be a pay phone or something. Trust me, it will be okay."

"Oh, will you stop saying 'trust me'? You sound like a Hollywood movie! This is *real!*"

I stare at Asim. This is the first time I've seen him angry.

250

At least with me. The stress is really getting to him. I wish he had a little bit of my power plant thing.

We start off again, trotting up the hill. We keep to the left weaving in and out of the trees planted sparsely along the concrete sidewalk. Asim stops at the edge of the car park. He's staring at the big neon sign that's shouting down the daylight.

"See those white steps?" I say. "We'll have to run up those full tilt. We'll be pretty exposed but I don't know the back way. Speed will be everything here because we can't hide." We look at the mountain of steps and the big glass doors at the top. "There's no one around at the moment. And the car park is pretty empty. This is probably our best time."

Asim gulps. He's still panting. "Do you know where to go when we get inside? Where the pay phones are? You've been here before, haven't you?"

I stop breathing. Somehow, I hadn't quite got to this bit in my plans. I'd sat in the car waiting for Mom lots of times, but I'd only been inside once. That was two years ago.

"Yeah, sure," I tell Asim. "Follow me."

We sprint between the cars and then before we get to the path that leads to the steps, I stop. I grab Asim, and we crouch down behind a red Ferrari. A man in a suit and a Stetson hat is coming out of the glass doors. We wait for him to stroll down the steps. He's so busy looking at the roll of bank notes in his hands, he probably wouldn't have seen us anyway.

"One, two, three, four, go!" I whisper and we hurl ourselves up the steps. We push open the big glass doors and come to a screaming halt.

"Which way?" whispers Asim.

"Um." This doesn't look familiar at all. My mind has gone blank like a map written with invisible ink. The

251

electric feeling is ebbing away and I'm standing in a small pool of fear.

"Someone's coming!" hisses Asim and we start to run. I have no idea where we're heading but the instinct to just move, anywhere, pushes us down the corridor. We're pounding along when I hear the *ping!* of the slot machines and suddenly I remember this big room full of machines and Mom's description of the bar around the corner. There was something about the bar she used to laugh at, something really false like a stage set.

"What is that smell?" asks Asim.

I stop a second and sniff. It's sweet, making my saliva glands work. Banana, maybe, or no, there's something beachy about it, gritty. A tingly feeling starts at the back of my nose and I see sand and palm trees.

"Coconut!" and the map in my head appears as if it's been dipped in lemon juice. I pull Asim along and we race toward the bar. I try not to slow down as we pass the palm leaves billowing in the air conditioning, but I catch a glimpse of someone sitting on a stool and a woman behind the bar. The woman's eyes meet mine for just a heartbeat and I see they're blue and horrified and widening with surprise.

"Hey!" she yells, but we're gone, around the corner and hurtling toward the elevators.

"Who was that? Did you know her?"

"Yes, but we can't stop now." The electric energy is flooding back and I have such a certainty in my guts that we only have minutes left. You can't stop to chat or explain when there's no time and only *you* can save your girlfriend.

I press the button on the wall twenty times. Come *on*! I tell it, bashing my fist against the steel. Girlfriend. That's what she is. That's what I'd like her to be. For the first time

I let myself put that word with Esmerelda Marx. Suddenly I can no longer live with the idea of my girlfriend being trapped in a cellar even for another minute.

"I hate elevators," says Asim. "I always try to avoid them. Are there any stairs?"

Just then the doors open and I grab Asim and pull him inside.

I stand staring at the row of numbers as the doors shut.

"Press something!" shouts Asim wildly.

"I don't know, I can't remember!"

"Just press anything. We're not going to Tony's office alone, are we? We have to find a phone first."

I'm staring at B1, B2 . . . Something oddly familiar. That's it! "Bananas in Pajamas," I shout. "The second one!"

Asim stares at me. "Now I'm really worried. You've lost it completely."

I press B2 and in two times four we're there.

We creep up the red carpet. Asim is whispering in my ear, his feet dragging. "Can't go in there by ourselves . . . this is crazy . . . we'll be kidnapped, too . . ." but I'm not listening to him. Every cell in my body is alert, concentrating. We are so near, I can feel it. Behind one of these doors, there is my girlfriend, Esmerelda.

And then I see it. The plaque on the third door. TONY SERENO. I stop, and put my finger to my lips. Asim draws in his breath.

The door is open just a little way. Maybe ten inches. We freeze against the wall. I creep forward like a spider, slow, si-lent. I can feel Asim tugging at my shirt, trying to pull me back. I shrug him off and put an eye in the narrow doorway.

There's the room, just as my mother described. I can see

a table and a large Persian rug and at the back of the room a couple of chairs. Empty. Opening the door just a fraction, I peer at every corner of the room to make one hundred percent sure no one is there.

"Now!" I hiss at Asim. I go straight to the rug. "We've got to look under here for the opening to the cellar. Ez will be in there—I'm certain of it. You pick up that end."

But Asim is just standing in the middle of the room, gaping. He keeps making a clicking sound in his throat, as if he's starting to say something but can't get it out. But it's all right because when I pick up the corner closest to the table, I see a panel of wood with grain running in a different direction. I pull back the rug further and see it's a door in the floor and there, almost under Asim's feet is the lock set deep into the wood like a plug.

"This is it," I whisper to Asim.

He nods, still speechless. His mouth hangs open like one of those clowns you see at fairs.

"It's okay," I say. "We'll be quick now. But I'm going to have to yell. Go and close the door, lock it if you can."

Like a robot he goes to the door and does as he's told.

I put my mouth right near the floor and shout, "ESMERELDA!"

I wait, cupping my ear to the boards. Nothing. I yell again, shouting my name, too. "CAN YOU HEAR ME?"

Asim is kneeling down now, too. "They're not *there*. Oh, what will we do? Maybe they've gone. Maybe they were never here."

The confidence in my gut is beginning to melt away. I could dissolve into a puddle on this floor. I study the dial on the lock of the trapdoor—it looks like the lock on a safe, with numbers etched into the steel all around the face of it. We'll have to find the right combination of numbers. Oh, God, I didn't think of that. I didn't think of any of this. I don't know how I could have been so stupid. I look at Asim's white face. And now it's not just me in this mess, I've got my best friend in it, too.

I start to twist the dial. A last spurt of hope makes me think maybe, like the door, it won't be locked, maybe it will just spring open. Under my fingers it twists all around, clockwise and anticlockwise, but nothing happens. It's locked all right.

"It must work like a safe," I say, "you know, it'll only respond to a certain pattern of numbers."

I yell again, my voice cracking on the last syllable. The loudness scares me to death.

"Jackson, quick, did you hear something?" Asim has his ear to the floor. "Listen."

There's a thumping right under our knees. Then a familiar angry voice comes through the floorboards. "Jackson, you nerd, is that you?"

Asim and I whoop like at a soccer finale, falling over and hugging each other.

"Badman, you maggot!" I shout. "Have you got Esmerelda there?"

"Yeah, but she's hurt. Broken her arm. Get us out of here!"

"Where's Tony?"

"What? We've only got a minute, less. That Tony guy and Rocky, they said they'd be just five minutes. They must have already been twenty. We're gonna be cooked unless you hurry."

"Okay, okay. But this door is locked. We need to know the combination."

"You're the math genius, you figure it out!"

We're all silent a minute. Odd or even, prime, composite, rational, squared? How do you choose? Where do you begin? Favorite number patterns must be one of the most personal things on the planet. Wouldn't the combination of your safe express your personality? For instance, if I had to pick a combination, I'd choose even numbers ascending by four. Or maybe you'd choose your birth date. But none of us knows what preferences Tony has, except for kidnapping, extortion, and drug dealing.

"Jackson?" I nearly fall over again. It's Esmerelda!

"Are you okay?" I screech at the floor. "Oh, it's so good to hear your voice!" But now I can't think at all.

"Jackson," she calls, "Rocky told us that Tony's favorite game is blackjack."

"What has this got to do with it?" Asim says. "Mine is Scrabble. So what? Look, they will be back any minute. We should go and get help."

"The object of the game is to be the first to twenty-one," I tell him.

But Asim has gotten up and is prowling around the room. I hear him stop at the desk and scrape back a chair.

"You're really distracting me—" I turn around and see him give a little jump of delight. He's looking at the phone on the desk.

"Thank God, call 911."

He nods, his eyes dancing.

I try to go back to thinking about twenty-one. That is a real clue. Such an ugly number, twenty-one. The optimism of two followed by the disappointment of one. I shake my head. I'm going nowhere. Just crazy. The sweat is dripping off my forehead. I twist the dial to twenty-one. Nothing.

Think, Jackson.

A low moan makes me turn around.

Asim's face is grey as ash. "The phone is dead." His voice has no emotion in it. It's as lifeless as his face.

"Okay, let's work with what we've got. Twenty-one is not a prime number, that must give us some clue. What are the multiples of twenty-one?"

"Twenty-one and one, three and seven—" Asim stops suddenly and comes over. He kneels down on the floor, his knees cracking in the silence. "777, does that remind you of anything?"

"Yes! Rocky's license plate."

I wipe the sweat off my forehead. My hands are slippery and they're shaking so much I couldn't even hold a pencil.

"Do you want me to do it?" Asim asks gently.

I nod and we change places. He wipes his hands on his shirt and settles his knees directly behind the dial.

"Hurry!" comes a yell through the floorboards.

"Take your time," I tell Asim.

Carefully, he positions his fingers so he has a good grip. He turns it to seven. He waits a beat then turns it again. Another beat and he turns to seven for the last time. We wait. I close my eyes and open them. I can't bear it. Can't bear the waiting.

Nothing happens.

"Okay, we'd better get out of here and see if we can get help," I say. I start to get up. My knees crack in the silence. I feel like an old man.

"There must be something else," says Asim. "If there is seven, there must be a three and a one. They are the factors of twenty-one."

"Try it."

He takes a deep breath and stretches his fingers. He places them carefully around the dial.

"Jesus, just do it!"

One, two, three. There is a loud click and in one amazing moment the lock snaps open and Badman's ugly head bobs up.

"Glory be to God!" shouts Asim and falls on Badman's neck.

I can't stop grinning. I could damn well kiss him, too, he looks so good.

"Get off, you crazies, and let me up!" As he steps up onto the floor I can see he can't help the smile on his face either. It's like a giant crack in a rock.

"Never thought I'd be happy to see you nerds," he says, and cuffs me so hard on the shoulder I stagger. "Where's the cops?"

"Well," Asim begins but I'm busy lowering myself down the stairs.

"Hi, Jackson," says Esmerelda, "I knew you'd come to save me." There are tears on her face and she's in her pajamas. Her black hair is all mussed around her cheeks, sticking to her tears. My throat is choked and I'm not thinking anymore.

"I love you," I tell her, and bend to kiss her.

"Quick, get her out of there!" Badman's face appears at the top. "What are you doing? There's no time for that!"

"You're always in the way, aren't you?" I say. But he's right. I don't know what came over me.

"Can you walk?" I ask her.

"Yes, just help me up. *Aagh*," she winces, "not that arm. It's killing me."

Her eyes fill with tears from the pain. I wish I could take

the pain from her and have it myself. I have such a flood of wanting to protect her forever, so that she never has to feel this hurt again.

"Come on!" comes the shout from above.

Gently I put my hand under her other arm and lift. She stands, tottering a little, then climbs slowly up the steps.

"Ez!" cries Asim and throws his arms around her.

"Careful!" She holds her hurt arm at the elbow, at a small distance from her body.

We all look at her arm. It's twisted around so that the inside is facing out. An acid bile shoots into my throat.

"Who did that to you?" I ask. I want to break something, smash something to smithereens.

"Who do you think?" says Badman.

"They threw us down the stairs," says Ez. "Where are the cops?"

I wish people would stop asking that. Seeing Esmerelda like this, I can't quite believe I came here without them. A weight of guilt falls like a boulder into my stomach.

Then the scrape of a key in a lock makes us freeze.

The door opens and a tall man in a suit walks in. Another built like a gorilla comes in behind him. They stop dead, staring at us from the other side of the table.

"Well, well, well, what have we here?" says the tall man, looking from one to the other of us. "I could have sworn we left just two children here, isn't that right, Rocky? And now there are four. They must have multiplied while we were gone, how very peculiar."

"Like bacteria, eh, boss? Their cells divide real quick and next thing you know, you've got a full-blown army on your hands—"

"Oh, go and sit on *yours* why don't you, you useless

259

gorilla." The tall man's voice drops its smooth tone and he goes over to the desk and picks up a whiskey bottle.

"Tony Sereno," I say. I'm surprised to hear my voice. I thought I was just thinking his name to myself.

"Jackson Ford, I presume," says Tony. "At last."

We stand and look at each other. I try to balance my weight equally on my two legs. A gym teacher told me once you can feel your center of gravity running in a straight line if you do that. I need something now to center me, or I could float off like a particle of dust into the air. My heart is racing so fast I can hardly breathe. Let alone think what to do.

"Have you come to rescue your little friends? Well, you're a bit late. You were my first choice, I'll have you know, but Rocky here made a small error. So now we'll just have to reconsider the situation." Tony's voice is light, as if he's considering buying apples or pears.

I watch him pour the whiskey and put the glass back down on the table. He takes a cigar from a pack marked Cuban Best and picks up a gold lighter. He holds the flame to the cigar, puffing rhythmically until the cigar is burning, then throws the lighter down on the table. It makes a loud metallic thud, scattering ash in a small pile, like snow.

Every detail seems important somehow, like a puzzle. I feel I have to watch carefully because if there's any little space between one event and another, it might be enough to wriggle through and escape.

"We were going on a journey but we can't fit you all in the backseat I'm afraid," Tony is saying. "So we may have to reduce our numbers."

Badman catches my eye with a small movement of his hand. I glance his way without moving my head and see that his hand is sliding into his pocket. His eyes are focused

260

on the gold lighter Tony threw down on the table. I can feel Badman building up to something; there's an unusual stillness to him, a ferocious kind of concentration.

"The cops will be here any minute," I say to Tony. "You'll get fifty years for kidnapping and grievous bodily harm to a minor, let alone stealing years off the lives of all our mothers." I say the first things that come into my mind, just to make them focus on me instead of Badman. It works, too well.

"You little cretin," hisses Tony. He turns to Rocky. "Do something about this garbage."

"What do you want me to do, boss?"

Badman is taking something out of his pocket. His other hand darts toward the gold lighter, so quick it blurs. Suddenly I know exactly what he's going to do.

I pick up the first thing I see and hurl it into Tony's face. The glass smashes against his nose, whiskey dripping off his chin.

Rocky cocks his gun, pointing it straight at me when suddenly there is the most deafening explosion. *Ba- ba- ba- ba-bang*—it goes on and on in staccato bursts, a chain of sound that lights up the room and at first I think I've been shot.

Then I see Tony is holding his face and Rocky has dropped his gun and there are a string of burned firecrackers lying scattered at Tony's feet.

"*Run!*" screams Badman and we grab each other and make for the door. We blast into the hallway, and a shot whistles past my ear. Feet are thudding down the red carpet behind us. Another shot makes a hole the size of a tennis ball in the wall beside me.

"We're not gonna make it!" Someone is crying and I look around for Esmerelda's hand.

That's why I'm not looking when I run straight into a man coming the other way.

He stops me like a brick wall. My teeth graze against brass buttons. Finished.

But I'm staring up into a dark blue uniform.

"Oh, thank God almighty," I hear Esmerelda say and she sinks quietly into the thick soft carpet. In her white bathrobe she looks like a neat curl of cream lying on the red.

I bend down to stroke her face and the policeman rushes past me, into the office. I hear crashing sounds and swearing but I'm trying to listen for Ez's pulse. It's there under that milky skin, strong and steady. I feel Asim's hand on my shoulder. And Badman. More police are running up the hall and with them is someone I recognize. Her blue eyes are wide and shining.

"Bev!"

She picks me up and wraps me in her arms and I can smell the sweet sickly flavor of coconut on her apron.

"Jackson, who do you think you are, Superman?"

"*You* called the police!"

"Of course. I knew neither you nor I could tackle those gangsters alone."

"We nearly did. Nearly." I could sink into the soft safety of her and fall asleep, just melt away forever. But I can hear Badman talking, right next to my ear, and he's taking one of Bev's hands and pumping it up and down.

Badman and I look at each other.

"Thanks, buddy," says Badman. "That was one brave act."

"I couldn't have done it without Asim."

Badman puts out his hand. "Thanks, Asim. I owe you," and he shakes his hand.

"You did the quick thinking," Asim replies.

We're quiet, watching the police prod Tony, then Rocky, down the hall. Their wrists are cuffed, their faces dark as storms. The left side of Tony's face is black with gunpowder, and he's lost one of his eyebrows. We all shrink against the wall as they pass, not wanting any part of us to be close to them.

"We make a good team," Badman says hesitantly. "The three of us."

I'm just about to correct him when Esmerelda does that.

"Four," she pipes up weakly from the floor.

16. Esmerelda

"Are you nervous?" asks Lilly.

"Not really," I tell her.

"I guess after what you've been through, this puny concert is nothing."

"No, Lilly, it's everything."

We smile at each other. Although we've known each other since we were little kids, it feels like the first time we've really seen each other. A lot of that has been my fault. Not saying what I felt. Not telling the truth. Often it's just easier to go along with what someone else wants—but you never get close that way, never be yourself. It was Badman who made me see it. That night in the cellar, when he asked me why I didn't sing rock if I liked it so much, I sounded so pathetic in my own ears. "But you're stronger than that!" he said, and I thought for the first time, maybe I am.

"You know, I really like 'A Different Door,'" says Lilly, smoothing out her pink dress. "I think it's very—well, in*tense*. I hope Mrs. Reilly doesn't notice the swearing. But you know what I like best? Being a backup singer and getting to dance on stage. And wearing this pink dress."

Catrina comes up, and puts her hand on Lilly's shoulder. "Me, too. If you hadn't decided to change everything, Ez, and sing with the Badman, I wouldn't be about to go up on stage with Lils. What do you think of the dress on me? Is it too tight?"

"No—shows off your curves. Are you wearing a push-up bra?"

"Yeah, it's pink, too."

Lilly sits down beside me. She looks at the writing on my cast. "*Walk on the wild side*," she reads aloud.

"That's Badman," I laugh.

She nods. "You know, this is all kind of a relief, to tell you the truth. I always got too nervous trying to carry the tune. And, well, I hated depending on you, but having to pretend that I didn't." She looks down at her pink lap, the sequins practically shouting in the footlights. "But I love all the other stuff about performing, you know, the glamour and the dancing and the *clapping*! I didn't want to give that up." She pauses a moment. "Me and Catrina, we won't be standing *too* far back though, will we? I mean, we're backup singers and all but we'll be right next to you in the front, right?"

"Yeah. I don't mind where you stand as long as we're singing that song."

"Oh, Ez, none of it matters anyway—I'm just so glad my oldest friend is okay!"

She gives me a hug. There've been so many hugs in the last three weeks I'd have sore arms even if one wasn't broken. But like ice cream, each hug has a different flavor.

Under the cast, my skin itches like a million mosquito bites. Especially down near the elbow where I can't scratch. I've got three pins in there holding my bones together. But I can put up with that. I can put up with anything. Right now, I feel invincible—that's a line from a famous song, Valerie told me last night: "I Am Woman." Valerie loves it.

She looks so happy out there in the audience. Jackson said she cried for two days nonstop when Bev brought him home. And when he told her she had to stop crying because if she went on for another day that would make three and it would be bad luck, she started all over again. But since she's dried up, I've never seen her look sunnier. It's as if she's put down a heavy package and now she can stand up with her back straight.

Next to her is my family. Wow, look at Mom in her black dress. She went out and bought it especially for the concert. And tonight of all nights there was her annual Bank Banquet. There would have been speeches and awards like at the Oscars, and Mom was marked for a special mention as Achiever of the Year. I saw the invitation. But she didn't even mention it. She probably bought the dress for the Banquet but wore it tonight, instead.

I remember the argument she and I had before all of this happened. Our words still run through my mind, clear as a tape on rewind. I remember how I fantasized about her saying, "If only I could have this day over again!" It's weird because when she came to the hospital, she practically said that same thing. She said sometimes one day is like a whole life and when the day is ending, it's like dying. You lie there and think about how you've spent your life and what you might have done differently. Even though it was such a terrible day, she said she was lucky to have had it because it gave her a second chance. She could start again. And there were going to be changes! Dad looked nervous when she said that, but he gave me *another* hug and said, "Mother knows best."

One change I have noticed is that neither of them even ask anymore if I've done my math homework. Funny thing is, I don't mind doing it now. None of it seems like such a big deal (even those percentages) because I'm doing what I love, as well.

I'm taking singing lessons with Valerie. We go together to see Ms. Juanita Perez—she's wild, with those Roman soldier kind of sandals that lace up the leg and a vocal range that is mind-boggling. She says Valerie and I will catch up with her; she can extend anyone's range and power with her exercises. You have to breathe in a special way and make weird noises in your throat like a wounded animal. It tickles, and at first it seems impossible but she says the throat is like any other muscle, it needs to be exercised and toned to be at its "olympic" best. I believe her, because I've reached at least a couple more notes on the scale and Valerie has almost half of another octave.

Mom suggested the lessons. I couldn't believe it. We had a long talk and she told me stuff about her childhood and how poor her family had been. It ruined her father's life, she said. Even though her mother kept telling him that they had all the important things—each other, and food on the table and healthy kids, his heart was broken. So when Mom grew up she decided she would take control of her family's finances. But she was so busy being in control, she forgot anyone else might be different. She said she was kind of jealous of Valerie—having the guts to risk everything for her passion in life. Jealous, too, of how much time I spent with her. "But you're my *mother*!" I told her. "No one could replace you." We had this big hug and I felt like I'd suddenly grown four inches. Daniel came in then and wriggled his head up between us like a puppy. You could practically see his tail wagging.

"Esmerelda, come now and put on your costume," Mrs. Reilly is breathing over me, "and your . . . er . . . make-up.

Why do I always have to tell you people twenty times? The concert is starting in ten minutes."

I look down at my jeans ripped at the knee, my black T-shirt, the cast on my arm scribbled all over in different pens. "But I'm already dressed," I tell her.

Two bright red spots flare on her cheeks. She flicks her eyes over me and shakes her head. "Why do you always insist on starting a sentence with 'But'?" She doesn't wait for an answer. "Have you made up your mind to sing this 'Different Door' song?" Her nose wrinkles on "door" as if she's just smelled something bad.

"Yes." I stare back at her. I try not to blink, keeping my eyes level. It's like staring down a witch.

"Well, I'll tell you one thing, Esmerelda *Marx*." She says my name as if the smell has returned. "If you lie down with dogs, you get up with fleas."

I just keep staring at her. She says the stupidest things. Once, in front of the whole school assembly she shouted, "Every time I open my mouth, some fool speaks!"

She takes one step nearer, and jabs me in the chest. "Have you ever heard of Plato, girl?" She doesn't wait for me to answer. "No, of course not, he was only the most famous philosopher of ancient Greece. Well he had a sign above *his* door: *Let no one ignorant of mathematics enter here.* That's the kind of door you should be concentrating on, Miss Marx."

In one way Lilly was right—after what I've been through, Mrs. Reilly's sneers are as easy to flick away as sand from my feet. Anyway, I know a bit about old Plato. Valerie told me. Plato hated any new music coming out of Greece. He said change would break down the rules of their society. He sounded just like Frank Sinatra. Well, I'm sure Plato knew tons about math and philosophy, but there are a few things I'd like to discuss with him about music and the human soul.

Muttering to herself, Mrs. Reilly hurries off to meddle with the kindergarten. She's taken to muttering a lot lately, ever since the principal, Mr. Phillips, talked to her. He called her into his office on the day after we returned to school. We saw her coming down the steps with her back all stooped and her mouth turned down.

You see, after the kidnapping, Badman and I decided to make an appointment with Mr. Phillips. Badman gave this wonderful speech—about how he'd woken up to himself, lifted his game, pulled up his socks, and straightened his tie. He used every expression he'd ever heard Mr. Phillips shout at him over the last year. His manners were so polished with politeness and respect you could have slid him like a piece of soap across the floor. He pleaded with Phillips to let him participate in the concert—his first real live audience! He wanted a chance to make a new start, he said, his eyes moist, to make a contribution to the school. Phillips was pretty moved, you could tell.

We walked out of there floating on air. "Maybe we can stop calling you Badman now," I said as we came out of the principal's office.

"Nah," he replied, "I'm too used to it. And anyway, Dad thinks it's a great stage name for a rocker."

I look over now at Badman. He's been checking his strings for the last half hour. He's standing guarding his own space, snarling if anyone comes near. He's as nervous as a cat, but he'd never admit it. He sees me looking and his frown lifts. I nod at him. I'd be nervous, too, if I were him. There's a lot at stake. His dad is supposed to come tonight. When we went missing, his mother totally freaked. She couldn't find his father and she spent the dawn hours at the police station. When the police finally tracked down his dad in New Zealand, we were already home. That really shook up Mr. Bradman. That he hadn't even known his son was missing. Badman talked to him on the phone and he thinks his dad must have "woken up to himself." Anyway, he promised to get back in time for the concert.

I peep around the corner of the curtain and search the audience. There's Mrs. Bradman sitting next to Mr. Norton. He's talking to her, nodding a lot, with a sympathetic expression on his face. He's looking after her. He's all right, Mr. Norton. You know what he said to us when we returned to school? He said he used to play air guitar in his bedroom. He'd pretend he was Elvis Presley and jive around in his *blue, blue, blue suede shoes* . . . He showed us his whole air guitar routine in the coat room. It was a riot! If you get a chance to do that for real, he told us, you should take it.

"Can you see him?" Badman's looking out over my shoulder at the audience.

"Who, your dad? Not yet. But he'll be here, he promised you."

"Yeah, but he's never on time. Mom told him he'll be late for his own funeral. *He* said he hopes he's so late he misses it."

"What, the concert?"

"No, his funeral."

"Well, he's not the only one who's late. Have you seen Asim, or Jackson? I wish the four of us were here together right now. It's our first concert at high school. There'll never be another like it."

"Yeah," says Badman. "Maybe next year I'll be rippin' it up in Auckland!"

"Hey look, there's Asim's dad. He's slipped in beside Valerie."

"He looks pretty pleased with himself . . . Hey, did you see that? Was that a kiss?"

"Well, whatever, I'm just glad he's here. There are Asim and Jackson coming up the side. I was beginning to think we might have to do without a drummer."

"No way. Rock *is* drums."

Asim hurtles up the stairs of the stage and comes panting over to us. I give him a hug, seeing as they're more common than colds around here.

"You got your sticks, drummer?" says Badman.

"Yes." He wrings his hands. "But I don't know about this. We haven't rehearsed much—"

"Only every day and night for three weeks!"

"Yes, but I've never had any proper lessons or . . ." Suddenly he gives a huge grin. "I've got some news—"

"Oh, *Jackson*, look everyone, how *cute* is that puppy!"

We all look to where Catrina is pointing and see Jackson holding something out in front of him. Kids are crowding around until he's entirely lost in a wriggling mass of arms and legs. I decide just to wait until all the excitement has calmed down. But a deep thump of happiness pounds in my stomach. Now we're all together, just as it should be.

Two weeks ago, when Badman and I decided to do our own song, Valerie said we would need a place to rehearse. She cleared out the garage and put matting down on the floor. She worked for days, with Jackson and me helping after school. Asim's dad repaired the broken windows and tiles on the roof, and checked the electrical wiring. And that's how we became a garage band. Valerie moved in like a one-woman army and took over the musical arrangement.

She convinced Asim to be our drummer, helped us with the lyrics, and brought over a guitarist she knows to go through Badman's solo with him.

Badman loved those jam sessions. He kept falling over himself to be helpful. And he smiled so much I think his jaws must have ached. Funny, every time Asim got low in confidence, Badman was there to back him up. I think it was Badman who actually convinced him to keep going. He kept beaming like a flashlight around the garage saying, "If we can defeat the friggin' Mafia, we can do anything!" He gave Asim such encouraging pats on the back that once he fell clean off his stool.

It's so strange, if I hadn't spent that incredible night in the cellar with him, I'd think his evil twin had flown away and a good guy has come in his place. But Valerie just shrugs about it. "Everyone wants to belong," she says. "You kids are like a family now. And besides, as John Lee Hooker says, 'Let that boy boogie woogie, 'cause it's in him, and it's gotta come out!'" Someone ought to have told old Plato that.

We've all been practically living in that garage. On the same night Valerie brought home the puppy, she brought in the keyboard. She didn't show any of us the puppy at first. She hid it in the laundry. But you could tell she had a secret. She cornered Jackson and told him he was going to play keyboard for the concert. She'd teach him an easy bass part, and that way he could be part of the band.

"It's really only nine notes you've got to learn," she said.

"Make it an even number and I'll consider it," he said.

"Oh, stop counting," she said, "and let yourself go! God knows what I've done to make you so *anal*!"

"I thought musicians had to count to stay in *time*," he argued.

They fought till we started playing to drown them out. But they just moved off to the garden. Sometimes they can go on for hours. I think Jackson does it just to prove a point. Make himself different from her. He thinks when you battle Valerie you have to use every weapon you've got to resist her. But when she brought the puppy out of the laundry, Jackson melted like ice cream in the sun.

"He's always wanted a pet of his own," Valerie told me, "but you can't keep an animal in an apartment. You watch, he'll want to build a dog kennel now, just like he built that possum house."

"Have you given him a name yet?" I ask Jackson as he pushes his way toward us.

"Yeah. Eight."

"He's got eight names?"

"No, just Eight."

"So guess what," Asim tries again. He doesn't wait for anyone to say *what*? "Our visa came through! It was so sudden. It has been extended for another three years, which means we can probably get our permanent residency here in this beloved land." He puts his hand on his heart and grins like a maniac, but I know he means it.

"That's fantastic!" I give him another hug. Then I turn to Jackson. "Have you told Valerie yet?"

"Yeah."

Asim is laughing and punching Jackson's shoulder. I've never seen him look so happy. Almost out-of-control happy. He looks, for once, like he doesn't have a care in the world.

"Valerie was mad as hell," Jackson tells me. "She says funny, isn't it, how there was an election coming up and suddenly all the kids are let out of detention centers, and look, hey presto, a visa is granted. Mehmet had to take her by the shoulders and tell her all over *again* and then finally it sank in and she cried. When she hugged Asim he couldn't breathe for about two minutes. I counted the seconds."

More hugs!

"What are you all DOING up here behind the curtain?" Mrs. Reilly stalks up to us like a snapping crocodile. "And what on Earth is that creature doing hiding in your shirt, Jackson Ford? It's made a wet spot right there under your collar!"

"I'm taking him out now, Mrs. Reilly."

She stalks off to yell at other kids, and Asim and the others make for the stairs at the side of the stage. But Jackson stands still, reaching his hand out to me.

"I just wanted to give you this," he says. He holds out a little package wrapped in green tissue paper. Inside is a silver necklace, with a heart carved out of a stripy golden wood.

"From the sassafras tree," blushes Jackson. "I carved it myself. Well, with a bit of help from Mehmet ..."

I run my finger over the smooth shiny surface. It feels warm.

"Turn it over," says Jackson.

On the back there is carefully carved writing: EZ/JF 4 EVER. The infinity sign curls underneath.

I put it around my neck. "It's beautiful."

"You're beautiful," he says.

I look at him standing there, a big pleased smile on his face, the puppy poking out of his shirt, his dark eyes shining, his hard brown boy's hands stroking the dog. *He's* the one who's beautiful, inside and out. I take the puppy and put it on the floor. Then I take Jackson's face in my hands and kiss him full on the lips.

274

I don't feel scared anymore. I don't want to run away. His lips are cool and dry. He tastes of chocolate milk. He puts his arms around me and my heart says *this* is the flavor I choose. I stand there for this moment breathing in his skin and feeling his hug seep into me like sunlight. It's warming all the cold places under my skin.

When we go up on stage, you can hear a pin drop. This is partly because Mrs. Reilly announces us as if she's introducing the plague. It's also because Badman looks like a zombie from a horror film. Out of the corner of my eye I can see little Robbie Mason inching onto his mother's lap. I don't think Homeland High has ever seen an act like ours. But as soon as Badman starts his first riff, and Asim comes in, right on time, with Jackson's bass rhythm backing the guitar, I forget to look at the audience. I'm listening for Badman's chord change and there it is, perfect, like a question I'm ready to answer. The music flows up through my belly and out into the air, easy as breathing.

I close my eyes and it's like swimming down under a wave. Instead of silence there's only sound, this one conversation we're having here on Earth. I can hear Asim pushing the drums, playing on top of the beat like Valerie showed him, a little faster than the real rhythm. Badman is pulling against him, laying back just a heartbeat, playing with the pulse of the song. It's as if we're all talking, expressing who we are, pulling and pushing the rhythm and making this pattern that I don't ever want to stop.

When I open my eyes I see the pink dresses swishing beside me and they're a surprise, like sudden flowers against our black. I love them! The girls' voices slide into the chorus with mine and we belt it out, smiling like maniacs. We can't stop smiling. Each of us is a part weaving the pattern, and now I can feel the groove Valerie described—we've clicked into this place where we all belong, where the energy is flowing and we could go on forever, easily, without effort, just like the planets doing their thing, like the cycles of night and day. Asim still looks kind of delirious, almost cross-eyed with delight. I grin back at him. It's as if we're all connected up here inside some divine bubble of happiness, just doing what we were meant to do.

Badman takes off now with his solo. His fingers are working their way up the neck, the high notes spurting light as spray, then crashing like bombs into the dark. Badman's flying way out there, improvising his way into some other galaxy. His notes have flung past the pattern we were making, discovering notes and sequences we'd never heard in our garage band. I realize I'm holding my breath, going where he's going and for a moment I think maybe he'll never come back, but like Led Zeppelin he catches himself and Asim is there to meet him, drumming us back into the main rhythm. We fall into the groove, but it's a new journey, and as the beat takes over I try to make my larynx into drums the way Juanita taught me. We're listening, talking, soaring, and now I see that the front rows of the audience are on their feet, clapping and swaying, and then everyone's up, catching the wave we're on and Badman is taking us higher.

I'll never forget tonight even if I live to be a hundred. Even though Daniel got sick and threw up on Mom's lap and she had to take him home before we finished our number. Even though Eight ran out into the audience and Mr. Phillips nearly stepped on him. And even though Badman's dad arrived late, only after Badman had finished his solo.

"He got here, didn't he?" Badman said. "And all the way from New Zealand!"

Up there on stage, nothing could touch what we had. It was like Valerie's perfect harmony—keeping your own tune while listening to others. Usually that's hard. Takes a lot of concentration. But tonight it was natural, the only way to be.

Jackson says he won't forget tonight either, and if we can do this happy stuff more and stop disabling our immunity systems with anger, maybe we *will* live to be a hundred. When he said "happy stuff" he smiled in a funny way, so I don't know whether he meant the music or the kiss. Maybe it was both.

The last three weeks, there's been more "happy stuff" than I ever thought possible. Which is pretty amazing, since it all came right after the most *un*happy experience in my entire life. But the singing took me away. Practicing every afternoon in that garage—it was like having a bubble of happiness inside. Once you've felt that, Jackson says, no one can ever take it away. It's a part of you.

You know how Frank Sinatra said rock was the end of civilization? Well, I think it's what helps keep everything going. You've gotta hear the music that sets you free. Then you've got the glory inside you. If you didn't have that there'd be no point in getting up in the morning and brushing your teeth. It'd be like being in jail. Or dead.

Maybe I'll write a song about it.

17. Jackson

I just have to add something that I haven't told you. It won't take long. But do you know what? When I kissed Esmerelda on the night of the school concert, I forgot to count. No challenges, no numbers. Absolutely nothing happened in my head. For me, that's about as rare as snow in summer. It was the best feeling. When I listen to Ez talk about singing, I think kissing must do the same thing. Hypnotize you.

I couldn't help thinking afterward, though, about exactly how long the kiss lasted. I went through it all in my mind, and I even tried to kiss the mirror, to get it right. The glass was really cold. Ez and I, we didn't dislocate our jaws or anything, but we did have our lips open a bit. I figure it went for about sixteen seconds. That one kiss was so good, I didn't even need to ask for another to make it even.

A kiss like that could change a guy's whole attitude to life.

I told Asim that, and he could see it. He thinks he'll have his first kiss in eighth grade. I'm just glad I got mine out of the way in seventh grade.

Mom says I'll really enjoy the rest of high school. She thinks I'll grow into myself, like finding the right-sized suit. I hope so—before I moved to Homeland I felt empty a lot of the time, with too much loose space inside.

"Life is either a daring adventure or nothing at all," said Helen Keller. Well, I think I've had about enough adventures to last a lifetime. But then again, maybe this is only the beginning.

You never know.